The One You Love

MB

PAUL PILKINGTON

The One You Love

CORONET

First published in Great Britain in 2014 by Coronet
An imprint of Hodder & Stoughton
An Hachette UK company

First published in paperback in 2014

3

A CIP catalogue record for this title is available from the British Library

ISBN 978 1 444 78484 8

Printed and bound by Clays Ltd, St Ives plc

Hodder & Stoughton policy is to use papers that are natural,
renewable and recyclable products and made from wood grown in
sustainable forests. The logging and manufacturing processes are
expected to conform to the environmental regulations of the
country of origin.

Hodder & Stoughton Ltd
338 Euston Road
London NW1 3BH

www.hodder.co.uk

For my family

Prologue

He watched from the boat as they sailed past the sights of London – the thrusting steel spires of Canary Wharf, the domed O2 Arena, then Tower Bridge and, finally, the London Eye and Westminster. The sky was deep blue and the sun's heat intense, so the cooling river breeze was heaven.

After disembarking, he headed for the tube. The day in the capital had been enjoyable. But now the holiday was over, and the real business was just beginning.

It was time.

Soon she would know just how bad it felt.

Part One

I

'Em, it's Will. Where the hell is that fiancé of yours? He didn't turn up at the meeting place, and he's not answering his phone.'

Emma Holden pressed her mobile into one ear and cupped her hand over the other, but still struggled to hear what her brother was saying over the chatter of the busy London pub. The Irish theme bar was heaving with twenty- and thirty-somethings – mostly City workers celebrating the end of the working week and the beginning of a long, sunny August Bank Holiday weekend. Emma, however, was celebrating something far more important – her wedding, due to take place in just over a week's time. And while this place wouldn't usually have been her first choice for a night out – it was so busy that it was difficult even to turn around – somehow it seemed perfect for a hen party.

'Hang on a minute,' she shouted into her phone, reaching around a group of people and handing her drink to her friend, Lizzy. She nodded and smiled as Emma gestured that she was going outside. 'I'm going somewhere quieter,' Emma shouted into her mobile as she began to weave her way through the crowds. 'Can't hear anything in here.'

After a monumental effort she reached the door and exited into the sultry night air, leaving the rest of her ten-strong hen party inside. The distinctive central London summer smell hit her: a mixture of fast food, beer and exhaust fumes. For the first time that evening she felt the alcohol going to her head, somehow ushered on by the waning sunlight.

'Sorry about that,' she said, stepping out onto the crowded pavement – the heat wave that had baked the country for the past two weeks had really brought out the revellers. 'That was my fault – Lizzy persuaded the barman to turn the music up. Now it's so loud my eardrums feel like they're about to burst. I only noticed your call because I had my mobile out, showing Lizzy and the girls some photos from last week.'

'Em,' Will said. His serious tone made Emma check herself, as though he'd just issued her with an order. 'Where's Dan? He didn't turn up in Covent Garden, and he's not answering his mobile or your home phone.'

'What?' Emma absorbed the news as she watched a garish, white stretch limo cruise past. A group of laughing girls, heads out of the window, toasted passers-by with glasses full of champagne.

'Yee ha, cowgirl!' one of the girls shouted from the limo window. For a second Emma was confused, before remembering what she was wearing. The Wild West outfits had been Lizzy's idea. And dressing up was compulsory, especially for the bride-to-be. She took off her cowgirl hat and held it under her arm.

Will was out with a group of Dan's friends – a mixture of university mates and colleagues from the web company where Dan worked. 'We even went over to your flat,' Will continued. 'Thought he might be running late, but he's not answering the intercom. We're all standing outside there now. I also tried to reach Richard, but he's not picking up either. They're not with you lot, are they?'

'No.' Emma raked her fingers through her shoulder-length, brown, glitter-sparkled hair. Richard, Dan's brother, had been due to rendezvous with the group in the centre of town later that evening. *Why would they both be out of contact?* 'Last I saw of Dan was when I left to go out, about two hours ago. You sure you didn't miss him in Covent Garden?'

'Positive. We stuck around there for over an hour. All we needed was a tambourine and collection basket and we'd have made a fortune.'

'I don't understand,' she said, beginning to pace up and down outside the pub, suddenly forgetting the party going on inside. 'He was about to go out when I left to come here. He wouldn't have been more than a few minutes behind me.'

'It's a bloody mystery, then.' Will paused. 'You don't suppose he got cold feet, decided to head off to LA with Cameron Diaz?'

'Screw you, William.'

'Just joking,' he said with a laugh, breaking the tension. 'The man would be mad to turn down the chance to marry my little sister.'

'That's better.'

'Seriously, though, Em. What if he's had an accident or something?'

'An accident?'

'He could have been in a road accident.'

'Aren't you being a bit melodramatic?'

'Probably, but these things can happen.'

'Do you have to be such a pessimist?' said Emma, watching as two police officers attempted to cajole a homeless man from a shop doorway opposite: a sad but familiar London sight. 'He's probably stuck on the tube – that's why he can't answer his phone. You know what the Underground's been like this week. I was stuck on the Northern Line for half an hour on Wednesday. Signal failure or something.'

'Maybe,' he replied. 'I was thinking of breaking your door down, though, just in case.'

'Don't you dare! You'd hurt yourself. Anyway, I'm the black belt, not you.'

'Okay, Bruce Lee.' Will feigned disappointment. 'I'm just looking out for my little sister.'

'I know. And you always have done.'

'Hey, that's why older brothers were invented. Tell you what, I'll wait here and see if he turns up.'

'No,' Emma said, moving away from the pub door as what appeared to be another hen party pushed inside; this group was dressed as cheerleaders, with ultra-tight tops and mini-skirts. At least Lizzy hadn't gone for *that* idea. 'Go back to Covent Garden in case he turns up there. I'll try and call him myself.'

'The others can go back, but I'd rather stick around here,' insisted Will. 'This is all pretty strange, Em. You don't think—'

'Don't even say it,' Emma interrupted. 'Just don't.'

'You're right. This is totally different from last time.'

Once Will had rung off, Emma tried several times to contact both Dan and Richard. But it was no good – neither was answering their phones. She returned inside, her party spirit completely wiped out.

'Hey, there you are!' said Lizzy, throwing a semi-drunken arm around her as she returned to the group. 'Wondered where you'd got to. Thought you might have sneaked off for a crafty last snog with some hunky stockbroker before it's too late. After all, you're still twenty-eight, free and single – for the moment.'

Emma didn't meet Lizzy's smile. Instead, she looked down at her mobile phone, still grasped tightly in her hand, hardly hearing what her best friend was saying. All she wanted to do was get out of there as quickly as possible and find out what was going on.

'Get this down you,' Lizzy ordered, forcing a cocktail into Emma's free hand. 'You're far too sober for my liking. I'm in charge tonight, and whatever I say, goes. And I say drink! Cheers!'

'Cheers,' Emma said half-heartedly, clinking glasses.

She watched as a beaming Lizzy took a swig of her drink. She'd met the ever-cheerful Lizzy, a pretty strawberry blonde with a big heart and even bigger voice, at an audition three years ago. Since that initial meeting the two had become good friends and had flat-shared for a time, until eighteen months ago when Emma had moved in with Dan. A classically trained singer, Lizzy was now plying her trade on the West End stage, where she had a role in *Like We Did Last Summer*, a new romantic musical based around popular tunes from the Swinging Sixties.

'You okay?' Lizzy finally noticed that Emma seemed distracted.

'I'm not sure.' Emma played with the straw and ice cubes in her drink. 'It's Dan. He's gone missing.'

'What?'

'That was Will on the phone. He said Dan didn't turn up for the stag party. And now no one can get hold of him. I just tried to call him now. His mobile sounds like it's turned off, and there's no answer on the home phone.'

'But wasn't he about to leave when I arrived at yours?' Lizzy said.

'Yeah. That's what worries me.'

'Maybe he's stuck on the tube?' Lizzy raised an eyebrow.

'That's what I thought. But it's been two hours, Lizzy.'

'I'm sure he's fine,' Lizzy offered, lightly touching Emma's arm.

'You don't think he's had second thoughts, do you?' Emma's hitherto buried insecurities found a voice. 'You know I said he's been acting weird over the past few weeks. Maybe he's decided that I'm not what he wants.'

'Don't be silly. Dan's a great guy, and he's crazy about you, Em. Anyone can see that.' Now Lizzy squeezed her arm. 'Men act weird now and again – it's genetic. He's probably just sitting on a park bench somewhere, feeding the ducks and contemplating his final days of bachelorhood. Trust me, my brother was the same before his wedding – had some kind of crisis and thought about travelling around Australia for a year instead. And this is the guy who can't stand insects or heat.'

'I sound hysterical, don't I?' Emma smiled, taking a nervous sip from her drink. It wasn't like her to get worked up – she was usually calm and controlled. But tonight was different. The thought had been weighing on her mind for months – whether this wedding was really the start of something much better, or the point where everything fell apart at the seams.

Just like last time.

'You're under a lot of pressure,' Lizzy said. 'You're getting married a week on Sunday, for heaven's sake. Plus, you've got the biggest audition of your life coming up next week. Big things are happening, girl!'

Lizzy was right. An upcoming wedding would be enough to unsettle anyone, but adding a potentially career-making movie role audition into the equation really cranked up the tension. Emma was desperate to get the part in the new British romantic

9

comedy – it would be a major step up from the daytime soap she'd spent two years on and her recent appearances in a variety of London stage plays. It was the break she'd been working so hard for, and had never dared hope one day might arise.

'I know it'll turn out to be nothing,' she said, 'but why disappear tonight, of all nights?'

'You want to go back to the flat, check if everything's all right?'

'Would you mind?'

'Not at all.' Lizzy took Emma's drink off her and handed it to Sarah, another one of the hen party, who was sporting not just a cowgirl outfit but also a holster complete with water pistol, which she was using to fire vodka into the other hens' drinks. 'We can leave this lot here. We'll catch up with them once we've found that fiancé of yours. Bloody men, eh?' She wrapped an arm around Emma's shoulders and gave her a motherly hug. 'Always want to be the centre of attention.'

'Yeah,' Emma said, trying her best to smile. 'Bloody men.'

During the taxi ride to Marylebone, Emma tried Dan's mobile another three times. Each time the phone went straight through to voicemail. She also called Will, who confirmed that Dan still hadn't appeared or answered the intercom.

As the taxi twisted and turned through the bustling streets of the capital, a sickening feeling of loneliness swelled inside her, refusing to go away. 'Please, God,' she whispered to herself, resting her forehead against the taxi window, trying to stop her mind from racing. 'Please don't let it happen again.'

2

'Still nothing?' Emma asked, as she climbed out of the taxi and approached Will.

Will was sitting on the apartment block steps with his arms folded. He was wearing black Calvin Klein trousers and a bright white shirt that contrasted dramatically with his thick, dark hair. He shook his head. Although he was only a few months short of thirty, he looked like a little boy waiting for Mummy to come home.

'I'm sure there's a perfectly reasonable explanation, Em,' Lizzy said, joining them as the taxi drove off.

Emma looked up at the top window of their rented flat, which overlooked Marylebone High Street. For a second she thought she saw a figure looking back at her, but decided it was just a trick of the light. She'd calmed down a lot during the taxi ride – the circular breathing taught to her by her karate instructor when she was a youngster had helped her refocus away from those overly negative thoughts. Okay, it was weird, Dan not turning up. But, as Lizzy said, the likeliest thing was that there would be a perfectly reasonable explanation.

'She's right.' Will got up from the steps and dusted himself down. 'I was thinking about it while you were on your way over here. I'm over-reacting. And if it wasn't for that bloody intercom security system, I'd have been able to go up there and check for myself.'

'Couldn't you have sneaked in when someone came out?' Lizzy suggested.

'That was the plan,' he replied. 'But no one's come in or out since I got here. Bloody annoying. I also pressed all those buttons' – he pointed at the intercom on the wall – 'but nobody answered.'

'It's deserted in there at the moment,' Emma explained, searching in her bag for her keys. 'A lot of people are on holiday, I think – I've hardly seen anyone on the stairs in the last couple of days, and the post is building up.'

'Someone's in there, though,' Will countered. 'You can hear music when you open the letterbox.'

'Really?' Emma found the keys. 'We'd better get inside and take a look.' She pulled out her keys but as she did so, they slipped from her grasp and fell into the gutter, narrowly missing a drain.

Will picked them up. 'That was lucky. Hey, Em, your hands are shaking – are you okay?'

'I'm fine,' Emma lied, taking the keys. Although mentally she had recovered her composure, her body was still in overdrive. 'I'm just a bit on edge, that's all.'

'Come on,' Lizzy said briskly. 'Let's get up there and sort this out. He's probably flat out on the bed and has slept through the calls.'

They could hear the music as soon as they entered the foyer to the building. It seemed to be coming from one of the upper floors, travelling down the wooden staircase. Judging from the bass vibration, it sounded like it was set on maximum.

'U2, if I'm not mistaken,' Will said. 'Sounds like the band is actually up there rehearsing.'

'Dan was playing that album when I left,' Emma said, beginning to hurry up the stairs, with Will and Lizzy following close behind.

She took the steps two at a time; with each step the swirling music from above got louder. Something definitely didn't feel right about this. Her imaginings flooded back, but now they weren't about whether Dan had got cold feet – they were of something more sinister, more tragic. Maybe Dan had fallen and hit his head, and he'd been lying on the floor while she'd been out partying?

As she reached the middle floor, Mr Henderson, her elderly downstairs neighbour, blocked her path. Judging by his expression, it seemed he had been waiting for her. 'What do you think you're playing at?' he asked, poking a wrinkled, liver-spotted finger in Emma's direction.

'Excuse me?' Emma was taken aback by his unusually aggressive tone: normally he was so placid. He and his wife had been living in the flat below theirs for over twenty years, and had welcomed them with offers of help when Dan and Emma had first moved in. Emma hadn't seen much of Mrs Henderson in recent months; some time ago, while looking out of the window, she had seen her being helped into an ambulance, but she didn't know what had been wrong and felt it might seem overly nosey to ask.

'That music,' Mr Henderson said angrily, gesturing upstairs. His face was bright red and his eyes burned in a way that Emma had never seen before. 'Your boyfriend's had that on full blast ever since I got back from the shops. Edna's trying to get to sleep in here; she's not well, you know. She gets distressed easily. She was crying when I got back home, sitting in the corner of the room, covering her ears. People think just because you've got dementia that you don't matter. But she matters to me. I love her.'

Tears welled up in his eyes as his anger faded. 'Doctor says she's dying,' he added. 'Please let her rest. Please get your boyfriend to turn the music down. He won't even answer the door for me. I've been up there three times, but it hasn't done any good.'

Emma looked at Will and Lizzy, who returned anxious glances.

'Sorry,' she said, feeling desperately bad for the old man but also wanting to get to the top floor without delay. 'I'm sorry,' she said again, side-stepping him and heading for the next set of stairs, almost launching herself at the first step.

'I'll call the police if you don't turn it down,' Mr Henderson shouted, before breaking into a bronchial cough. But Emma had already turned the corner at the top of the stairs.

She reached her front door, fumbling with the keys. Dan never played music that loud, and the thought only intensified her sense of foreboding about what lay inside.

'Dan!' she shouted. 'Are you in there?' The key wasn't going into the lock, so she began banging on the heavy wooden door with her fists. 'Dan!'

'Come here, Em,' Will said, taking the keys gently from her. 'Let me do it.'

Emma stepped back, surprised to find that she was crying.

Lizzy hugged her. 'Everything's going to be all right,' she said. But she didn't sound convinced any more.

Will unlocked the door and a crescendo of guitars and drums swept out onto the landing. 'Danny, you in here?' he shouted, moving into the flat. He turned left towards the living room from where the music was coming, while Emma and Lizzy headed for the kitchen.

'Dan?' Emma neared the kitchen. 'Where are . . . oh my God!'

'What is it?' Will shouted, his voice sounding even louder in the silence after he'd turned off the stereo.

'Something's wrong,' Lizzy replied.

Emma stood next to her in stunned silence, taking in the scene. She placed a steadying hand against the fridge-freezer. The kitchen was smashed up: broken plates and dishes littered the floor, the bin had been overturned and emptied, the blinds were half torn down, and the water was running in the sink.

'My God,' Will said, as he appeared breathlessly at their shoulders and surveyed the damage.

'What the hell's happened?' Lizzy asked, of no one in particular.

'The other rooms,' Emma said, pulling herself out of her shock.

She turned and headed for the bedroom, flinging open the door, expecting to find something horrible inside. But there was nothing. The bed was immaculately made, just as she had left it; everything was in its right place. A faint hint of Dan's aftershave hung in the air. Emma turned to head for the bathroom, the last remaining room of the flat.

'Oh, shit!' she heard Will shout from behind her. 'Shit! Call an ambulance! Somebody get an ambulance!'

'What's wrong?' Emma rushed out into the hallway.

Will appeared from the bathroom, his hands covered in blood.

'Oh, no,' she said, covering her mouth and shaking her head. She backed against the wall. 'Please say he's okay.'

'It's not Dan.' Will's face was pained as he held his blood-soaked hands out in front of him. 'It's Richard. I think he's dead.'

3

'Do you think Dan did that to Richard?' Emma asked, as the three of them sat in the hospital waiting area.

Ever since they had found Richard, Dan's brother, unconscious on the bathroom floor, his head and face bloodied and battered, Emma had been desperate to ask that question. But she had been afraid of what the other two might say.

Lizzy hadn't said anything, either in the flat while they waited for the paramedics to arrive, or in the taxi on the way to the hospital. Will hadn't commented either, but Emma knew him well enough to sense that something was troubling him.

'No, no, of course not,' Lizzy said, snapping out of her reverie. 'Dan couldn't have done something like that.'

Will sat with his head resting in his hands, staring blankly into space.

'Will,' Emma said, noticing his silence. 'You don't think he did it?'

'I don't know what to think,' admitted Will.

'Dan would never hurt Richard!' Emma said, turning on him. 'Dan always says they've never fought in their lives. They couldn't be closer.'

'Could you try and keep the noise down, please,' said a passing nurse. 'We've got patients who are trying to sleep.'

Emma apologised, feeling suitably chastened.

'I'm sorry, Em,' Will said, 'but it doesn't look good, that's all.'

As much as Emma hated to admit it, Will was right – it didn't look good. The paramedics had made it pretty clear to the arriving police that they believed Richard had been attacked, rather than just falling and hitting his head. The injuries indicated that someone had used a blunt instrument, and had smashed it into his head more than once. It was no accident. And Dan had now disappeared. It was little wonder that most of the police questioning at the scene had centred on Dan's likely whereabouts, and the relationship between him and his brother.

'He couldn't have done it.' Emma refused to believe that the man she had fallen in love with could be capable of carrying out such a violent attack. 'I can't believe you'd ever think he could.'

'I hope you're right,' Will said. 'I really do.'

'I am right. I believe in him.'

A tense silence descended for a few seconds.

'Do you think the police will want to talk to us again?' Lizzy asked.

'They'll definitely want to talk to us in more detail,' Will said. 'Those were just preliminary questions before. We're talking about possible attempted murder here – or even murder.'

'I really thought he *was* dead back there,' Lizzy said, reflectively. 'When you couldn't find a pulse, and there was all that blood, I thought that was it.'

'I can't get those images out of my head – of Richard lying there against the bath,' said Will. 'The way his head was twisted. I thought he'd broken his neck. You never expect to experience something like that. Thank God the paramedics got there so quickly.'

'You saved his life,' Emma said, 'doing the first aid.'

'I'm not sure I did anything, really.' Will deflected the compliment. 'But at least he's got a chance now.'

Emma touched Will's arm. 'Sorry I shouted at you just now. None of us are thinking straight.'

'Don't worry about it, Em. I probably deserved it. Look' – Will got to his feet and exhaled – 'I'm going to nip outside, call the others and let them know that the celebrations are on hold. They'll be wondering where we've got to.'

'What are you going to say?' Emma asked.

'I don't know,' Will admitted. 'That there's been an accident?'

'Just don't tell them where we are. I don't think the hospital would appreciate cowgirls and stags descending on the ward. And, anyway, I couldn't handle it, not yet. Not until I've had time to let this all sink in.'

'Understood,' Will replied. 'I'll be suitably vague.'

Emma nodded her thanks.

'I won't be long,' he said, 'and hopefully you'll have had some good news by the time I get back.'

'I hope so,' Emma replied.

'Will's been gone a while.' Emma watched a team of medics wheel past an elderly man, an oxygen mask held over his face. The man seemed to look right at her, as if trying to communicate something with his watery eyes. The smells and sounds of the hospital took her back again to a time she had tried to forget, and she shivered.

'Twenty minutes,' Lizzy confirmed. 'Maybe he's having trouble getting in touch with the others.'

'Maybe,' Emma said, as the man on the trolley disappeared around the corner. She looked at her friend. 'I really hate these places. It just brings back all the bad memories.'

'Of what happened to your mum?' Lizzy asked gently.

Emma nodded. 'This is the hospital where she died. I came here every day for four weeks, watching her change from being the most energetic person I ever knew into an empty shell.' She swallowed the lump that had come to her throat. 'It's hell what breast cancer can do. When she died, I said I'd never come back here. I guess I thought it would be too painful.'

'I can understand that. It's always painful being reminded that someone you love is gone, no matter how long after the event.'

'It's her birthday tomorrow.' Emma gave a painful smile at the thought. 'She would have been fifty.'

'Oh, I'm so sorry, Em.' Lizzy reached over and put a hand on her back. 'No wonder this is all bringing back bad memories. If there's anything I can do – tomorrow, that is – let me know. You need to be with people at a time like this.'

'Thanks,' Emma replied. 'Back when Mum was dying, Dan was a massive help. When Dad sank into his depression and didn't want to know, Dan stuck by me. It helped me realise just how special he is. He carried me through it all. But where *is* he?'

'He'll be back.'

'I'm really scared, Lizzy,' Emma said, lowering her voice. 'What if Dan and Richard did have a fight, and Richard fell and hit his head?' She looked at Lizzy. 'What if Dan killed Richard by mistake? I mean, I don't even know what Richard was doing there – he wasn't supposed to be going to the flat.'

'Emma,' Lizzy said, reaching across again to comfort her. 'We don't know that Richard is dead. We've got to hope for the best. And you've got to believe that Dan couldn't have done this. You said it yourself.'

'But if he didn't do it, then where is he?'

'I don't know,' Lizzy admitted.

'Emma Holden?'

Emma looked up and saw a fresh-faced man, dressed in a blue shirt, tie and smart trousers. He didn't look much older than she was. It was only the stethoscope around his neck that told her he was a doctor.

'Yes, that's me.'

'Dr Chantler.' He held out his hand. 'I'm the registrar looking after Richard.'

Emma shook his hand, her heartbeat quickening in anticipation. 'Is Richard . . . ?'

Dr Chantler maintained his poker face. 'I think it's better if we talk in private,' he said, leading the way to a small room.

'There is some good news,' he began, once they had all sat down. He was perching on the very edge of his chair, leaning forwards and glancing at the door every few seconds, as if readying himself for a hasty departure.

Emma scrutinised him for clues, but his expression gave nothing away. She and Lizzy waited for a painful moment while Dr Chantler gathered his thoughts, steepling his fingers so that the point they formed touched his top lip. The air in the room was stiflingly hot and stale, and the orange plastic chairs were sticky.

'Well, Richard is alive,' announced the doctor, without a hint of celebration. 'It was touch and go for a time, but the team worked very hard and, fortunately, Richard also did his fair share of fighting, which always helps.'

'And the bad news?' Emma prompted, not really wanting to know the answer but desperate to find out everything and get it over with. She watched the doctor ready himself.

'I'm afraid the bad news is that Richard has slipped into a coma.'

'Right.' Emma wasn't surprised by the revelation. Although she'd hoped they wouldn't be that serious, the extent of Richard's injuries and the fact that he had remained unconscious throughout the journey to hospital had pointed to possible coma. At least he was still alive.

'The CT scan showed that Richard has suffered a subdural haematoma – a bleed between the surface of the skull and the brain. The pressure that this puts the brain under can lead to coma.'

'But he is going to be all right?' Lizzy asked in an anguished voice. 'He'll come out of it?'

'We've operated to remove the clot and deal with the bleeding, but we'll just have to watch and wait,' stated the doctor. 'I'm afraid it's impossible to predict what's going to happen with any certainty. But it's worth saying that a large proportion of patients recover well from coma.'

'But some never do,' Emma said flatly.

'Some never do recover, that's true,' he admitted. 'But a lot do. I know it's difficult, but you must try and be as positive as possible. The first few weeks are crucial, really.' He looked at Emma. 'I hear that Richard has no immediate family, apart from his brother?'

Emma nodded. 'His parents died when he was young.'

'Well, it's good that he's got friends to be by his side. There's plenty of research that shows patients in a coma respond to external stimuli: familiar voices, smells. You could help greatly in his recovery. As I said, just try and stay positive, even if you don't feel like it.'

'We'll be there for him,' Emma said. 'Can we see him?'

'Not just yet. He'll be in recovery for a few hours at least. But as soon as we move him, we'll let you know.'

Will watched from the hospital car park as an ambulance swung into the drop-off area. The back opened and a young woman was rushed into the hospital on a stretcher – yet another human being with their life in the hands of strangers.

He took a last, long drag on his cigarette before dropping it to the ground and stamping it out. He hadn't had a cigarette in over a year, but he'd needed one tonight. Looking up at the clear night sky, he tried to spot the Orion constellation. His father had shown him it when he was little, during a camping trip in the Lake District. But here in the city, light pollution obscured the celestial view.

He thought back to the item he had found next to Richard's body.

What the hell am I going to tell her?

Pulling out his mobile, he pressed the speed dial button and took a steadying breath, feeling light-headed and nauseous.

The phone was answered on the second ring.

'Hi, it's me – Will,' he said, leaning back against the wall of the hospital for support. 'Something terrible's happened. And I don't know what the hell I'm going to do about it.'

4

He had watched from across the road, sunk down in his car seat, as the ambulance arrived. Emma had looked so vulnerable, tears flowing down her cheeks, as she was comforted by that back-stabbing brother of hers. How he had longed to move closer. But he knew that now wasn't the right time. Things had to be planned carefully – they couldn't be rushed.

Now, back in the house, he entered the living room and picked up the photograph.

'Don't worry, Em,' he said to the image.'Everything is going to be okay.'

'Will, where've you been?' Emma said, as her brother appeared from around the corner of the hospital waiting area. It had been over an hour since Will had left. He looked exhausted.

'I went for a walk.'Will slumped into the seat beside her with a thud. 'I didn't plan to, but I just ended up walking off down the road. Before I knew it, I was up near Euston Station.You know, I never realised just how many really strange people there are around the streets of London – maybe I'm just on edge, but it didn't feel safe out there. If it wasn't a homeless guy, it was a potential drug dealer or mugger.Then, on the way back, I nearly walked under a bus – think I was in some kind of trance.'

'You do look pretty rough,' Lizzy commented.

'Thanks,' he said, deadpan, staring at the ceiling.

'Have you been smoking?' Emma asked, sniffing the air.

'Busted. I only had the one, though – I succumbed to tempta-tion but then threw the rest of the packet in the bin. Promise.' He did a mock Cub Scout salute.

'You got hold of the others okay?' Emma said, letting the cigarette issue drop.

'Yeah,' he replied, still looking up at the ceiling. 'It took me a while to get any sense out of them – both groups are pretty drunk, of course. They thought it was all a big wind-up at first. Sorry, Em, but I ended up having to tell them the truth. Well, as much as we know, anyway.'

'That's okay,' Emma replied. 'They had to find out sometime.'

'They wanted to come to the hospital, but I told them there're enough drunks here already in A&E. Now everyone's going home.'

'You did the best thing,' Emma said. 'We can keep them up to date with what's happening from here.'

'No news about Richard, then?' Will rubbed his eyes as if he were trying to scoop out his eyeballs.

'There is,' Emma replied. 'The doctor came along before. He's alive, but he's in a coma.'

'Shit.' Will shook his head. 'Is he going to be okay?'

'They said they're still doing tests and won't know how bad it is for a while yet. The doctor said something about a bleed on the brain.'

'Bloody hell.' Will blew out a gust of air from deep in his lungs. 'You know, even though it didn't look good, I thought he was going to be all right. I thought we might have done enough.'

'The doctor said there was every chance,' Lizzy said.

'I hope so,' Will said. 'I really do. And I assume you haven't heard from Dan yet?'

Emma shook her head.

'Come here, sis.' Will put an arm around her and pulled her close. 'No matter what happens, we'll be here for you.'

'Like last time,' Emma muttered.

'Yeah,' he said. 'Like last time.'

'Emma, wake up,' Lizzy said. 'They've brought Richard back from recovery.'

Emma opened her brown eyes. It took a few seconds for

reality to break through. She glanced around, first at Lizzy, then at the hospital reception desk opposite, where a couple of nurses were filling out forms. Realising where she was, and why, was a terrible feeling.

'What time is it?' she asked, kneading her stiff back.

'Nearly one o'clock in the morning,' said Will, flattening down strands of hair at the back of his head – a sure sign that he, too, had been unable to stay awake.

'By now, we should officially have been completely plastered in one of London's tackiest nightclubs, dancing to Kylie,' Lizzy said. 'I had it all planned.'

'I know,' Emma said, 'you worked so hard. Where's Richard?'

'A nurse just came by,' Lizzy replied. 'She said we can go in and see him. They've put him in the private room over there.' She pointed to a door quite close to where they were sitting.

'Did they say how he is?' Emma stood up.

Lizzy shook her head. 'She didn't say anything.'

But the nurse hadn't had to say anything – just one look at Richard lying in the bed, hooked up to a ventilator that controlled his breathing, told its own story.

In many ways he looked more ill now than he had done back at the apartment: his head was bandaged, hiding the injury and subsequent operation, and his face was ashen.

'Can he hear things?' Emma asked the nurse, a rather rotund lady in her fifties with a kindly face and a Scouse accent.

As Emma approached the bed, she half expected his closed eyes to snap open like in a horror movie. But of course they didn't.

'We don't know, really,' the nurse admitted. 'But people who have come out of coma do say that they remember things from when they were unconscious, so it's always better to assume that they can hear everything you say. We recommend that all conversation in the room includes everyone, don't we, Richard?'

'Sorry,' Emma said. 'I didn't realise.'

'It's okay,' the nurse said. 'You'll find it strange at first, but you'll get used to it.'

'How long have we got with, um, Richard?'

'You can have five minutes, but then I'm afraid the doctor will need to come back in. Sorry.'

'That's okay.' Emma stepped close to the bed and grasped the handrail that ran all the way around it; Lizzy paused just behind her, while Will stood at the foot of the bed, his face solemn. 'It's just good to see him.'

'I'll leave you to it,' replied the nurse, leaving the room.

'Thanks,' Emma said, keeping her gaze on the motionless figure in the bed. 'Hi, Richard,' she said. Despite talking to someone who was unconscious, she didn't feel at all awkward. It was as if Richard was awake and alert, listening to every word, making eye contact. 'It's good to see you. We thought you might be—'

Suddenly, unexpectedly, she broke down.

'It's okay, Emma,' Lizzy said, but her voice was also cracking with emotion and she had tears in her eyes.

'Maybe this isn't such a good idea,' Will said, still keeping his distance at the bottom of the bed, as if Richard were infectious. 'Maybe we should come back tomorrow. It's been a tough day for all of us.'

Emma turned to look at Will and held his gaze. He was right. There was too much going on in her head, too many thoughts swimming around.

What happened to Richard?

Where is Dan?

Did Dan . . . ?

'You're right,' she agreed. 'We'll go.' She turned back to Richard. 'We'll see you first thing tomorrow,' she promised. She placed a hand on his cheek and held it there for a few seconds. His skin was worryingly cold.

Richard was going to be Dan's best man.

What the hell has gone so wrong?

'Thanks for letting us see him,' Emma said, as they walked back past the nursing station.

The nurse who had accompanied them into Richard's room looked up from the desk. 'That's okay. It was the least you deserved after waiting there for so long.' She smiled kindly. 'It's not as bad as you think. I've been working here for nearly twenty years and I've lost count of the number of people who weren't really given a chance, but then recovered against all the odds. I always used to wonder why people who have the worst injuries recover, while some who don't seem as badly hurt don't make it. And do you know what I realised?'

'What?'

'That love can make the difference between life and death. I realise it sounds sentimental, but I *know*. I've seen how powerful love can be. And that's why having you there is so important for Richard. It's just a shame that his brother couldn't be here, too.'

Emma kept quiet, wondering whether the police had told the nursing staff about the circumstances surrounding Richard's condition, and Dan's possible role in it.

'He called about five minutes ago,' the nurse continued, 'to ask how Richard was. Must be hard for him being so far away from home at a time like this.'

'Far away?' Emma queried, confused. She was having trouble grasping this sudden turn of events.

'He's out of the country on business, isn't he?'

'Are you sure it was Dan who called?' Emma asked, desperately.

'That's what he said.'

'Did he say anything else? Did he pass on any messages to us?' Emma's head was spinning with possibilities.

'He just told me to tell you that he was sorry,' said the nurse. 'He was sorry that he couldn't be there with you all.'

5

'Thanks, Lizzy,' Emma said, as her friend handed her a cup of tea. 'It's lovely of you letting me stay here. I just can't face going back to the flat. Not yet.'

'It's no problem, really,' Lizzy replied, sitting down on the sofa next to Emma. Lizzy brushed back her own hair around her ear. The new, shorter, bob cut suited her, Emma thought. It made her look older, but in a good way. 'It's nice having you back here. Pity it's under these circumstances, though.'

'I know.' Emma stared into the tea and let the steam drift up into her face.

It was Sunday morning, more than twenty-four hours since they had found Richard nearly dead in her flat. They had returned to the hospital on Saturday, as promised, and Emma had stayed there for most of the day, watching Richard. They had also spoken to the doctors – thankfully there hadn't been any further internal bleeding. And although they still couldn't say whether he was going to be okay, their tone seemed more positive.

'Sleep any better?' Lizzy asked.

'Not really,' Emma admitted. 'I must have woken up over twenty times – I probably slept for about three hours or so in total. Every time I woke up, I just kept replaying seeing Richard in the flat and the hospital. In the end I came in here and watched some telly.'

'I didn't hear you,' Lizzy said. 'You should have woken me. I'd have kept you company.'

'I didn't want to ruin your sleep as well.'

'Nonsense. Next time, wake me up. I'll expect you to make the hot chocolate, though.'

They smiled at each other, the kind of smile that only happened at times of anxiety.

'Emma,' Lizzy said, tucking her legs under her body, 'what do you think really happened?'

Emma shook her head. 'I really don't know. But I still can't believe that Dan would hurt Richard. Like I said, they've always been more like best friends than brothers. I just can't imagine any way they'd fight.'

An uncomfortable silence fell.

'I've been thinking about what the nurse said,' Lizzy mused. 'About Dan calling the hospital to see how Richard was. Why doesn't he just get in touch with us, if he really is innocent? I don't mean that I think he did do it,' she added quickly, 'but it just doesn't make sense.'

'Maybe he's afraid of what we might be thinking,' Emma offered, not admitting that she had thought the very same thing ever since the revelation that Dan had called the hospital.

'Or maybe he's hiding from the person who really did that to Richard?'

'I've thought that, too,' Emma said. 'Maybe they'd got into some kind of trouble – I don't know, gambling or something, and someone came looking for them.'

'Dan was a gambler?'

'No, but maybe Richard was. Oh, I don't know.' Emma shook her head in exasperation. 'I still can't believe that this is happening.'

Lizzy shifted on the sofa; she clearly had something more on her mind. 'Emma, just tell me to back off for being insensitive, but I was wondering what you're planning to do about your second reading, your second audition, tomorrow.'

Emma exhaled. 'I can't go. Not while Dan's still missing and Richard is in hospital. I just couldn't do it; it would be so selfish.'

'I understand,' said Lizzy, taking a sip of her tea.

'You think I should go to it?' Emma asked, reading her friend's face.

'Well, it's a fantastic opportunity,' Lizzy said, slowly. 'After all these years of hard work, it's what you've always wanted, always dreamt of – having Guy Roberts, the famous casting director' – she rolled her eyes and waggled her hands in a showbizzy fashion at Emma, who gave a weak chuckle – 'call out of the blue and ask you to come for an audition for a potentially blockbusting movie. And to think that someone actually recommended you to him for the part! It's amazing! So it's a real shame to turn your back on something that could change your life.'

'But—?'

'But,' Lizzy continued, 'I think that you're doing the right thing.'

'Thanks, Lizzy.' Emma smiled gratefully. 'I don't know what I'd do without you.'

Will woke up with one hell of a hangover, courtesy of a bottle of Jack Daniel's. He'd spent the evening drinking in front of the TV and had fallen asleep fully clothed on the sofa. Although he'd woken up several times since, he hadn't had the balance, energy or inclination to make his way to the bedroom. Now, he struggled to his feet and staggered towards the window. Pulling open the curtains, the shock of early-morning sunlight set off what felt like a nuclear bomb in his head.

Turning back towards the living room, grimacing at the sour taste in his mouth, he focused on the photograph lying on the table.

Why didn't I tell her about it when I had the chance?

Somehow he'd managed to regain his composure in the hospital, even joking with Emma and Lizzy. And the phone call from Dan had seemed to indicate that maybe it wasn't all as he feared.

But who was to say that the person calling really had been Dan?

He moved over and picked up the photo.

'If you had anything to do with this, I swear I'll kill you,' he said, his eyes burning at the man in the shot.

Will showered, dressed and headed outside into the sunshine, needing to escape the stale smell of alcohol that seemed to have soaked into every part of the flat. He decided to head towards Regent's Park – maybe amongst the crowds of picnickers and sunbathers he could try and forget about the mess he had got himself into, if only for a couple of hours.

'What did he say?' Lizzy asked, as Emma replaced the handset. 'Was he okay about it?'

'Surprisingly nice,' Emma replied, not quite believing what the casting director Guy Roberts had just said to her. 'He said he understood why I'd decided not to go, but he was really disappointed as I'd been the standout candidate from the first reading. He also said that I have real talent.'

'Wow, Emma, that's great! And you said there were loads of people going for the part.'

'He probably says that to everyone.'

'No way. Why would he? People like him have got enough wannabe actors bothering them without encouraging people who aren't good enough. I'm so proud of you!' Lizzy enveloped Emma in a congratulatory hug.

'Thanks,' Emma said, 'but it's not really important now, is it?'

'I guess not,' conceded Lizzy, pulling away. 'Not right now, anyway. But everything will work itself out, Em, I'm sure of it. Then maybe you can contact this guy later, see what else he's working on. If he likes you that much, he'll be interested in seeing you again for another part.'

'Maybe.'

'Let's get out of here.' Lizzy was trying hard to sound cheerful. 'You need to take a walk, have some time away from that hospital. We'll go and get a coffee or something.'

'Okay,' Emma said. 'That'll be nice.'

Just then her mobile rang.

She spun around, looking for the phone, and saw it on top of the breakfast table. As she dashed over to get it her heart leapt when she saw the caller ID.

It was Dan.

'It's him,' she shouted, hope filling her voice as she grabbed the phone. 'Dan, where are you, are you okay?' she spluttered, not giving him a chance to say a word.

She forced herself to stop talking and listen, but was met with silence.

'Dan, are you there?'

Again there was nothing.

'Dan?'

Then the line went dead.

She looked across at Lizzy, a million thoughts chasing through her head, but before she had a chance to say anything the phone rang again.

'Dan?' she said.

'Hi, is that Emma Holden?' a deep, male voice asked.

'Yes, yes,' she replied, taken aback by the fact that it wasn't Dan on the other end of the line.

'Detective Inspector Mark Gasnier here. I'm part of the team investigating the serious assault on Richard Carlton. I was hoping to speak to you today . . . ?'

'Sure,' she said, meeting Lizzy's concerned gaze.

'Is this morning okay?'

'That's fine. Do you want me to come down to a police station?'

'That won't be necessary. We'll come over to you.'

He stood on the opposite side of the street, looking up at the window of the flat. It had been risky to call, especially while he had been standing only metres away, but he just had to hear her voice, if only for a few seconds.

He could sense the anxiety, the desperation.

It was all worth it.

A double-decker rumbled past, its sides plastered with an advertisement for *Buddy: The Buddy Holly Story*, and briefly obscured his view. He took one last look at the flat before heading for the tube, making his way towards the hospital.

6

Will sat down on the grass, closed his eyes and let the warmth from the sun bathe his face. A gentle breeze wafted his shirt, and amongst the shouts and laughter of fellow visitors he could hear birdsong. He had been wandering around a bustling, vibrant Regent's Park for more than an hour, already completing a couple of circuits. He knew what had brought him here – this place harked back to happier times. It was the place his parents had taken him to, when he and Emma were children – he'd seen the photos, with the four of them sprawled out on a picnic blanket, surrounded by treats.

Even Dad had looked happy in those days.

He lay there for a few minutes, watching the brightness of the underside of his eyelids. But he couldn't just shut out the world and its problems.

He opened his eyes and scanned the park. The sun had really brought out the crowds, especially the families. The park was one huge playground, with kids running around, playing football and tag. He focused on a small boy who was trying to launch a kite, but there really wasn't enough wind, and the kite kept crashing down and bouncing along the ground.

As he watched the boy pick up the kite to try again, he saw the man, sitting on the grass, looking in his direction. The hairs on the back of Will's neck bristled, and his pulse quickened.

It can't be.

He stared across at the figure, who still seemed to be staring back. It was just too far away to make out the man's face properly.

Will's first reaction was to turn and run, or at the very least pretend he hadn't noticed the attention. But then he was over-come by anger. Anger at what had happened to Richard, and to Emma. Instead, he stood up and began striding towards him, dodging kids as they weaved across his path.

By the time he reached the man, the guy had his back to him, sitting on the grass, leaning on his hands.

'What the hell are you doing here?' Will demanded. 'Are you following me?'

The man turned.

'Excuse me?' He looked puzzled, shielding his eyes against the sun. 'Do I know you?'

It wasn't him.

'Oh, I'm so sorry,' said Will, holding up his hands and step-ping back a couple of paces. 'I thought you were a friend,' he said, trying to explain.

'Right . . .' the man said, warily. 'That's fine. Don't worry about it.'

'Sorry,' Will said again, turning and pacing away in the oppo-site direction.

'What the hell am I doing?' he muttered to himself as he walked away, his face flushed with embarrassment. He only stopped walking once he had put enough distance between himself and the stranger. He leant against a tree and put a hand to his head.

Why did this have to happen?

He thought back to how the man had looked at him. As if he were some kind of maniac, ready to pull out a knife and attack him.

My God, he was really cracking up.

Then his thoughts turned to Emma and, not for the first time, he felt intense, painful shame. She thought he was the perfect brother, the one who had supported her through every-thing. And he had revelled in playing that part.

'You're a bloody impostor,' he shouted to himself, just as a family with two young children walked around the corner. The father shot him a glance.

'Come on, kids,' he said, shepherding them away from Will. 'Let's go over to the zoo.'

'Yay, Daddy!' the little girl shouted excitedly, tugging at her father's trousers. 'Can we see the monkeys?'

'Sure we can,' he said, ruffling her hair.

'Yes!' she said, jumping up and down on the spot. 'I love monkeys!'

Will watched them as they walked away, the two children leading from the front, unable to curb their enthusiasm, the man and woman holding hands just behind. Faced with a scene of such love, Will felt lonelier than he had ever felt in his entire life.

But, worst of all, he realised with disgust, he was beginning to empathise with the man who had caused all these problems. 'Please,' he said, looking up into the deep blue sky, 'don't let me become like him.'

'Emma?' the man at the door said.

Emma nodded.

'Detective Inspector Mark Gasnier,' he continued, holding out a hand and flashing a surprisingly white, movie-star smile.

'Hi.' Emma took his hand and met his firm but fair grip. The guy certainly wasn't what she had expected. He was a towering figure, his hair gypsy black and his skin summer-tanned. She'd expected someone scruffy, even hangdog, but this guy was wearing a designer suit.

'This is Detective Sergeant Christian Davies,' added Gasnier, nodding towards his companion.

'Pleased to meet you,' said Davies, also shaking hands. He was at least a foot shorter than his partner, rounder in stature, with a fatter face and cheeks ruddy from the sun. They looked quite an odd pairing.

Emma smiled and waited.

'So, can we come in?' asked Gasnier, smiling again. This time it seemed more businesslike than friendly.

'Oh, sure, yes, come on in,' Emma said, embarrassed that she had forgotten herself. She led them into the living room, where Lizzy was waiting nervously on the sofa.

'Hi,' Lizzy said, getting up to welcome them. 'Would you like a drink? Tea, coffee?'

'It's okay,' Gasnier replied, sitting down without invitation. 'We've just had one back at the station. And we won't be here for long, you'll be glad to hear.'

Lizzy smiled nervously. She'd never been involved with the police before; she'd never even so much as spoken to a policeman in her life. But now she had two detectives from the Met sitting in her flat. It was just too crazy.

Emma joined Lizzy on the sofa, facing the two officers. Gasnier, with his long frame, made the sofa look toy-size.

'This must be a really difficult time,' he began, looking across at Emma.

She stared straight back at him, noticing that his eyes were an unusually pale blue, as if someone had inserted two tinted marbles into the place where his eyes should have been.

'I hear that you're due to be married in a week or so.'

Emma was surprised by the start of the discussion, and could only manage a nod.

Gasnier looked down at his notebook. 'We've got a lot of details here from the preliminary questioning. I hope the police constable treated you well?'

'Yes, he was very nice,' Emma replied.

'Good to hear it,' he replied with a grin. 'That was my nephew.'

'Oh, right.'

'I tried to persuade him not to go into the force, but he wouldn't listen. He'll learn, though.'

Davies bit back a smile, but Gasnier's comment seemed more like an accidentally voiced internal thought than a genuine attempt at humour.

'You said that you last saw Dan when?' asked Gasnier, getting back to the questioning.

'It was about seven. Seven o'clock on Friday, just before I went out.'

'To . . . ?'

'To my hen party. Well, we were going to have a night out in London – me and some friends.'

'And when did you notice that something was wrong?'

'I got a call from my brother, Will. He said that Dan hadn't turned up for the stag do. So we all went back to the flat to see if we could find him.'

'All?' Gasnier said, raising an eyebrow.

'Lizzy and me.' Emma gestured to the silent Lizzy. 'Will was already there, waiting for us.'

'Your brother was already at the flat?'

'Yes.'

'Talk me through what happened next.' Gasnier sat back and folded his arms.

'Well,' began Emma, 'we went into the hallway to the apartments and we could hear music playing from upstairs. When we got to the top we realised it was coming from my flat, so we went in looking for Dan. And that's when we found Richard, in the bathroom. We thought he was dead at first, but Will did some first aid on him until the ambulance arrived.'

Gasnier paused, looking unblinkingly at Emma. It was as if he was trying to read her, deciding whether she was telling the truth.

'How was Dan in the days, weeks before he disappeared?'

'Okay,' she said. 'A bit on edge really, but we both were, what with the wedding coming up.'

'Does Dan have any enemies that you know of?'

'No. At least, I don't think so.'

'No one with a grudge – an ex-girlfriend, someone who he owed money to?'

'Not that I know of.'

'Have you ever suspected Dan might be having an affair?'

'Never,' Emma said, aware that she was perhaps sounding a bit too defensive.

'I'm sure you're right,' Gasnier said. 'But I have to ask, you understand. So there's no reason you know of to explain why he might want to just get up and leave without saying anything to anyone?'

'No.'

Emma resisted the temptation to say what she feared: that he had left because he didn't want to marry her.

'Are Dan and Richard close?'

'They're really good friends. Richard was going to be Dan's best man.'

'Was Richard at your flat before you left to go out?'

'No.'

'Did you know Richard was coming over to the flat?'

'No, I didn't.'

'But he was coming to the stag party?'

'He was supposed to be meeting them all later in the centre of town.'

'So what changed?'

'I don't know.'

'Who do you think attacked Richard, Emma?'

'I don't know.' She looked at him in mute appeal. 'Maybe someone broke into the flat looking for money. We've had some problems around here with druggies.'

'You don't believe Dan did it?'

'No, I don't.'

'You do realise that we are treating the attack on Richard as attempted murder?' Gasnier asked. 'And if Richard does die, this will become a murder investigation?'

'I realise that, yes.'

'So if you know anything, anything at all that might help with this investigation, then you would do well to say so now.'

'I don't know anything else,' Emma replied. 'I've told you all I know.'

Gasnier waited a beat.

'A witness has come forward,' he said. 'They saw Dan on the staircase, running away from the flat, about an hour before you arrived there and found Richard.'

7

He spent some time waiting outside the hospital entrance, watching visitors and patients going in, their faces telling a thousand stories of hope, pain and anguish.

He knew just how they felt.

When he felt ready, he entered the building and headed for the ward. He knew where Richard was; the nurse had been extremely helpful in that respect, once he had explained that he was a close family member. They'd even said he could see Richard outside the official visiting hours. And to think people criticised the NHS for being inflexible.

As he reached the ward, the nerves really kicked in. Would he be challenged? But he pushed such concerns aside. He was doing this for the right reasons, and that was enough to dispel any fears he had.

8

'They think he did it, don't they?' Emma said, looking across to Lizzy, who was sitting, staring into space, on the other end of the sofa. 'They really think Dan tried to kill Richard.'

'It did sound like it.' Lizzy nodded slowly in agreement. 'But I suppose if I was in their shoes, and someone had come forward saying they saw Dan running from the flat, then I'd probably be thinking the same thing. I don't think they've got anything else to go on, apart from that witness statement.'

'But he could have been running to get away from someone else!' Emma was trying to convince herself as much as Lizzy. 'Like the person who really attacked Richard.'

'He could have been,' Lizzy said. 'The trouble is,' she went on, turning to look at Emma, 'we just don't know, do we? Nobody knows what happened, except for Dan. And he's not contacting us.'

In unison they looked at Emma's mobile, which lay silent on the table.

Emma shook her head. 'I don't understand why he would try and call, yet keep his mobile switched off.'

'Me neither.'

'It just doesn't make any sense.'

'Why didn't you tell the police that Dan called?'

'I don't know,' Emma admitted. 'I guess I thought that it might make them even more convinced that Dan was guilty.'

'I can understand that.'

'You think I should have told them?'

'I think it's a bit weird that you didn't.'

Emma nodded. 'You're probably right, but it's too late now. If

I told them, they'd wonder why I'd kept it from them in the first place.'

'But what if telling the police about Dan's call might actually help?'

'How?'

'I don't know, maybe they could trace his mobile or something.'

'But maybe telling the police isn't the right thing to do?' Emma responded. 'Dan must have run for a reason – what if telling the police makes things worse? I mean, they're not really concerned about Dan's safety, are they?'

'You didn't like that Gasnier guy, did you?' Lizzy looked with concern at her friend.

'Not really. There was something about him, something that really grated.'

'Actually, I didn't particularly like Gasnier. He came across as being arrogant. And I really don't like arrogance.'

'It was the way he made it look like I was protecting Dan.'

'But you are,' Lizzy said.

That home truth stopped the conversation dead; they spent a minute or so contemplating the situation in the kind of silence that seems deafeningly loud.

'I'm getting worried,' Emma admitted, breaking the quiet. 'I still don't think Dan could have done this, but the more I find out, the less sure I'm getting.'

'It's understandable.'

'I mean . . .' – Emma's words suddenly stuck in her throat – 'I haven't exactly made the best choice of boyfriends in the past.'

'You mean Stuart?' Lizzy ventured.

Emma nodded.

'You've never said much about what happened between you two.'

'It's something I want to forget, really. I don't think it's healthy to wallow in the past. What happened with Stuart is ancient history.'

'But you're afraid of . . .'

41

'Dan is different to Stuart,' Emma said abruptly. 'I know what you're getting at – the fact that Stuart and I were engaged and then he just upped and left. But it's such a different situation, Lizzy. When Stuart left me, it wasn't a surprise – it was more of a relief, really. I could see it coming for months – ever since we'd moved down to London. Dan is different. He's never showed any signs of wanting to end our relationship.'

'Who do you think it was that saw Dan running away?' Lizzy asked now, slipping out of her sandals and putting her bare feet up on the table.

'Could have been anyone. Maybe it was someone passing by on the street, someone who lives in the building, a visitor?'

'It would be good to know who the witness was, and exactly what they saw, wouldn't it?'

'It would,' Emma said. 'It would be good to know anything that could help to explain all this. Maybe then I'd be able to start thinking straight.' She looked at her friend. 'Lizzy, will you go over there with me?'

'Pardon?'

'The police said I can go back to the flat, now they've concluded their forensic investigations. Will you come over with me? I need to go over there. We might find something to explain what happened.'

'But the police have already searched the place.'

'I know, but they might have missed something. There might be something personal that only I know is important.'

'You sure you're ready to go back there?' Lizzy looked at her doubtfully.

'I can't say I'm looking forward to it,' Emma admitted, 'but if it helps to find Dan, and clear his name, then it's worth it.'

'This might be harder than I thought,' Emma said, as they arrived. It seemed much longer than two days since they had been standing on the pavement outside the building, wondering where Dan was.

'We don't have to do this,' Lizzy said, standing by her side. 'We can still leave and come back when you feel ready.'

Emma mustered up some courage. 'No, it's okay. If I don't go in there now, I'll regret it later.'

She looked up at her window, and noticed the curtains twitch on the floor below: the Hendersons' flat.

Lizzy had also noticed. 'We're being watched.'

'Looks like it,' Emma agreed, steeling herself for the journey inside.

They made their way up the stairs, memories still fresh in Emma's mind of how they had run up there two days previously, music blaring in the background. She was so lost in reminiscence that the sight of Mr Henderson waiting on the landing, just like last time, was a real shock.

'Hello,' he said, noticeably sheepish. He looked down at his battered brown shoes, a small hole visible in the front of one of them, before meeting Emma's gaze. 'I want to apologise about the other night,' he continued, clearing his throat nervously. 'About what I said. It's just that I was upset, about Edna. I'm not usually so . . . we'd just got some bad news from the specialist, you see. He says that she hasn't got long left – I don't really understand everything he told me, but that was the sum of it. She'll be gone in months, maybe weeks.'

'I'm so sorry to hear that,' Emma said gently. 'It must be really difficult.'

Mr Henderson just stood there, biting his lip. For a moment she thought he was going to break down, but he seemed to steel himself.

'I jumped to conclusions the other night,' he said. 'I should have done something.'

'It's okay,' Emma said. 'Really.'

'If I'd thought that something was wrong,' he lamented, 'I would have tried to help. I know it's not like you to play such loud music. I should have done something when he didn't answer the door. I just keep wondering if I'd done something sooner, whether it might have made a difference.'

'Really,' Emma said, trying to think how to reassure him, 'I don't think there was anything anyone could have done.'

If only she really believed that herself.

'Edna only told me what she'd seen last night,' he said, through tear-bright eyes, 'while we were watching television. At first I wasn't sure whether to believe her. Sometimes we can be sitting in front of the TV and she starts telling you stories about what she's seen or heard that day, but it just turns out to be part of the TV programme she's been watching earlier. So when she told me, I thought she'd seen it on television.'

'Sorry,' Emma said, 'I'm not sure what you're trying to say.'

'Sometimes she's quite lucid,' he said, continuing his monologue as if he hadn't heard Emma's remark. 'You wouldn't think anything was wrong with her. She talks about things that happened when she was a child, and about when we first met.' He looked at Emma, helplessly. 'All those memories are still fresh for her, you see. When she's talking about old times I forget about the dementia, and I just enjoy talking to my wife again. I have her back with me. Not just a hollow shell – the real Edna. The woman I fell in love with and married. But then she's gone again, lost in her own world, talking about the television.'

'What did Edna see?' Emma said, trying to curb her eagerness for answers, for fear she might scare him off. But it was already starting to make sense. 'Did she see Dan?' she pressed. 'Did you tell the police that she saw Dan running away from the apartment?'

'We didn't tell the police to try and get your boyfriend into trouble,' he protested. 'Please believe that. But when Edna told me what she'd seen, we felt we had to tell them everything we knew. I was going to talk to you about it, but I didn't know how to get in touch with you.'

'It's fine. I understand. You had to tell them anything that might help.'

'I'm sorry,' he said.

'What did Edna say she saw?' Lizzy asked, joining the conversation.

44

'Well,' he said, 'not a great deal, really . . .'

'Harry, where are you?'

They heard a frantic shout from within Mr Henderson's flat, and Emma knew at once that the chance for explanations had slipped away.

'Harry?'

'I'd better go and see what she wants,' he said, glancing back towards his front door. 'Won't be a second, love!' he shouted loudly.

'Is she sure that it was Dan she saw?' Emma said, trying to recover the situation.

'Harry, where are you?' shouted Mrs Henderson again.

'I really had better go,' he said. 'She needs me.'

'Please, Mr Henderson,' Emma begged, 'it's really important. The police came to see us before. They think that Dan was the one who attacked his brother. They think he tried to kill him. And I think it's mostly because of what your wife told them. So is she certain it was Dan? Or could it have been someone else? You said that she gets confused – maybe she did see someone, the person who really did this, but just not Dan.'

'I don't want to talk any more about it,' Mr Henderson replied, backing towards the door now, avoiding her gaze. 'I've told you all I know, and I really don't want Edna to be bothered about it. She can't take this kind of upset in her condition. I'm really sorry for your fiancé, and his brother. I'm sorry. I'll pray that his brother gets better.'

'Mr Henderson, *please.*' Emma's voice cracked on the last word.

But he had turned and shuffled back into his apartment.

She moved up to the doorframe, but resisted stepping inside and violating his personal space. 'Please, if there's any doubt about what your wife saw, then we really need to know about it. The police need to know.'

Mr Henderson ignored her pleas. As he went to close the door, Emma's first reaction was to put a foot in the doorway. But she decided against it.

She let him close the door in her face.

9

This was going to be a special meal, a new start. Once they had been so close, but they hadn't even spoken in the past few years, not since he had just upped and left, without so much as a goodbye.

But now he was coming home.

She had made a special trip to the butcher's in the high street, to pick up a quarter of best quality steak. It had been so long since she had cooked him a meal. The house had been so empty since he left.

But, no matter, because he had returned when she needed him the most.

When she had first heard his voice, she'd cried. He'd apologised for just disappearing the way he had, said that he had had to get away, get his head sorted. He'd been having problems with his girlfriend; she knew that, although he'd never confided in her about those sorts of things. But she'd never realised that things had got so bad – that it was this girl who had driven him away from his loved ones.

What gave her the right to drive a boy away from his mother?

At first he had called her on the telephone, ringing in the early hours. She didn't mind being woken at two or three in the morning, not for the chance to speak to him – she would have stayed up all night if that was what had had to be done. He said that he missed home. And although he was still far away – though she didn't like to ask him where he was, in case it scared him off – he promised her he would be home soon. But she wondered where he had spent all those years. What job had he been doing? Where had he been living?

Then, after numerous phone calls, he had announced that the time had come for him to return home. And that was today.

She looked at her watch; he was fifteen minutes late. What if he'd changed his mind, decided that he could do without his mother? She pushed that thought aside, bending down to the hob, checking that the meat was not overdone. She then turned the gas down and reached for her glass of wine.

She had never been much of a drinker, but this was a celebration. She emptied the glass and poured herself another, again glancing at her watch.

Where is he?

She moved out of the kitchen, through the drab living room and across to a bay window. She scanned the street, half expecting him to be standing there, just waiting to be invited in. But there was no one there.

'Please come back to me,' she whispered. 'I love you so much.'

She stared out of the window for a few minutes. Then she remembered the meal, dashing back into the kitchen. The pans had boiled dry, ruining the vegetables and potatoes, and the meat was crisping up, dry at the edges. How long had she been daydreaming?

Where is *he?*

She grabbed an empty pan from the draining board and hurled it across the kitchen. It slammed into the wall and bounced across the floor. The sound of steel against floor tile reverberated around the room, hurting her ears.

She finished another glass of wine and then reached for the knife block, pulling out a six-inch blade. She watched her own reflection in the knife, warped as though in a fairground house of mirrors, and suddenly wondered what the hell she was doing. As if shocked into sense, she abruptly pushed the knife back into the block.

He wasn't coming, and it was that stupid girl's fault.

10

'What are you thinking?' Lizzy asked, as Emma stared at the closed door.

Emma had knocked a couple of times, but didn't want to risk antagonising her neighbour too much. Now, she turned and stepped away from the door, beckoning Lizzy to the other side of the landing, out of earshot. For all she knew, Mr Henderson was standing on the other side of the door, trying to listen to them.

'I think he might be hiding something.' Emma lowered her voice. 'I might be wrong, but it just didn't seem like the full story.'

'You really think so?' Lizzy replied in a whisper, glancing over at Mr Henderson's door.

'Look how he reacted when I started asking him whether it was definitely Dan. He looked like he was hiding something – protecting his wife.'

Lizzy thought it through. 'Maybe that's all he's doing, protecting his wife. You heard what he said, about her being ill. He might just want to be left alone.'

'Maybe,' Emma conceded. 'But I can't just let things go without trying to find out for sure.'

'So what are you going to do? Kick down the door?'

'Very funny,' Emma said, meeting her smile with a small roll of the eyes.

'Sorry,' Lizzy said. 'Not the time for a joke.'

'Don't be silly. The day you lose your ability to make me laugh, I'll know that life isn't worth living.'

'So? What are you going to do?'

Emma grew serious again. 'Well, I know we can't just force our way in there. I've had enough contact with the police to last me a lifetime – I don't want to get arrested.'

'How about speaking to Mrs Henderson directly? Maybe she'll be prepared to speak about what she saw.'

Emma mused on that possibility. 'Could be worth a try. Obviously we'd have to wait until Mr Henderson goes out. But even if we do get to talk to her, she might not make much sense. And the other problem is that if Mr Henderson found out that we'd spoken to her behind his back, he'd go crazy.'

'Worth the risk, though,' Lizzy ventured. 'After all, what she told the police could get Dan sent to jail.'

'I know,' Emma acknowledged. 'You're right. But it'll have to wait. Come on,' she said, steeling herself and heading for the stairs, 'let's get this over with.'

'You sure you want to play detective?' Lizzy asked, as they stood in front of Emma's door. 'We can let the police get on with the investigation – they're used to dealing with things like this.'

Emma considered that. But they already seemed convinced that Dan was guilty, and she felt it was up to her to convince them otherwise. 'I'll be okay,' she replied, bringing the key up to the lock.

But she didn't feel okay – she felt terrified again.

'You don't know that. Who knows how you'll react to going back in there so soon after . . . well, after everything?' Lizzy put a hand on her arm. '*I*'m scared, Em, and I'm not as personally involved as you. You don't have to pretend that you're not afraid.'

Emma turned to her friend. 'I am scared, Lizzy. But I still have to do this.'

'Promise me that if it gets too much, you'll tell me, and we'll be out of there right away.' Emma nodded.

She turned the key and stepped into the flat, feeling like she was crossing some forbidden threshold.

The first thing that struck her was the temperature – despite it being warm outside, the flat was cool, almost cold. Emma didn't believe in ghosts but, as she moved into the hallway, the thought struck her that the place now had a sinister feel. The place didn't feel like her home any more – it was tainted and, for the first time, Emma wondered if she would ever live there again.

She could sense unease from Lizzy, too – she was sure she was holding her breath.

Emma flipped on the hall light switch and glanced down the passageway towards the kitchen, which was shrouded in darkness.

'You okay?' Emma said, turning around to Lizzy.

Lizzy nodded, but she looked anything but okay.

They moved towards the living room, passing the closed bathroom door.

'We won't go in there,' Emma said.

'Fine by me.' Lizzy's voice was cracking with nerves.

As they walked past the door, Emma thought for a moment that she heard a scratching sound from behind it – like someone clawing at the wood, lying stricken on the floor. But she reasoned that it was just her mind playing cruel tricks, and pushed away the irrational thought that Richard was still in there, waiting for someone to save his life.

She moved into the living room, half expecting to see Dan on the sofa, watching the football. But the sofa was unmanned, the television off. She looked around the room, but it was difficult to see clearly – the only light was leaking in through the curtains, which the police must have drawn after they had concluded their investigations.

'Looking for anything in particular?' Lizzy asked.

'Just checking to see if anything's missing – something I might have missed when we first spoke to the police.'

'You still think it might have been a burglary?'

'I know I'm clutching at straws,' Emma said, turning to her, 'but if I do find that something is missing, then it might help to explain what happened.'

She moved across to the window and threw back the curtains, letting sunshine flood in. The room looked a whole lot better. Again, she scanned the room. All the expensive equipment was where it belonged: the television, DVD player, stereo system, games console.

Satisfied, but disappointed that nothing was missing from the flat, Emma went to the bedroom to pack some extra clothes. Lizzy put the kettle on for a cup of tea, having discovered that there was still some milk in the fridge.

'Here you go,' Lizzy said, handing Emma a cup as she walked back into the living room. 'The milk is just about okay, but you might want to drink it quickly.'

'Thanks.'

'This is a nice photograph,' Lizzy noted, nodding at a photo frame she held in her hand. 'Dan looks really young there.'

'He is,' Emma said, admiring the photo Lizzy had picked up from the window sill. 'It was when he was at university. I don't know why I've always liked it so much – I didn't even know him then. Maybe that's it, though – it shows me what things were like before we met.'

Lizzy watched Emma stare into the photograph as if she were looking at some faraway object. 'You won't just have those memories. You've both got a great future.'

'I hope so,' Emma replied. 'But who knows.'

Lizzy put an arm around her. 'You and Dan will be fine.'

'I just need an explanation, Lizzy. I can't take not knowing.'

'I know.'

Emma looked up towards the television, and that's when she realised that something *was* missing.

It was a framed photo of her and Dan, which they had taken on a recent holiday to Rome. It showed them standing in St Peter's Square, the famous basilica rising in the background. Usually the photo was on top of the television, but where it had been there was now just a big, blank space.

She got up and searched behind the set, to see if it had fallen down the back, but it wasn't there.

It can't be him again, can it?

Emma moved out of the living room and hurried down the

hall towards the bedroom, the terrible thought nagging at the back of her mind.

'You okay, Emma?' asked Lizzy, following her.

'Just checking something,' she called, not slowing her pace.

This time she knew what she was looking for. She surveyed the bedside table and the wall opposite the bed. Her suspicions were confirmed.

She'd been focusing so much on the expensive items that she'd missed it completely.

'They're all gone,' she said, as Lizzy entered the bedroom. 'All the photos of Dan and me. They're gone.'

11

'Why would someone take those photos?' Lizzy asked, as they were sitting on the sofa in Emma's flat.

'I don't know. But I do know that the police will see it as more evidence that it was Dan who did that to Richard.'

'You think?'

'I can just imagine what they'll say,' Emma said, thinking back to how the detective had announced that someone had seen Dan running from the apartment. 'They'll say he took a couple of reminders of me and him, before running away.'

'They might not,' Lizzy offered.

'They will, Lizzy. You saw for yourself – they're convinced Dan did it.'

Lizzy looked at Emma, gathering herself. 'But what if he *is* guilty?'

'You can't mean that,' Emma replied, shocked at the suggestion. 'You can't think Dan could be capable of doing that!'

Lizzy turned away somewhat apologetically. 'I'm sorry, Emma, but we just don't know, do we?'

'I don't believe you. I thought you of all people would support me – and Dan.' Emma's voice was full of tears.

'I do.'

'Then don't give up on Dan, please!'

But as they sat in an uncomfortable silence, it became harder and harder for Emma to ignore the voice in her head: the voice suggesting that Dan *was* guilty.

'Look, Emma,' Lizzy said, after almost a minute of silence. 'I'm sorry. I want to believe that Dan is innocent, and I do believe it really. But there is a chance, no matter how much we don't want to think it, that Dan did do that to Richard. We just don't know what happened, do we?'

Emma couldn't find the words. To admit that she agreed with Lizzy would feel like a terrible betrayal. In a strange way, she felt that to even entertain the possibility that Dan was guilty would make it more likely to be true.

'Maybe Dan had a really good reason for doing what he did,' Lizzy continued. 'Maybe he did it in self-defence. What if Richard came round to the flat and for some reason they started to fight – I don't know why – and as they fought, Dan hit Richard just that bit too hard?'

Emma shook her head. 'No.'

'I read a story last year about a man who got into a drunken fight in a nightclub – he bumped into the back of somebody's girlfriend and the guy took offence, something like that. The guy threw one punch and the man fell and hit his head on the floor – fractured his skull. He died on the spot and the other guy was charged with manslaughter. It can be as easy as that. A trivial thing, but you catch a person in the wrong place, or they fall and bang their head in a certain way, and they end up in hospital or dead. What if that happened, for whatever reason, and Dan just panicked? You wouldn't blame him, would you? And maybe now he's hiding out, knowing that he should turn himself in, but scared of what might happen to him. It would be completely understandable, and it wouldn't make Dan a bad person.'

Lizzy waited nervously for a response, while Emma mulled over what she had just said. Part of her hated Lizzy for even suggesting that Dan might be responsible, while another part loved her friend for daring to risk their relationship by exploring all the options, no matter how painful.

'I can see where you're coming from,' Emma acknowledged, picking up the photo of Dan from the coffee table. 'And if we'd been talking about anyone else except Richard then I might believe it could be true. But,' she said, looking across at Lizzy, 'I just can't believe that Dan would ever fight with his brother. Not after what he's told me about their relationship – and not after what I've seen when they're together. They're not just brothers, Lizzy, they really are best friends.'

'Even best friends can fall out,' Lizzy responded.

'Yes,' Emma said. 'But not those two. Dan told me once how when they were on a family holiday – Dan was about eight and Richard was six – Richard was taken to hospital after falling and injuring his leg. Dan was so upset that he wouldn't leave the hospital – he stayed at his bedside for two days solid. I know that was a long time ago, Lizzy, but I don't think things have changed – Dan would be the same now as then. That's one reason why I need to go to see Richard as much as possible. Because I know that Dan would be there day and night if he could be.'

'But doesn't the fact that the photos are missing put any doubt in your mind?'

Emma shifted uneasily. She felt bad that she had never felt able to tell Lizzy about what had happened before, and what she feared may now be happening again. 'It makes me more convinced that it wasn't him.' Emma nodded to herself. 'Okay, say Dan did attack Richard, and he decided to run away. Why would he take the trouble to grab the photos above anything else? I've looked around the flat, and he hasn't taken anything else of his – clothes, bags, passport, even his wallet with all his bank cards. Of anything, those are the things that he would need if he were going on the run – not five framed photos. Whatever way you look at it, it doesn't make sense for him to have done that.'

'Okay.' Lizzy smiled, holding her hands up. 'I'm convinced. I just think you need to explore all the options.'

'I know, Lizzy, and I do appreciate it. I don't want to delude myself, but on this point I'm so sure.'

'So we still have the mystery of the missing photos,' Lizzy announced. 'Are you going to tell the police about them?'

'I will. But not right now.'

Again there was a silence, this time interrupted by Lizzy's mobile phone. As she answered the call, wandering into the hall clutching the phone to her ear, Emma climbed off the sofa and moved across to the window. She looked down at the busy high street below – business people strode past at London pace, while tourists ambled by, moving in and out of shop fronts.

Then, for a horrible second, she thought she saw *him*, peering up at her from across the road, a camera dangling from a strap slung around his neck.

It *couldn't* be him, could it?

Instinctively, she twisted out of view. And for a few seconds she just stood there, flattened against the wall, her heart racing.

She could hear Lizzy talking in the kitchen but it seemed so far away. Thoughts ran through her head, of a time when she'd never felt safe, of a time that she'd tried her best to forget.

But then she scolded herself for being silly. Breathless, she edged out from behind the wall and gazed out of the window again. Where she thought he'd been standing was a middle-aged man in a smart suit reading a newspaper.

It was just her imagination, playing tricks again.

Then she did see someone she recognised. Mr Henderson had exited the apartment building and was walking off down the street, pulling a wheeled shopping bag behind him. She watched him as he paused at the bus stop, just seconds before a double-decker arrived. When it moved off again, he had gone.

'Emma,' Lizzy said, approaching from behind.

Emma jumped; she was really on edge. 'Hi,' she said, turning away from the window and forcing a smile.

'You okay?' Lizzy asked.

'Fine.'

'Emma, that was the theatre on the phone. One of the leading ladies in the play has had to pull out of the show because of a family illness, and they want me to take her place.'

'That's great news!' Emma said, forcing her smile yet wider. 'But the performance is only a week away, isn't it?'

'I know. That's why they called. They want me to go over there now and start rehearsing.'

'You'd better get over there then! What are you waiting for?'

'I'm not leaving you here on your own. I told them I wasn't sure I could do it.'

'Don't be stupid, Lizzy,' Emma replied. 'I really appreciate what you're doing, but you can't let this go. Get over there now.'

'You let your chance go,' Lizzy countered.

'That's different, Lizzy, and you know it.'

'It wouldn't feel right. You shouldn't be on your own.'

'I'm not on my own. I've got Will, too.'

'Call him, now,' Lizzy insisted. 'Ask him to come over.'

'I'll go over to see him,' Emma promised. 'But I'll just stay here for a bit. Put some extra clothes in a suitcase.'

'I can help you do that.'

'No, you go,' Emma insisted, shepherding her friend down the hallway, towards the door. She knew that the more time Lizzy had to think about this, the less likely she would be to take up the offer. 'I'll be fine, honestly.'

'Promise you'll call Will.'

'Yes, I'll call him.' Emma opened the front door. 'Now, you get going.'

'You sure, Em?' Lizzy backed out of the flat as if being physically pushed. 'I wouldn't have thought you'd want to hang around here. Not on your own, anyway.'

'Just for a while, then I'll go to see Will.'

'Okay,' Lizzy said, 'as long as you're sure. And I'll always have my mobile on. If you need anything, just call and I'll come over straight away.'

'Thanks,' Emma said. 'I'll only be here for another couple of minutes.'

As she closed the door she let down the pretence. In truth, she had wanted Lizzy to stay – the thought of being alone scared her witless – but she wasn't going to let Lizzy give up her big chance. This was her problem and, ultimately, she had to deal with it. Within seconds she had buried the feelings of fear, if only temporarily. She was thinking about what she would ask Mrs Henderson.

12

'Hello, Richard.'

He moved closer, towards the edge of the bed, watching Richard as he lay there motionless. Richard was in a better state than he had expected – more asleep than seriously injured. The doctors had obviously done a good job. But it was possible to make out the damage that had been done, just under his hair-line, above his left eye – a purplish, inky bruise that seemed to leak into the surrounding skin.

'You're free to stay as long as you like,' said the pretty Filipino nurse who had shown him to the private room. 'The doctor has already been around this morning, so you won't be disturbing anyone.'

'Thank you,' he said, watching Richard's face for signs of life. It was weird thinking that he held his life in his hands.

'So, you are cousins?'

'Pardon?' he said, caught in a daydream, transfixed by the bleeps of the life-support machine and the thoughts of imminent death. 'Yes.' He smiled, taking care to show it was in a pained fashion. 'Although we're very close – more like brothers.' He'd produced the forged driving licence at the nursing station, which was enough to get past the enhanced security that had been put in place around Richard. 'This is the first chance I've had to come and see him. I've been away, you see. But I really wanted to come and see how he is.'

'That's nice,' said the nurse, checking the clipboard at the bottom of Richard's bed. 'He's had a lot of visitors since he arrived here. It's nice when someone is obviously loved so much.'

'Yes, it is. The problem is,' he added, 'that the more you love someone, the harder it is to let them go.'

'Yes,' the nurse said, nodding. 'But please try to think positively. Richard can get better.'

He smiled at her, while thinking about how Richard's loved ones would react to the news – and especially how Emma would feel. She would certainly take the news hard, and he was looking forward to watching the drama unfold.

'I'll leave you to it,' the nurse said, smiling sympathetically. He barely noticed that she had left, only registering he was finally alone with Richard when he heard the door close.

'So,' he said, sitting down and leaning in towards Richard, placing both hands on the bed's guardrails. He felt the bed give under his weight, seeming to symbolise the power he had at this moment.

'It's funny how things work out,' he whispered into Richard's ear. 'You know,' he said, as he looked at the tubes and wires spiralling from Richard's body, 'if there was any other way of doing this, then I would do it. But you shouldn't think of this as a bad thing, Richard. It's all part of the wider picture, the greater good. I hope you understand that.'

He moved a hand towards the ventilator and grasped one of the tubes. He was shaking, and a bead of sweat tickled his face as it snaked down past his ear. This was going to be harder than he had expected.

'You see, she needs to know,' he said, pulling back again and letting go of the tube. 'And you're going to help her understand.'

13

Some months earlier

The call had come out of nowhere. Shocked to hear his voice again after all that time, his first reaction had been to hang up and hope he would go away. And then the threats had started coming, so he had had little choice but to go over there and find out what was going on.

When he'd arrived at the flat, it had been a stomach-churning sight. The place looked like an indoor rubbish dump; he had struggled even to open the door, pushing past unopened post and unread newspapers. Then there had been the living room, which was strewn with plates of mouldering, half-eaten food and open bottles of whisky and beer. The kitchen stank to high heaven. The smell, something that he could only liken to stale vomit, mostly came from the bin, which had attracted a number of fat, black flies.

It was like a scene out of a horror movie.

He had found him in the bedroom, unconscious on the unmade bed with the telephone off the hook next to him. The room reeked of alcohol. His cheek was resting in a pool of crusted vomit and at first he had wondered whether he'd choked to death.

And he was ashamed to admit that, for a split second, he had actually been pleased to think that was the case.

But he was alive, and he'd done the right thing, calling the ambulance and even accompanying him to hospital. He had stuck around just long enough to know that he was going to be okay. Not that he really cared. All he really did care about was that this guy would leave him alone and let him get on with his life. But he wasn't sure that was ever going to happen.

14

Present day

Will had sworn that he would never ring his number again. Just the idea of talking to him, somehow inviting him back into his life, made his stomach turn. But what if his suspicions were true? He'd never be able to forgive himself if he just stood by and did nothing to help.

He stood away from the crowds in a more secluded part of the park. He'd been there for a while now, enough time for the back of his neck to start reddening in the sun. The earlier case of mistaken identity was still playing on his mind, freezing him into inaction. It wasn't so much the embarrassment at accosting the stranger, or the way he had looked at him. It was more the realisation of how fragile he still was when it came to anything to do with that man.

He stared at his mobile phone, willing himself to call. He found the name and rang.

The call went through to voicemail.

He rang off, taking the inability to get through to him as some kind of heavenly reprieve, and spent another ten minutes or so wandering around Regent's Park in the sunshine. But it was just putting off the inevitable.

He stopped again, just outside the entrance to London Zoo. Throngs of families passed in and out, smiling and happy. Again he reached for his mobile and this time he called the landline number.

Again there was no answer.

Where the hell is he?

Will tried the mobile number again. This time he decided to leave a message. 'It's Will. I want to know, did you attack Dan's brother, Richard Carlton? Did you go to Emma's flat and do that to him?' He turned and moved away as a family approached. 'If you are responsible for this, I want to know.' He spoke under his breath. 'And I swear, I will tell the police everything if I have to. I'm not bluffing – I mean it. I want to know if you have Dan. You promised that you'd keep Em out of this.'

He rang off and spent another half an hour or so pondering his next move. When his phone rang he scrambled for it, thinking it could be him calling back. But it wasn't.

'Hey, Em, you all right?' he said, glad to hear Emma's voice, but unable to banish the feelings of guilt that now flowed every time he spoke to his sister.

He listened as Emma talked him through the police visit, the disappearance of the photos, the revelation that Mrs Henderson had said she saw Dan running from the flat, and the strange behaviour of Mr Henderson when they had questioned him.

She was trying her best to sound positive, but Will knew her too well not to notice the strain in her voice. She was alone in that flat. How bad could it get? While he was wallowing in self-pity, worried about how all this would impact upon him, his sister's life was falling apart.

'I'll be over in an hour,' he promised, glancing at his watch. 'I just have to do something first.'

He said goodbye and headed straight for the tube. If the guy was ignoring his calls, the only option was to confront him face to face. He owed it to Emma.

'Oh, hi,' Will said, taken aback when an attractive, twenty-something girl opened the door. It was the last thing he had been expecting – maybe he'd found a new girlfriend? 'I was looking for—'

'He doesn't live here any more,' she interrupted, in a Scottish accent. 'He moved out, and I'm the new tenant.'

'Oh, right. You don't know where he's gone, do you?'

The girl laughed. 'Know where he's gone? I feel like his

personal secretary, the amount of mail I've forwarded in the past two weeks. I wouldn't care, but I haven't even met the bloke.'

'Lucky you,' Will said, joking but serious at the same time.

'Are you a friend?' she asked, leaning against the open door. Will noticed a tattoo just above her jeans waistband as her shirt rode up.

'Yes,' he lied, 'although obviously not close enough for him to tell me that he was moving. So, you've got a forwarding address?'

'Sure,' she said. 'Come on in – I'll just get it.'

Will followed her into the flat.

'You've done this up nicely,' he noted, as he surveyed the living room. He hadn't planned to comment on interior design, but the difference compared to his last visit there was amazing. The place looked so much better – cleaner for a start. Before it had been dreary, even foreboding, but now it was inviting, homely.

'Thanks,' the girl said, rummaging around on a bookcase. 'I try my best.' She handed Will a piece of paper and three letters. 'I thought you might like to deliver these by hand,' she said with a smile.

'Sure.' Will looked at the address on the paper. He knew that part of Southwark well, as a friend and colleague at work had lived there for a time, and he'd visited their flat on a number of occasions. Like many London boroughs, Southwark was a real mix of good and bad. He recognised the road as being in one of the grubbier parts.

'You know,' the girl said, 'it's really sad when the former tenant not only gets more mail than you, but more visitors too.'

Will looked at her. 'I find that hard to believe. You don't have lots of visitors?'

'Only moved down here two weeks ago from Edinburgh. I don't know anybody here yet. Well, apart from some work colleagues – they seem okay.'

'It takes time,' Will replied, looking at the letters, which he suspected were all junk mail of one kind or another. 'London can be a pretty lonely place. But, trust me – you'll make many more friends than the guy who used to live here.'

Will arrived at the block of flats half an hour later. He paused on the grassy area outside and looked up the full twenty floors. It was a concrete monstrosity. Balconies were decorated with satellite dishes, washing lines, even bicycles. It was like a vertical jumble sale. The walk from the tube had confirmed Will's opinion of the area – it wasn't a place in which he felt particularly comfortable.

He took a deep breath and approached the main doors. It was another intercom system. He pressed the right button but there was no reply.

'Fantastic.'

But this time he got lucky. As he paced around at the bottom of the steps, a young woman carrying several bags of shopping passed by and entered the building. He reached to hold the door for her as she struggled to edge through the gap, and then followed her inside. She didn't question him, instead heading up the stairs to their left.

Will tried the lift, but it was out of order. Not welcome news, as the flat was on the sixth floor. The climb was tiring, but it gave him time to think about what he was going to say.

He reached the door and knocked, but no one answered. His polite raps were just turning into full-blown thumps when the door opposite opened, and an elderly woman interrupted him.

'He went out,' the woman said, eyeing him suspiciously.

'Do you know where?'

'I'm not his housekeeper,' she countered. 'He only moved in a few weeks ago.'

'I know,' Will said. 'How long has he been out?'

'A few hours, maybe. Are you a policeman?'

'What makes you think that?'

'Because you're asking a lot of questions, and he looks like the sort.'

'No, I'm not the police. Just a friend.'

'I thought I recognised you,' she said, softening up. 'It's just that he's had a few people visiting him that don't seem too friendly, and he asked me not to talk to people.'

'I'm worried about him,' Will said. 'I can't get hold of him on his mobile.'

'Probably because he's at the hospital. You can't use your phones in there, can you?'

'He's gone to the hospital, this morning?'

'That's what he said. Passed him on the stairs carrying a bunch of flowers and that's the explanation he gave me – said he's got a friend in there at the moment.'

Will hailed the first taxi he saw. He stewed in the back of the cab, wondering whether he was just being paranoid.

Surely he wouldn't do such a thing?

The cabbie made polite conversation, mostly about the weather and traffic, but Will wasn't in the mood to chat. He considered calling the hospital, just to check that everything was all right, but then decided not to.

At the hospital, he paid the driver and raced towards the entrance, checking his pace as he got a few sideways glances from hospital staff. He headed for the lift but then decided the stairs were a quicker option, taking them two at a time.

By the time he reached the right department he was seriously out of breath. Gasping for air, he strode past the nursing station and headed for Richard's private room. He heard a nurse calling out behind him but he didn't stop.

The door to Richard's room was closed but, through the blinds, he could see someone standing over the bedside.

It couldn't be, could it?

He flung the door open, and it bounced back on its hinges with a clatter.

'Hello, William,' said the man, stepping back from Richard's bedside.

'Dad,' Will said, taking in the scene. 'What are you doing here?'

15

Emma said goodbye to Will and resumed packing. It was so good to hear her brother's voice; he was always such a comfort. She finished packing the rest of her things and zipped up the suitcase, hoisting it off the bed and onto the floor with a thud. Then she reached up to the top of the wardrobe and pulled down the box that was stored there. She carried it into the living room, placing it on the table, and flipped open the lid.

Inside was all the material related to their wedding: eighteen months of mementos, starting with the batch of engagement cards from family and friends, to the cut-outs from various wedding magazines of potential dresses and other wedding paraphernalia, and, finally, copies of the wedding invitations, and receipts for the wedding ceremony, which was due to take place a week today.

'Get a grip,' she said, closing the box. This wasn't doing any good.

She knew that all this reminiscence was just a diversion tactic. And it wasn't like she had time to waste – Mr Henderson had already been gone for ten minutes or more, and could be back at any time.

'Mrs Henderson, I was hoping to have a chat with you. Are you in there?'

Emma knocked on the door again. She'd been trying to get an answer for over a minute now, but despite knocking several times, there hadn't been any sign of life within the flat. She wondered whether Mrs Henderson was asleep, or maybe worse.

'Mrs Henderson? Edna?'

This time she heard someone moving within the flat.

'Mrs Henderson,' she said, surprised to suddenly have some success. 'I just want to ask you about what you saw the other day. I'm looking for my fiancé and you might be able to help me.'

Now she could hear shuffling footsteps as someone moved right up to the other side of the door. She moved to the corner of the door, trying to find any gap through which to talk.

'Mrs Henderson? Edna? Is it okay for me to talk to you for a few minutes? It's Emma, Emma Holden, from upstairs.'

She heard a chain slide across and stepped back as the door edged open.

Mrs Henderson eyed her nervously. She was dressed in a pink dressing gown, her feet adorned by a pair of pink slippers. It looked like she was ready for bed. Her wrinkled face was a mass of confusion, scrutinising Emma. Then suddenly she broke out into a broad smile.

'Jane,' she said, reaching out and stepping into the corridor, cupping Emma's face with bony hands and giving her a moist kiss on the cheek. 'I didn't recognise you at first,' she continued, stroking Emma's cheeks, 'but I haven't got my glasses on, you see.'

'No, I'm not . . .' began Emma, stepping away from the embrace. But Mrs Henderson had already turned to go back into the flat.

'Come on in,' she was saying. 'I've just made a cup of tea, and I think there's a piece of cake in the cupboard. Can't have my sister going hungry, can we?'

Emma waited for Mrs Henderson to return from the kitchen. She felt guilty and nervous: nervous that Mr Henderson might come back at any time and react very badly at finding that she had gone against his wishes and approached his vulnerable wife; and guilty at taking advantage of Mrs Henderson's dementia by playing along with her delusions that she was her sister, Jane. But if pretending to be her sister for just a few minutes meant that she could find out what Edna had really seen that night, then maybe the end justified the means. There were enormous things at stake here.

Mrs Henderson returned with a cup of tea and handed it to Emma. 'Here you are, Jane.'

'Thanks.'

It seemed she'd forgotten about the cake.

'So,' Mrs Henderson said cheerfully, sitting down across from Emma on a stiff-backed chair. 'I want to hear all the details.'

'Details?'

'Yes.' She smiled conspiratorially. 'Are you looking forward to the big day?'

Emma just smiled back. Maybe this had been a big mistake. Why did she think she would be able to get any sense out of this poor woman, who was so confused that she didn't even know who she was talking to?

'The wedding!' Mrs Henderson said. 'I don't know,' she added, shaking her head in genuine bemusement. 'You've been looking forward to this for nearly two years, and suddenly you forget that it's even happening!'

'Oh, the wedding! It's going fine,' Emma said, suddenly unsure about whether Mrs Henderson now thought that she was talking to her sister or to Emma herself. Maybe that was what her condition was like – swinging between reality and fantasy.

'I'm so glad. I was getting worried after the argument and him just running out and leaving you like that. I thought that might be the end of it.'

'I didn't realise you heard the argument,' said Emma, still wondering whether Mrs Henderson was referring to the real-life events of Friday night, or her own fantasies.

'Of course I did. I heard you clattering around up there, fighting like cat and dog. It's a wonder you didn't wake everyone up. I even went out to find out if you were okay, but—'

Suddenly her face closed down, her features froze. It was as if someone had just pulled the plug, all the animation in her face draining away.

Emma rose from the chair. 'Mrs Henderson, are you okay?' She moved towards the old woman, taking in her face with concern. Her body was motionless, her skin wax-like, resembling one of the models in Madame Tussauds.

'Get away from me!' Mrs Henderson screamed loudly, suddenly filling with life again. She thrust her bony arms in Emma's direction, throwing her momentarily off balance as she ducked away from her reach. 'Get him away from me, stay away from me!'

Tears were streaming down the old woman's face as Emma watched from a safe distance, backed up against the wall, not knowing what to do.

Then, just as suddenly as Mrs Henderson had erupted, she shrank back into her seat, gripping its arms like she was on a roller coaster. Her blue eyes fixed on the wall opposite, filled with what looked like horror.

'I'm sorry if I upset you,' Emma said, edging closer. She was beginning to understand why Mr Henderson had been so protective of her: the woman was obviously forever on the cusp of distress. Emma got within a foot or so of Mrs Henderson and knelt down in front of her. It was a risk to get so close, but this time she was ready for any sudden movements. 'I didn't mean to upset you.'

Mrs Henderson blinked and looked across at her. 'I'm sorry too,' she said, tears still running down the wrinkles in her face.

Emma placed a comforting hand on her cheek, trapping one of the tears. 'You've got nothing to be sorry about.'

'I promised him I wouldn't tell anyone,' said Mrs Henderson, hardly able to look at Emma. 'He said he was doing it for love – because of you. You're a lucky girl, Jane, to have a man fighting over you like that.'

'Mrs Henderson,' said Emma, getting her to meet her gaze, 'who did you talk to? Who did you see out in the corridor? Was it Dan? Was it my fiancé, or did you see someone else? You know who Dan is, don't you? You've seen him – he lives with me upstairs.'

The old woman muttered something under her breath.

'Pardon?'

'I promised,' she whispered.

'What did you promise?' Emma pressed.

'He's doing it all for love,' she repeated. 'He's going to help you understand.'

'Understand? Understand what?'

'He'll help you understand,' she reiterated.

'Who said this?' Emma begged. 'Was it Dan, or someone else? If you can remember who you spoke to, then please tell me.'

'He's your number one fan,' she said.

This stopped Emma dead in her tracks, making her catch her breath.

The phrase was a shocking blast from her past.

'Did he say that to you?' Now her questioning took on more urgency, despite her trying to be gentle with the old woman. 'Is that what he said?'

'He's your number one fan,' Mrs Henderson repeated, as if someone had taken possession of her body, and was just using her as a mouthpiece.

'Did the person who said this have brown hair, quite scruffy?'

Mrs Henderson didn't respond.

'Did he tell you his name?' Emma was only dimly aware she was speaking more and more desperately. 'Was he called Stephen? Mrs Henderson, was the man you spoke to called Stephen Myers?'

'Would you like another cup of tea, Jane?' Mrs Henderson smiled, seemingly oblivious to the important conversation she had just been engaged in.

Then Emma heard the sound of a key being put into the lock of the front door.

She got to her feet, not knowing whether to go into the kitchen and hide, but she decided to face up to Mr Henderson as he entered the flat.

At first he didn't notice her, but he did a double take as he was closing the door. Her adrenaline was pumping, just like it used to do all those years ago in the karate competitions. But this situation needed tact, not physical force, and it seemed all the harder for it.

'What are you doing here?' he said, looking more afraid than angry. 'I told you not to bother us. I told you to stay away from my wife.'

'I've been having a good chat with Jane,' Mrs Henderson said.

'She's not Jane,' he rebuked, with surprising disdain. 'Jane's been dead for almost ten years.'

'Just let me explain—' Emma began.

'Get out and leave us alone,' he demanded, his voice rising. He seemed bolder now, but Emma still sensed he was being driven by fear more than anything.

What was he so scared of?

'Your wife said she'd made a promise to someone. Has she told you anything? Please, Mr Henderson, I really need your help.' Emma's desperation made her push her luck.

'My wife says lots of things,' he said dismissively, 'and most of the time they don't make any sense at all. Can't you see that she's not well? She can't help you.'

'She helped the police,' Emma countered. 'She told them that she saw Dan on the staircase, running from the flat.'

'Well, I told the police the same as I told you,' he replied, as he began unloading shopping from his bag. 'She doesn't know what she's saying. How can you take the word of someone who believes she's just had a discussion with her dead sister? If it were up to me, I wouldn't have even let her talk to the police.'

'But I thought you must have been the one who came forward?'

'No, I did not. The police invited themselves in here, and then when they found out Edna had been in the flat during the fight, they just started asking her question after question, until she told them whatever came into her head.'

'Are you sure Edna didn't say any more about what happened on the staircase? Did she give any description of the person she spoke to?'

'Please,' he implored, 'leave us alone. We didn't ask for any of this.'

'Any of what? What did Edna tell you?'

'Go,' he demanded, 'before I call the police.'

16

For a few seconds father and son eyed each other across the hospital bed. Will was still trying to catch his breath, relieved that his worst fears hadn't been realised.

Edward Holden had just opened his mouth to say something, when the door to the room flew open.

'It's okay.' Edward turned to the nurse as she barrelled into the room. 'He's my son.'

Will turned and smiled apologetically. The nurse scowled back, obviously not happy at the way he had just barged into the room without showing identification first. And he could under-stand that. You couldn't be too careful given all that had happened.

'You can stay,' she said, 'but next time, please report to the desk first. I don't appreciate having to chase people through my ward.'

'Of course,' Will said. 'I'm really sorry.'

'Well, I'll leave you to it,' the nurse said, unable to manage a smile. She closed the door, leaving Will with his father again.

He looked at his father. Edward was dressed in fashionable clothes that to Will looked more suitable for a twenty-something than a man of sixty. And then there was his new, trendy, boy-band haircut – close-cropped and messy. Will wished he could be happy that his dad had found a new lease of life, but it was just so difficult.

'I thought I'd come and see how things were going,' his father explained, finally answering his son's question. 'The nurse told me that Richard hasn't improved.'

'He might never wake up,' Will said, regretting his choice of words as he remembered what the nurse had told them about always being positive in front of the patient. 'Although a lot of people do recover, so we shouldn't give up hope,' he added, for Richard's benefit.

'I was worried about you, too,' Edward added, 'after what you said on the phone. You sounded really upset.'

'Just not worried enough to come and see me?' Will surprised himself at the bitterness in his voice. 'I needed your support; you had to be able to see that.'

'Will,' Edward said. 'I'm your father, and you know that I'd do anything for you. But you've got to understand that I can't just come running all the time. I have my own life.'

'Yes, with your girlfriend.'

Edward was living with a woman nearly thirty years his junior. She was a doctor – they'd met when he had been visiting his wife as she was dying of cancer in hospital. The thought of romance blooming over the bedside as their mother was pumped high with morphine never failed to make Will furious: he suspected that the relationship had begun even before his mum had taken her last breath, although Edward always denied that was the case. His story was that they had met by chance some months later, when Edward, a self-employed accountant, had filed a tax return for one of her friends. Whatever the story, Will hadn't visited since she'd moved in with Edward eleven months previously, unable to stomach seeing someone his own age taking the place of his mother.

'Look, William,' Edward said, ignoring the jibe, 'I've done my best to help you, but you also need to realise I never wanted any of this.'

'You still resent me burdening you with my situation,' Will replied. 'You'd have been happier if I'd never told you.'

'I'd have been happier if none of it had happened,' Edward replied, 'but it did, and we have to make the best of it. I admit that sometimes I wish you hadn't told me.'

'But you're my dad. Who else was I going to turn to?'

'You could have spoken to Lucy, instead of pushing her away.'

'She would never have understood. How could she?'

'She was a lovely girl. And she really cared for you, William. Maybe you underestimated her.'

'I couldn't have dragged her into it. Letting her go was the best thing for her.'

'Maybe you're right,' Edward said, finally. He seemed to study Will's face, searching for something. 'You don't look well,' he added, noting the dark smudges under his son's eyes. 'Are you sleeping?'

'Not really.'

'The nightmares are starting again?'

'They never really went away,' Will said, simply. 'But they're getting worse again, yes. This has brought it all back. I dream of the same thing over and over again. And they don't feel like dreams – they feel real.'

He hated the way he felt so needy when he was with his father: like a little boy longing for everything to be made all right. He'd learnt from bitter experience that there were some troubles that parents just couldn't take away.

'Why did you come here, Will?'

'What? To see Richard, of course.'

'You burst in here like your life depended on it. You were out of breath, you'd obviously been running, and you didn't stop when the nurse asked you to. Why?'

'I thought he might be here,' admitted Will, feeling foolish now at his paranoia. 'I thought he might try and finish the job.'

'What made you think that?' Edward looked hard at Will.

'I went round to his flat,' Will explained. 'I'd tried to call him, to ask if he had anything to do with what happened, but he wasn't answering his mobile or home phone. Then I found out that he's just moved, to a really deprived area south of the river. He's living in this horrible block of flats. I think it might all be connected. Maybe it's all part of a plan, and I'm going to get a call from him soon.'

'You didn't speak to him?'

'He wasn't there. A neighbour said he was at the hospital visiting someone, and I just jumped to conclusions.'

'Trying to contact him was not a good idea,' Edward said, glancing through the window as a nurse passed by. 'The police are looking into this. Let them get on with their job – it's what they're paid to do, and I'm sure they'll find out who did this. In the meantime, concentrate on looking after your sister. She'll be going through a worse time than you, Will, believe me.'

'They're convinced it's Dan,' Will said. 'But they don't know the full story. I should have shown them the photograph I found next to Richard.'

'You're jumping to conclusions. Apart from the photo, for which there could be other explanations, there's nothing else to suggest he has anything to do with it. How long is it since you last heard from him?'

'Eleven months, two days,' Will replied, without hesitation.

'Jesus, Will, you've got to stop this.'

Will turned away from his father and watched Richard, willing him to open his eyes.

A sudden realisation dawned: if Richard did wake up, and Will's suspicions were true about why he had been attacked, years of lies might begin to unravel. He felt sick.

'You know what I think?' Edward continued. 'This is all part of your guilt trip. You're desperate to blame yourself for what happened, but think about it. If it *was* him, why attack Dan's brother?'

'I don't know.'

'William, you're reading too much into this.'

'I should have gone to the police in the first place,' Will stated, as he continued to ponder the possible ramifications of Richard's recovery. 'I should have told them everything right at the beginning. But I'm a coward.'

'You're not a coward.' Edward dismissed the statement. 'I don't want to hear you talking about yourself like that. It won't help the situation one bit.'

'Oh, I am a coward, Dad.' Will faced up to him across

Richard's bed. 'I thought you would have known that by now. Or are you still in denial at the way the son of the great Edward Holden has turned out?'

'Don't be stupid, William.'

'I mean it, Dad. Emma is out there, desperate to know what happened to Dan, and maybe, just maybe, I can do something about it. But I'm too busy worrying about myself, and how it will affect me.'

'You're being too hard on yourself.'

'How can you say that after what I've done?'

Edward moved around the bedside and placed a hand on Will's shoulder. 'William, you found yourself in a situation and you made a mistake. That doesn't make you a bad person. It makes you human.'

'But I deserve to be punished.'

'You have been punished. You've been punishing yourself for years now. Your life is falling apart, and you're just standing there letting it happen. But it's got to stop, before you lose everything and everyone.'

'I've been having thoughts recently, about whether it's worth going on living,' Will admitted quietly, with reluctance.

Edward exhaled, rubbing at his newly grown beard. 'Have you given any more thought to seeing a counsellor?'

'I can't. You need to be open and honest for those things to work. You can't go in there, keep a secret like mine and expect to come out cured.'

'Then you've just got to work through this. But please, Will, try and move on, for all our sakes.'

17

Some years earlier

'Excuse me, can I have your autograph?'

Emma turned to look at the rather scrawny, acne-scarred man standing by the studio gates, who was holding out a note-pad and pen in expectation. He looked about eighteen, but was dressed more like an old man, in grey trousers and a knitted jumper, with his brown hair combed into a side-parting. A camera hung around his neck, and Emma immediately wondered if he was a trainspotter.

Although a voice was telling her to politely refuse and walk on, no one had asked for her autograph before. What harm could it do?

She didn't notice the warning signs of desperation in his green eyes.

'Sure,' she said, moving back towards him. 'No problem.'

'Thank you so much,' the guy gushed as he handed Emma the pad and pen. 'I'm so grateful to you for doing this. I thought you might be too busy – I know you're busy – but it's great that you can take the time for me.'

'It's no problem, honestly,' Emma replied, holding the pen ready to write. The biro was about half its normal size; the plastic at the end was cracked and splintered. To her distaste she realised that the tatty, browning Sellotape wrapped around the top of the pen was damp with what she could only think was saliva. She used her best acting skills to maintain a neutral face and just put up with it.

'I'm your number one fan,' he said. 'I didn't watch the

programme that much, but since you've been in it, I haven't missed an episode. If I'm out when it's on I record it. Sometimes I record it anyway, so I can watch it back as much as I want.'

Emma waited to just write what she had to and then leave. She was already regretting the situation – the guy seemed harmless enough, but definitely weird.

'What would you like me to—?'

'I think you're a fantastic actress,' he interrupted.

'Thanks.' She was embarrassed by the compliment. She didn't look up at him, keeping her eyes on the pad, but he was ducking down to catch her attention.

'I'm your number one fan,' he repeated, as if looking for a response that hadn't come the first time he'd said it. He edged forward, invading her personal space. He almost had her backed against the wall. 'I know everything about you.'

Alarm bells rang.

'I hope not,' she tried to joke, but it came out sounding nervous. She glanced across at the gates, but the security guy who sometimes patrolled wasn't there.

'Your favourite meal is lasagne, your favourite film of all time is *Dirty Dancing*. You're a black belt in karate. You started training at your school when you were eleven, because a girl started bullying you in your art class. It only took you five years to get your black belt. This year you're fighting in the British championships in Birmingham, but you're finding it difficult to fit in the training now you're working on the show. You've always wanted to be an actress, and you'd love to work on a film, but you don't think you're ready yet.'

Emma shifted nervously. 'How do you know all this?'

'I read it,' he said. 'I always look for articles about you in the magazines. I never buy the magazines, though – I read them in the newsagents. They let you go there and read magazines for as long as you like – you can stand there all day and it's all free. I like going there, especially when there are articles about you.'

'Oh, the magazine article.' She felt relieved that there was a rational explanation for his in-depth knowledge of her personal history and preferences. 'You read the interview in *Celebrity Goss*.'

He nodded and smiled, revealing yellowing teeth with a waft of stale breath. It didn't look as if he ever brushed them. 'I like reading articles about you.'

She hadn't really wanted to do the damn magazine interview, but her agent had convinced her that such self-promotion could lead to better acting roles in the future. In the end, she had quite enjoyed the experience but now, looking at this grinning man, she realised she had opened up part of her private life to strangers. It felt weird.

'What would you like me to write?' she asked, holding the pen ready, still not wanting to look up at him.

'Whatever you like,' he said. 'My name's Stephen.'

'Okay, Stephen.' She wrote down a short note on the first available blank page, some three-quarters of the way through the notebook. The rest of the pages were full of autographs, some of which she recognised as being from fellow cast members.

She handed back the book and pen, wanting desperately to wipe her hand clean. She watched as Stephen studied her message intently, as if trying to decipher a World War Two code.

'"To my number one fan, love from Emma",' he read out loud. He looked up at her and smiled. 'Thank you,' he said, again with more than a hint of desperation. 'You're not just beautiful – you're really kind. I think we're going to be really good friends. I knew we would, from the first moment I saw you.'

'Thanks. Look, I'd better get going now.' By edging around him, she had managed to turn him so that now he was against the wall. 'Nice to meet you.'

'Just a second,' he said, bringing the camera up to his face.

Emma put a hand up to block the shot. 'No, Stephen, please don't.'

'It's okay, it's done now.'

She could have tried to protest, but all she really wanted was to get away from him.

'I have to go,' she said, turning and walking away.

'See you again soon,' he shouted, waving.

'Emma, over here!'

Emma shoved the change from the sandwich into her pocket and looked across the canteen to see who had just shouted to her. Claire Donovan, a fellow cast member who was sitting towards the centre of the room on her own, was gesturing for her to come over.

'Hi,' said Emma, sliding into the chair opposite her. 'What's up?'

She had never eaten with Claire before. The cast tended to break into cliques, mostly depending on how long someone had been in the show. While Emma had been on the cast for only six months, Claire had been around for nearly four years and was reportedly one of the most highly paid actors in the show.

'I saw you talking to Stephen Myers yesterday,' said Claire, putting down her knife and fork.

'The guy at the gate? He asked for my autograph, that's all.'

'And he took a photograph?'

'Well, yes, but I didn't give him permission to do that. I won't be speaking to him again, that's for certain. He made me feel pretty uncomfortable, but I think he's harmless, really. Why do you ask?'

'He isn't harmless,' corrected Claire. 'Stay away from him. He's bad news.'

'What do you mean?'

'He's been hanging around the studios for a couple of years, on and off, bothering the female cast. And it's always the girls. The guys can walk past him and he won't ever bat an eyelid. I know he seems harmless, Emma, but once you give him some encouragement, it's very difficult to get rid of him.'

'He's a stalker?'

'Karen Rodham had a lot of trouble with him a year back. She was nice to him at first, signed his little autograph book, and thought nothing of it. But then he started wanting to talk to her every evening after work, going up to her at the gates. After a few weeks he began turning up outside her house, ringing the doorbell in the middle of the night, shouting up to her window, telling her that he loved her. Karen nearly left the show because of it. So, yes, he is a stalker.'

'My God, that's terrible. Did she tell the police?'

'Yes, but it took a while before they treated it as seriously as they should have done. Eventually, though, they put a restraining order on him and that seemed to work, because he stopped following her and even stopped coming to the studio. Then I saw him talking to you yesterday. I'm really sorry I didn't come over and pull you away, but I just can't bring myself to be anywhere near the guy. I'm scared that if I go near him, he'll start latching on to me.'

'So what should I do now?' Emma's head was whirling.

'Just don't speak to him again,' advised Claire. 'I know it sounds horrible, but if he tries to talk to you just blank him, pretend he's not there. Hopefully he'll get the message. Whatever you do, don't give him any sense of encouragement; otherwise what happened to Karen might well happen to you. I'm going to warn the rest of the guys too, now I know he's back.'

'Okay,' Emma said. 'Thanks for telling me.'

'Emma,' he said that afternoon, as she exited the gates.

Her heart sank as she saw Stephen Myers approach, smiling as if he was welcoming a close friend.

Although totally against her nature, she took Claire's advice and walked straight past.

'Emma!' he shouted as she passed him. 'What's the matter?'

Despite knowing about his past, she felt uncomfortable blanking him, but she took a deep breath and hoped that was the end of it.

But he ran up behind her. 'I've got your photo,' he said, struggling to keep up as Emma tried to out-walk him. 'Here it is.'

She didn't stop to look at the photo he was holding out to her.

'I'm going to put it on my bedroom wall.'

'Please, Stephen, I need to get home,' she said, resisting the temptation to snatch the photo from his sweaty hand.

'Are you okay?' he asked, now starting to jog, the camera bouncing up and down on his pigeon chest. 'Has someone upset you? Did he upset you?'

'I'm in a hurry,' she said, not knowing what he was talking about.

'Getting home to your boyfriend?'

Emma stopped. Maybe if she reasoned with him, ended this now, she could avoid problems later on. She had always believed that if you could just connect with someone, even the most unreasonable people could be brought onside.

'Look, Stephen. You seem like a nice guy, but I've really got to go home. It's getting dark and I have to get back.'

'To your boyfriend, to Darren.'

'Darren?'

'Yes, Darren . . . Darren Clarke.'

He was referring to her boyfriend's on-screen character. He worked on the show, too – it was how they had met.

'His real name is Stuart,' she said, 'but I don't live with him.' Immediately she regretted telling him that.

'I think you can do better than him,' Stephen said. 'You shouldn't be going out with a criminal – not someone like Darren. What do you see in him?'

Stuart played the 'bad boy' of the show; Stephen Myers obviously had difficulty in determining fact from fiction.

'Please, Stephen, I have to go now.' She turned and began walking off.

'Emma, I love you!' she heard him shout. It took all her willpower not to break into a run.

18

'Sorry I took so long,' Lizzy said to Emma, as she sat down at the table in the pub, later on Sunday evening. The place, a traditional local, was just around the corner from Lizzy's flat, and a favourite haunt of theirs. It was the perfect place for chit-chat – never too busy, nor too quiet, to be heard or over-heard. 'It was tricky to get away,' she added, placing her bag on the empty seat beside her. 'It's complete mayhem there at the moment – the girl taking my place is having real trouble learn-ing the routines, and the director is in the process of having a nervous breakdown. They wanted me to stay for another couple of hours really, but thankfully I performed okay so they let me go. Eventually.'

'I'm sorry, Lizzy, for dragging you over here,' Emma said. 'I don't want to ruin your big break. They aren't angry with you, are they, for leaving?'

'Nah, they need me, Em. There's no one else who could stand in at such short notice. I like to think that gives me a bit of leeway.' Lizzy grinned, cheekily. 'Anyway, I told them my aunty was sick, and I had to go over and see how she was. I make a worryingly convincing liar, you know.'

Emma smiled. 'I'm lucky to have you on my side. You're such a good friend.'

'I know, I know,' joked Lizzy. 'So, what's this all about? When you called, I thought something might have happened with Richard.'

'I spoke to Mrs Henderson,' Emma said.

'I thought you might.' Lizzy didn't sound at all surprised. 'So, what did she say?'

'Not a great deal – but what she did say was potentially really important.'

'Go on, don't leave me hanging in suspense.'

'I think I know who attacked Richard. And he might have kidnapped Dan.'

'What?'

'It's a long story. Let's get a drink – I've got a lot to fill you in on.'

'It started when I was working on the soap up in Manchester,' Emma began, as they both sat cradling their gin and tonics. 'I'd only been on the show for a few months and, one day, as I was leaving for the night, a guy comes up to me and asks for my autograph. His name was Stephen Myers. I didn't really think much of it, although he seemed a bit creepy. But the next day one of the other girls on the show, Claire, warned me about him, saying that he had a history of following female cast members around, turning up outside their houses, saying he loved them. She warned me not to encourage him – not to talk to him again.'

'So he was a stalker?' Lizzy said, taking a sip of her drink but not taking her eyes off Emma.

'Yes. He'd already been warned by the police about his behaviour towards another girl in the cast and he'd gone away, until the day I met him.'

'So what happened?'

'I did just what Claire said. That night, he was waiting outside the studio for me, and I just tried to ignore him. I hoped he'd get the message.'

'But he didn't?'

'No, he didn't. Every day he'd be waiting outside the gates. Sometimes he'd tell me that he loved me, other times he'd shout abusive things about Stuart, whom I was dating at the time. He couldn't seem to distinguish make-believe from reality, always calling Stuart "Darren", that sort of thing. He'd warn me that he was a bad influence, but that was just part of the storyline of the show at the time.'

'My God.' Lizzy grimaced. 'He sounds deranged.'

'He was really into taking photographs, and he'd always have a camera with him. Even though I tried to walk past as fast as I could, every day he'd take pictures of me. The male cast members even started accompanying me on the way out, surrounding me, like bodyguards, but it didn't deter him. Sometimes he'd post the photographs to my agent, but mostly I never saw what he'd taken.'

'He was just storing them for his own benefit?'

'I assume so. I certainly never saw any of the photos in a newspaper or magazine.'

'What a freak,' Lizzy said. 'How long did this go on for?'

'Just over a year.'

'Bloody hell! That must have been a living nightmare.'

'It was. And it got worse. Somehow he found out where I lived – I'm not sure, but I think he must have followed me home one night. At first he just sent letters – love letters, I guess – telling me how much he loved me and valued our friendship. He started begging me to leave Stuart and go out with him instead. And then he began hanging around outside the flat, taking photos of me as I arrived or left. Sometimes he'd wait outside in the middle of the night. One night I got up to go to the bathroom, and when I looked out of the window he was there. It was three o'clock in the morning.'

'How did you cope with it all?' Lizzy looked sympathetically at her friend.

'Okay at first,' Emma replied. 'But, after a while, I started getting really depressed. I was on anti-depressants for a time, and the show gave me and Stuart a few weeks off at one point so that we could go on holiday. If it hadn't been for Stuart and Will's support, I think I'd have lost it completely. Will was great, actually – he used to travel up from London all the time to make sure I was okay.'

'And what did the police do? I assume you told them about what was happening.'

'I told them pretty much straight away – well, as soon as he started turning up outside my home. Because he'd done that kind of thing before, I thought they'd take it really seriously from the outset. But I felt they downplayed things at first. They spoke to Stephen, but it was quite informal and didn't put him off. And they gave me all this advice about what to do, how to act; but it was like they were putting the onus on me, and even intimating that it was my fault. I felt they'd let me down, really. It left me with a bit of a distrust of the police, unfortunately.'

'So then what?'

'We got a restraining order. The courts barred him from contacting me or speaking to me. They also banned him from loitering around outside the studio, and outside the flat.'

'And it worked?'

'Thankfully, it did. I didn't see him or hear from him at all after that. And by that time, Stuart and I had both decided that we needed a total change of scenery, to try and put everything behind us. The whole thing had put our relationship under pressure, and I knew that I couldn't bear to stay around Manchester. I even seriously considering quitting acting altogether, because I knew that none of this would have happened if I hadn't been on a television show.' Emma paused and took a sip of her gin and tonic. 'But Stuart convinced me that doing that would only let him win, so instead I decided I would try out for some stage shows – somewhere where I was more anonymous.'

'And that's why you came down to London?'

'Yes. We needed a fresh start. And of course it meant I was close to my family. Plus, there was always a chance that if we stayed up there I might run into Stephen on the street. I just wanted to be somewhere where I thought there was no chance of ever seeing him again. And I haven't seen him since – it's been four years.'

'So what makes you think that he might have attacked Richard?' Lizzy asked. 'After all this time?'

'It was something Mrs Henderson said. She said the person who she saw on the staircase said he was my "number one fan". That's what Stephen Myers used to say. I think she spoke to the person who attacked Richard. And I'm pretty sure that person was Stephen Myers. Do you think I'm jumping to conclusions?'

'No, I don't.' Lizzy sat back in her chair. 'It sounds like it could be him. But do you think he could be capable of doing that? I mean, was he ever violent to you before?'

'No,' Emma admitted. 'He never did anything physical like that – but I always had the feeling that he might be capable of doing something. In his letters, he certainly threatened to do things. But who knows how he might have changed in the time since I saw him last, or what mental state he's in?'

'That's true.' Lizzy thought for a moment. 'But why would he suddenly reappear now, after four years?'

'The wedding – maybe he found out about it and wanted to wreck things.'

'He could have done. But how would he have found out?'

'Who knows? Maybe he never really did stop following me.' Emma stopped suddenly, and shuddered. 'What if he's been watching me all these years, Lizzy?'

'You really think so? Wouldn't you have noticed something?'

'Maybe. I thought I saw him outside the flat before.'

'Really?' Lizzy looked shocked.

'It's okay, it wasn't him,' Emma reassured her. 'I just imagined it. But look around this place here.' She gestured at the drinkers scattered around the pub. 'And look outside – all those people. In London you can blend in, hide, watch people. He might be following me and I'd never notice.'

'This is really freaky,' Lizzy said. 'How much do you know about him?'

'You mean his character, his age, things like that?'

Lizzy nodded.

'Quite a bit. Mostly from what he told me in the letters he sent. I know that he's four years younger than me, and that he was still living with his parents in Oldham, just to the east of

Manchester. I even know his parents' address, because he always put it on the letters he sent me – probably hoping that I would reply. I never did, of course.'

'What about any mental illness?'

'The police told me that he was supposed to be taking medication for some kind of mental disorder. And just by talking to him you could tell that something wasn't quite right.'

'So you're going to tell the police now?'

'I already have done. I called Inspector Gasnier straight after I'd spoken to Mrs Henderson.'

'And they're going to check him out?'

'They said they would "look into it".'

'Well, that's good. So I guess we'll have to wait until they speak to Stephen, then.'

Emma sighed. 'I'm not sure they're going to bother. The way Gasnier sounded on the phone, I think he was just humouring me. They're sure Dan did it, Lizzy, and they've got me pegged as the delusional fiancée who's desperate to clear her future husband's name.'

'You're a lot of things,' Lizzy said, 'but I don't think you're delusional.'

'Thanks,' Emma replied, looking down into her now empty glass.

'What is it?' Lizzy asked. 'You're thinking of something.'

Emma looked up. 'Lizzy, what are you doing tomorrow?'

'Why?' Lizzy said suspiciously. 'Emma Holden, I know that look. What are you up to?'

'I want you to come with me,' Emma said, 'to see Stephen Myers.'

'You're serious?'

'Totally. If I'm right about this, Dan's life could depend on it.'

19

'Emma, I'm not sure this is such a good idea.'

'What do you mean?' Emma said, glancing across at Lizzy, who was in the front passenger seat of the car, early on Monday morning. They had been travelling up the motorway for two hours now, windows wound down due to the heat, just under halfway to their destination: Stephen's parents' house in Oldham.

Lizzy had taken a great deal of persuading, believing that they should let the police get on with the investigation, but Emma had insisted she would go alone if necessary, so finally Lizzy had agreed to accompany her.

'Are you sure about seeing Stephen Myers again?' she said now. 'I mean, from the way you were talking about it all yesterday, about moving to London just to get away from him . . .'

'I'll be okay,' said Emma, passing a slow-moving lorry before moving back into the slow lane. The rush hour wasn't the best time for travelling halfway across the country, but so far the traffic had been okay, and it was not as hot in the car as it would be later on in the day.

'It's just . . . I don't know, have you really thought it through?' Lizzy looked over at her friend. 'Have you actually wondered how you'll react if you come face to face with him, after all this time? If he does have something to do with what happened, confronting him could be really dangerous. And even if he doesn't, then you risk re-igniting his interest in you. He might start following you again.'

'I've thought about it a lot.' Emma kept her focus on the road ahead. 'But I'm trying not to think about it now, in case I change my mind. I'm hoping that he won't be living at home any more, so we can just speak to his parents.'

'But he might still live there. I just wonder whether it would be sensible just to let the police get on with it, and steer clear, that's all.'

'That's what Will would say,' Emma admitted.

'And that's why you didn't tell him that we were going to do this?'

'He would have tried to convince me not to go.'

'Maybe I should have tried harder,' said Lizzy. 'Tried to pull you back from doing something you might regret.'

Emma glanced across at her before turning her attention back to the road. 'Look, Lizzy, don't feel bad. I know this seems a bit crazy, but I have to do something. I can't just wait around, hoping that Dan will just call or turn up, and everything will be all right again. I need to take control. Even if this turns out to be nothing, then at least I've tried. And if that risks inviting Stephen Myers back into my life, then it's the chance I have to take.'

'Have you thought that maybe this is just what he wants?'

'What do you mean?'

'For you to come looking for him. Maybe that's exactly what he wants to happen – to get you to come to him.'

'I have thought about that. But I don't think he's that calculating.'

'Okay,' Lizzy conceded. 'I'll run with it, but if things start getting out of hand – if this Stephen guy starts following you again – we'll call the police straight away.'

'Sure,' Emma agreed.

'What's up?' Emma said, as she slowed the car in a sea of shimmering brake lights just after Birmingham.

'Nothing, I'm okay.' Lizzy peered out of the open window. 'Do you think it will be like this all the way to Oldham?'

'Probably.'

Lizzy blew up towards her forehead and fanned her face with

both hands. 'Even with the windows open, it's stifling in here. At least when wc were moving there was a breeze.'

'I might get air-con next time I buy a car.'

'Good idea.'

'Although if I did, we'd probably never get another heat wave again,' joked Emma, but Lizzy's face didn't register the humour. 'Lizzy,' she said, watching her friend staring into space. 'I can tell when you're brooding. What's the matter?'

'It's nothing really,' Lizzy said, rather unconvincingly. 'It's just that . . . oh, I don't know . . .'

'Spit it out.' Emma selected first gear as the traffic began to move again, albeit painfully slowly.

'I'm just surprised, really,' Lizzy said, 'that you've never mentioned anything about what happened before. I mean, we've been friends for three years, we've lived together, and you've not spoken about it once. Yet from what you've told me, it was a really significant part of your life.'

'I've nearly mentioned it, lots of times,' Emma said. 'But just the idea of talking about it felt like—'

'I'm sorry, Em,' Lizzy interrupted. 'You don't have to talk about it. I'm being really selfish. I can't believe I even brought it up – you don't have to justify anything to me.'

'No, I want to explain,' Emma said. 'To be honest, I was scared about how I might react if I spoke about it. For years I kept it buried, and I just didn't know what would happen if I started talking about it again – I was afraid of how it might affect me.'

'I can understand that.'

'You don't know how many times I've nearly told you. There was one time when we were out shopping, last Christmas. We were walking down Oxford Street and for a moment I thought I saw him on the other side of the road, watching us. I nearly told you then.'

'But it wasn't him?'

'No, it was just someone else with a camera, taking a photo of the Christmas lights. But for that moment I was really scared, Lizzy – really scared.'

'That's terrible, Em. You shouldn't have to go through that on your own.' Lizzy gripped Emma's arm briefly. 'I could have helped.'

'I know. You're helping now.'

Thankfully the traffic eased and for half an hour they enjoyed a good run up the motorway at a constant seventy. For a time Emma lost herself, listening to the radio and concentrating on the driving. But, every so often, the reality of what they were doing would strike again.

Emma and Lizzy hadn't spoken in twenty minutes when Lizzy finally worked up the courage to ask her question.

'Emma, you said that the thing with Stephen affected your relationship with Stuart.'

Emma nodded.

'Is that why you two split up? But you don't have to talk about it if you don't want to. Just tell me to butt out.'

'It's okay,' Emma said. 'Maybe this is the time to tell you everything.' She took a moment to gather her thoughts. 'It had some effect, but it wasn't the reason we split up. I don't think Stuart really settled in London, to be honest. When we first moved down we were both really hopeful. We'd put the bad things behind us and we thought that things were going to get better from then on. At first things were going really well. Stuart got a short-term role with the BBC and I picked up a part in a stage play. But then after Stuart's contract ended, he had real trouble getting work that he wanted. He started getting depressed and just seemed to lose interest, really.'

'With you?'

'With everything. He didn't bother going for auditions and started sleeping in all the time. Then, after about three months of that, he just said that he thought we should split up. Said it would be for the best. He left straight away.'

'Was it a surprise?'

'Yes,' Emma said. 'Obviously I knew he hadn't been happy, and that something had definitely been troubling him, but I didn't think it was because he was unhappy with our relationship. It was a complete shock.'

'It must have been hard.'

'It was. We were supposed to be getting married, and, as far as I was concerned, spending the rest of our lives together. I thought he was The One. So when he left, I was heartbroken. Suddenly there was this huge hole in my life. I'd never felt so empty inside. But, shortly afterwards, I met you and moved into your place, and that really helped.'

'And then you met Dan.'

'Yeah.' Emma smiled ruefully. 'And now *he*'s gone.'

'I'm sure everything will be all right,' Lizzy said.

'I keep telling myself that,' Emma replied.

'We're only about half an hour away,' Emma announced. 'We've made good time.'

'Twelve thirty,' Lizzy said, looking at the in-car clock. 'No wonder my stomach's rumbling.'

'Maybe we should have eaten at the last services we passed, but I was just desperate to get up here as soon as possible. That way, we can get back to London at a decent time – with all your rehearsals, you need early nights.'

'It all seems so unimportant,' Lizzy said, 'under the circumstances. Maybe I should have said no, like you did to your audition.'

'You shouldn't think like that,' Emma said. 'Let's just focus on what we're going to do when we get to Stephen's parents'.'

'Okay. So have you thought about how you're going to do this? What are you going to say to them?'

'I'm hoping that they might be able to tell us about what Stephen has been doing recently – especially if he's been to London.'

'Do you think they'll tell us things like that?'

'Not sure, but it's worth a try. His dad seemed quite reasonable, and I think if he suspects Stephen might have done something, then he might be willing to speak to us.'

'You've met him before?'

'I've never met him face to face. But he did send me a letter once, saying that he would speak to Stephen and try and convince him to stop following me. He seemed like a really nice person.'

'Nothing like his son, then.'

'No, thank goodness.'

'So you're going to tell them why you're asking the questions? About Dan and Richard?'

'I think so.'

'And what if Stephen is there?'

'Then I'll ask Stephen,' stated Emma, 'although I'm praying that it won't come to that.'

'Surely if he has done it then he's not going to tell us, is he?'

'Probably not, but as much as I don't like the idea, in his own deranged way he did care for me, Lizzy. I might be able to get him to tell the truth.'

20

'Still sure you want to do this?'

'Not really,' Emma said, as they both examined the terraced home of Stephen's parents from the pavement outside. Moss sprouted from the grey brickwork in places, and the windows were smeared with a layer of grime. Not even the blazing sunshine could brighten the dreary house. 'Now I'm here, I'm starting to think that I might have jumped to the wrong conclusion.'

'We could just turn around, go home,' Lizzy offered.

Emma exhaled. 'No, we're here now. Let's do it.'

'Besides, they might not live here any more.'

'There's only one way to find out,' Emma replied, as she stepped towards the front door. It was wooden, with green paint that was flaking. She knocked and they waited. Part of Emma prayed that Stephen wouldn't open the door; she didn't know how she would react. All those sleepless nights he had caused; what if just seeing him sent her spiralling back into the depths of despair? But another part of her wanted to face him down. To look him in the eye and ask whether he had anything to do with this.

She waited for a few seconds, then knocked again. Flakes of green paint stuck to her knuckles. As she brought her hand away from the door, she noticed that it was shaking.

Still there was no answer.

'Maybe they're out,' she said, more relieved than she was willing to admit, even to herself. Travelling back into the past like this was unnerving, and suddenly she wanted to get back in the car and return to her normal life.

Except she didn't have a normal life any more, not without Dan.

She glanced down the road as an old woman crossed it, pulling a shopping bag on squeaky wheels.

'No,' Lizzy said, suddenly. 'Someone's in.'

Emma spun around. 'Really?'

'I've just seen someone at the top window.'

Emma looked up at the yellowing net curtains, but saw no one. She took a step back from the door, keeping her eyes trained on the window. 'Did you see who it was? Was it a woman or a man?'

'A woman.'

His mother.

Hesitating for a few moments, she came to a decision. 'Mrs Myers?' she shouted up at the top window. 'Can you open the door, please?'

Before she had even finished her sentence, the door creaked open.

The woman who appeared reminded Emma of one of the undead from a zombie movie. She was wearing a shabby nightdress, and her face hung down as though it were being pulled on by invisible weights.

Emma knew straight away it was Stephen's mother, even though she had never seen her before. It was her eyes that gave her away – she had Stephen's vacant yet longing look in them, and the resemblance made Emma shudder. It was like looking at an older, female version of her stalker.

'Emma?' said the woman, speaking as though she'd just woken from a deep sleep, her eyes burning into Emma.

Emma nodded, taken by surprise. She had always wondered how much Stephen had told his parents about her, but she had never once imagined that after all these years his mother would actually recognise her. And instantly.

'It's so great to see you,' Mrs Myers said, smiling, revealing stained teeth. She moved off the doorstep and towards Emma. Before she could react, Emma found herself being smothered by a hug. 'Stephen will be so happy.'

Emma recoiled internally at Mrs Myers' pungent body odour. She fought the urge to push her away, and instead surrendered to her embrace.

'You both take sugar?' Mrs Myers called from the kitchen.

'None for me, thank you,' Lizzy replied.

Emma didn't answer.

'Or for Emma,' Lizzy added, noticing that her friend didn't seem to have heard the question.

Emma was sitting on a scruffy sofa on the opposite side of the living room to Lizzy. The room was unbelievably dark and dingy, the carpet sticky, and damp patches had spread across the ceiling. But it was the overpowering smell that made the experience so uncomfortable. Emma couldn't quite put her finger on what the nauseating stench reminded her of, but it was familiar.

'Here you go,' Mrs Myers said, bringing in a tray with three cups of tea and a packet of opened biscuits.

'Thanks,' Lizzy said, looking with concern at Emma, who still appeared to be in deep thought.

'It's such a lovely surprise to see you,' Mrs Myers said, handing Emma a cup of tea. 'After all this time.'

'Thanks,' Emma said.

'I've heard so much about you, and of course I've seen you on the television. But to meet you in person is something I've wanted to happen for a long time. But you know Stephen – he likes his privacy, and I didn't like to push it with him.'

Emma exchanged glances with Lizzy.

'You know,' Mrs Myers continued, looming over Emma, 'you're much more beautiful in person. Stephen is such a lucky boy to have a girl like you – beautiful, and a talented actress. I told Stephen, make sure you never let her go – never let her go.'

'Mrs Myers,' Emma began, 'you know Stephen and I never . . .'

But then she stopped. Maybe this wasn't the best time to talk about this: she had to keep in mind what she wanted from this visit. To deviate from her aim could be a big mistake. It could ruin everything.

'We came to see Stephen,' she said, trying to sound nonchalant. 'Is he here?'

Mrs Myers looked perplexed.

Emma tried again. 'Is Stephen here with you?'

'No,' said Mrs Myers, her face collapsing with shock, as if she had just received the most devastating news imaginable. 'I thought he was with you.'

'He's not with me, Mrs Myers.'

'I . . . I don't know where he is then,' she said, putting a hand to her mouth and taking a step back, as if struck by an unseen blow.

'Do you know where he's been in the last week or so?' Emma pressed. 'Has Stephen been to London?'

'London? He's never been to that place.' Her voice hardened into anger. 'I've told him, don't go to that disgusting place. It's so horrible and dirty.' She jabbed a finger at Emma. 'He would never have gone there. What are you saying, young lady?'

Emma wanted to stand up and leave. She felt exposed, and she didn't like where this conversation was heading or the way Mrs Myers was behaving. But she decided to stay where she was and try to turn down the heat. 'I'm not saying anything, Mrs Myers. I just thought you might know where Stephen is.'

'Well, I don't. Please, drink your tea, before it gets cold.'

Emma did as requested, trying to hide her grimace when she realised that the milk in the tea was badly off. She watched as Mrs Myers took a sip of her tea and didn't register any kind of discomfort. She looked across at Lizzy again, whose face revealed that she had already tasted the vile drink.

Emma tried desperately to think of another avenue of investigation, but struggled to find a way ahead. She wondered how Inspector Gasnier might have approached it.

'Would you like to see Stephen's room?' Mrs Myers said.

Emma gave up drinking her tea. 'Yes, that would be nice.'

'Just one minute,' said Mrs Myers. 'I need to check something first.' She exited the living room and went upstairs.

'She thinks you're seeing Stephen,' Lizzy whispered. 'She's not well, is she?'

'Something's wrong,' Emma said, her ears pricking up as she heard Mrs Myers talking to someone upstairs, although it wasn't loud enough to hear what she was saying.

Lizzy heard too, and her face fell. 'You don't think—?'

'Maybe,' Emma said. 'But you're right; she's not well at all.'

'You can come up now, girls,' Mrs Myers shouted. She sounded happy again, and Emma wondered whether she was suffering from some kind of manic-depressive disorder. It would explain the cave-like, gloomy house; the unkempt living room and kitchen.

'Come on,' Emma said to Lizzy, as she rose from the sofa. 'I'll go first.'

'I don't like this,' Lizzy said.

'Neither do I. I don't like any of it.'

'In here,' Mrs Myers said, beckoning them towards the room at the far end of the landing. 'Sorry to keep you waiting – I just wanted to make sure that everything was in order.'

Emma edged across the landing, floorboards creaking under her, past two closed doors. She wondered whether the person who Mrs Myers had been talking to was lurking behind one of them. It could be Mr Myers, or it could be Stephen himself. She kept one eye on Lizzy, who was following close behind.

'Come on in,' Mrs Myers said, her face bright and welcoming.

Come into my parlour, said the spider to the fly.

Mrs Myers stepped back and let Emma into the room. The scene took Emma's breath away. The walls of the bedroom were covered with photographs – overlapping photos, three or four deep. There were so many, she could only see the wallpaper behind them at the very corners of the room.

'I knew you'd like the photographs,' Mrs Myers said, as Emma glanced from one photo to another.

They were all of her. It was a scrapbook of her life in Manchester – photos outside the television studio, in the streets of the city, outside her flat, even through the windows of her home.

But one photo in particular stood out.

It was an image of her crossing the road. She recognised the shops and buildings in the background – it was at Oxford Circus, the busy intersection on Oxford Street, in central London.

Stephen Myers had followed her to the capital.

21

Desperate to discuss with Lizzy what they had just seen, Emma excused herself. They headed downstairs, leaving Mrs Myers sitting on the bed.

'Do you think she's talking to *herself*?' Lizzy said, as they re-entered the living room. They could hear Mrs Myers speaking from the room above.

Emma looked up towards the ceiling. 'I think so – unless there's someone up in one of the other rooms.'

Could it be Dan?

'I think I'd rather believe that she's talking to herself.'

Emma smiled nervously at Lizzy. 'Me too.'

'I couldn't believe his bedroom,' Lizzy said. 'It really gave me the creeps – like something you see in the movies. This whole house gives me the creeps.'

'I know.' Emma thought back to Stephen's room. She couldn't get the image out of her head: the wall plastered with photos of her, shrine-like; a sinister catalogue of her life, compiled by a delusional man who thought he loved her. And then the revelation contained in that one particular photograph – the photograph that could be the key to finding Dan.

'It must have been a real shock,' Lizzy said, looking shocked herself, 'seeing them all like that. It's really freaky. The guy must still be obsessed with you, to have all those things still on the wall after four years.'

'Stephen followed me to London.' Emma's voice was small in the room.

'What? How do you know?'

'I found this on the wall upstairs.' Emma handed the

photograph to Lizzy. She had managed to snatch it from the wall without Mrs Myers seeing.

'My God, that's Oxford Street!' Lizzy looked at Emma, her eyes wide. 'When the hell was that taken?'

'I don't know. The coat I'm wearing in the shot, I've had it for years, so it could have been anytime.'

'Em, we've got to get out of here, now, while we can.' Lizzy stood up urgently, picking up her bag from the floor. 'What if he comes back while we're still here? What if he's actually upstairs now, hiding in one of the other rooms?'

Emma hesitated, fighting the inclination to agree with her friend.

'What? C'mon, Em. What if he comes back? He could do anything, and it's not like she's going to stop him,' Lizzy hissed, gestured towards the ceiling. 'She's as crazy as he is. Plus, nobody knows we're here; no one can help us if something bad happens.'

'I've been thinking,' Emma said slowly, pushing aside her fears of what Stephen might or might not do, 'about what this smell reminds me of.'

'What?'

'I used to go to dance classes, and I had to walk past a butcher's on the way from the bus stop. Down the side of the shop was an alley where they kept the bins, and it used to stink. That's where I remember the smell from. Lizzy, the smell in this house, it smells like rotting meat.'

Lizzy looked at her. 'You don't think . . . ?'

Just contemplating the thought was horrifying in itself, but Emma felt sure she had identified the smell. Something was definitely rotting in the house.

'I have to check it out.'

'But we don't know where the smell is coming from,' Lizzy protested. 'And Mrs Myers will be back down any minute. What if she catches you?'

'Keep a look out,' said Emma, standing up and moving towards the kitchen. 'Let me know as soon as you hear her coming down the stairs.'

'Em, I don't like this.'

'Please.'

'Okay,' Lizzy conceded, but she looked less than happy.

Emma investigated the kitchen, but although the smell was stronger there, there was nothing to suggest anything sinister. The place was a food hygiene disaster area, however, with sponge-like mould growing on the numerous cups, plates and saucers littered around the room. She wondered briefly whether the cups they had been given also had mould at the bottom; the thought made her feel sick.

Quickly and quietly, she opened the cupboards one by one, each time wondering whether something horrible was lurking inside. Most of the cupboards were empty, save for a few cans of food, most past their sell-by date.

Just as she was about to return to the living room, wondering whether the smell was perhaps coming from outside, she noticed the door in the corner of the room. She hadn't seen it on entering the kitchen, as it had been partially obscured by the open door from the living room.

'Have you found anything?' Lizzy called quietly from the living room.

'I'll just be a minute.'

Emma opened the door and grimaced as the foul, pungent smell hit her like a tidal wave, rolling up from the dark abyss at the bottom of the stairs.

'It's a cellar. The smell's coming from down there.'

'Be careful,' Lizzy insisted.

Emma stood at the top of the stairs, looking down into the darkness. She looked to her right and found a light switch, but the bulb had blown. She would have to go down there in the dark, or give up.

Never a fan of the dark, she didn't relish it. But something drove her on.

'Are you okay, Em?'

Hanging on to the thought that Lizzy was only in the next room, Emma progressed gingerly down the stairs, brushing against cobwebs, not daring to answer her for fear that any noise would send something careering out at her from the darkness. With only the dim light from the kitchen providing any guidance, it felt as if the darkness were swallowing her up.

When she reached the cellar's concrete floor, the decaying meat smell was so strong she began to feel nauseous.

The cellar stretched back farther than the light from the top of the stairs could penetrate. It was impossible to tell where exactly the stench was coming from, but there was no doubt that the source was down here.

What the source was, she didn't like to think.

A number of cardboard boxes littered the floor, and she began looking through them, hardly able to see anything. The boxes contained a variety of household junk material: an old kettle, chipped cups and saucers, a tea tray. No putrid meat.

No body parts.

But the smell *was* coming from somewhere.

She moved deeper into the cellar, stepping around obstacles. Coughing now from the overpowering smell, she stumbled over a stray box that was so heavy it refused to budge even with her running into it. The smell seemed stronger than ever. As she ripped at the brown tape that snaked across the top of the box, she realised that its sides were wet.

'Em!' Lizzy shouted, from the top of the stairs.

Emma continued to pull at the tape. It was so difficult to see here, in the very back of the cellar. Then she had an idea. She pulled out her mobile phone and used the glow from the screen to brighten the darkness, if only barely.

'Em! We've got to get out of here! Quick!'

Finally, Emma managed to open the box, and she instinctively recoiled. The smell rolled around her as she held her breath and peered inside.

The box contained raw chicken, still in the supermarket packaging. It was in the latter stages of decay, but she didn't stop to look at it too closely.

She turned, coughing and spluttering, and headed back

towards the stairs. There was no time to investigate further. It hadn't been a pleasant experience, but at least her worst fears – that a body, Dan's body, had been down there – hadn't been realised.

Lizzy was waiting for her at the top of the stairs, her face anguished. 'Thank goodness you're all right. C'mon!' She pulled at Emma's sleeve. 'We've got to go, now!'

'What's the matter?' Emma closed the cellar door, feeling panicked.

Lizzy looked terrified. 'It's Mrs Myers. She's upstairs, screaming Stephen's name. It sounds like she's having some kind of a breakdown up there. Please, can we go?'

Emma nodded decisively, once. 'Let's get out of here.'

They passed through the living room into the hallway, counting the seconds until they could escape from this house of horrors and emerge into the real world.

But the sight of a crying, bread-knife-wielding Mrs Myers blocking their exit brought them to a sudden halt.

'You can't leave,' said Mrs Myers, holding the shaking blade towards them, tears spilling down her cheeks. 'Not until you tell me where my Stephen is.'

22

'You were going to leave, without even saying goodbye, just like he did,' said Mrs Myers, taking a tiny, faltering step towards them. Emma mirrored her movement and held up her hands, while gesturing for Lizzy to retreat into the living room.

'I'm sorry, we were just going for a walk,' Emma lied. Now was the time to tell Mrs Myers whatever she wanted to hear. Tell her anything to get out alive.

'No.' Mrs Myers shook her head and took another zombie-like step forward.

Emma used those milliseconds to evaluate what she might do to get the knife off her. But it was difficult – the hallway was narrow, with little room to manoeuvre.

'Let's sit down and talk about it in the other room,' Emma offered, trying out a smile. There would be more of a chance if she brought Mrs Myers into the living room. Taking the knife by force, however, would be a last resort – her karate instructor had always stressed that talking, along with body language, was often the most effective weapon in a dangerous situation.

'I love my son so much,' said Mrs Myers, her face contorted by grief. She was grasping the knife so tightly that her knuckles were ivory white, contrasting with the dirt of the rest of her hands. 'I miss him.'

'I'm sure you do,' Emma said, keeping her eye on the blade and stepping back, towards the living room. Mrs Myers followed her into the room, step by step, as if they were linked together.

Lizzy was standing against the far wall. Emma shot her a comforting glance.

'We're going to talk about this,' Emma said, to both Lizzy and Mrs Myers. 'Do you want to give me the knife?'

Mrs Myers was looking around the living room, bug-eyed, as if it were the first time she'd ever been in there.

Emma watched the woman's face for any sign of acceptance. 'Can you give me the knife?'

'When he called me a few weeks ago, I was so happy. He told me he was coming to see me – that he hadn't meant to go away like that. He was looking forward to seeing his mother.'

'Did Stephen say where he was?'

'I thought he was with you. He said he was with you.'

'He wasn't with me, Mrs Myers,' Emma said. 'I promise.'

The knife began to lower as Mrs Myers' head started to droop; it was as if her neck muscles had started to fail.

'Do you know what it's like to lose someone you love?' she asked, staring at the carpet. 'It feels like your insides have been ripped out – your heart stamped on.' Now she was fighting tears.

'I understand,' Emma said. 'My mother died.' She understood all too well what it was like to lose someone who you loved so much that it physically hurt to think about them not being there any more.

Mrs Myers raised her head and looked Emma directly in the eyes. Then she stepped forward.

Emma stood her ground as she approached.

'Em . . .' Lizzy said, concerned.

'It's okay,' Emma replied, bringing an arm out towards the knife, which Mrs Myers now held loosely. But before she could get it, Mrs Myers released her grip on it completely and the knife fell onto the carpet.

'C'mon,' Emma said, leading Mrs Myers to the sofa and sitting down with her. 'Just sit down for a while.'

As she did this, Lizzy moved forward and picked up the knife. 'What shall I do with this?' she asked, holding it by the very end of its handle, as if it were contaminated.

'Better keep hold of it for now,' Emma said.

Lizzy pulled a painful face. 'Shall we call . . . you know?'

'Please, don't.'

Emma and Lizzy started with shock as a bearded man carrying shopping bags appeared in the doorway.

'Please, don't call anyone,' he said, stepping into the living room. 'She has a mental health nurse. I'll call her.'

'Are you Mr Myers?' asked Emma, standing up.

'I am, but please call me Peter.' He held out his hand. 'It's nice to meet you, Emma. Well, I can't pretend I don't know who you are,' he said, noticing her surprise. 'Not with all those photographs up in that bloody bedroom.'

'Nice to meet you, too.' Emma took his hand.

'I guess you're here to see Stephen,' he said.

'We wanted to talk to him, yes,' Emma replied, noting that Stephen looked even more like Mr Myers than Mrs Myers did. It was the shape of his face, and those cat-green eyes.

Mr Myers sighed. 'I can take you to where he is,' he said. 'I'll just phone the nurse, and then we can get going. You'll be okay, here, won't you, Margaret? I won't be gone long.'

His wife just nodded, staring at the floor.

'I'm sorry you had to see Margaret like that,' said Peter Myers, a few minutes into the journey. His van was emblazoned with adverts for his handyman business: locksmith, electrical and computer repairs, plumbing – no job too small. 'I had no idea things had got so bad.'

They'd left shortly after the nurse had arrived and settled Margaret. He hadn't told them where they were going: just that he was taking them to see his son. And although Emma was still nervous about seeing Stephen, she felt comforted by Peter Myers' presence. While his father was there, she doubted Stephen would do anything stupid. And he might just be more likely to tell the truth about what had happened.

'You don't live there any more?' she asked, thinking too late that it was a terribly personal question.

'Not for a few months,' he said, turning the corner and

accelerating along the main road. 'Although I do pop in regularly, just to make sure that she's okay.'

'She seems really depressed,' Emma said.

'She is. She's not been well for a while, although it's been getting worse since I left, if I'm honest with myself. She used to be such a proud woman, especially where the house was concerned. But now, well, you saw what it's like.'

'At least she has the nurse to look in on her.'

'I know. But she stopped taking her drugs regularly and things got worse from then on. That's one of the reasons why I left – I just couldn't cope any more. I know it sounds selfish, but I just had to get away, for my own sanity.'

'Is it something to do with Stephen, her being depressed? Lizzy heard her shouting his name, and she was talking to me about how he had left her.'

'It all started with Stephen, but now it's taken on a momentum of its own. To be honest, if he walked through the door tomorrow, I think it would probably be too late.'

'She told me he called her a few weeks ago,' Emma said.

'She said that?' Peter Myers was clearly shocked, and for a second it took his attention away from the road.

'Yes, she definitely said he had called her.'

He shook his head. 'I really need to call that nurse and tell her something needs sorting out.'

'You don't think he did call her?'

'No,' Mr Myers said, turning right and then taking a sharp left into a country lane. They continued, in silence, down the lane for a few hundred yards, before pulling to a stop against the side of a low, dry-stone wall.

'We're here.' Peter undid his seatbelt and got out of the van.

Emma and Lizzy followed him as he moved towards the wall. As Emma looked over it, she saw that they had parked next to a cemetery; she gazed across at hundreds of gravestones running off downhill into the distance.

'Follow me,' he said, climbing over the wall and heading off, weaving through the gravestones. Emma and Lizzy followed, not speaking. Just a few metres from where the van was parked, Mr Myers stopped and waited.

When they caught up with him, he simply pointed at Stephen Myers' headstone.

Part Two

23

'I can't believe it's been four years,' Peter Myers said, staring at the headstone. 'The time has gone so quickly, but so many things have changed.'

Emma didn't know what to say.

'I'm really sorry, Mr Myers,' she said, finally, feeling like a complete fraud for standing in front of Stephen's grave and uttering words of condolence. But even though she had feared Stephen, and learn to hate his puppydog-like attention, there had always been a part of her that had felt compassion for him. He had been a sad, pitiful figure – the sort of person who seemed destined never to be truly happy.

She wondered whether destiny was set in stone that way.

'I always thought it could end up like this,' said Peter, as if reading Emma's thoughts, 'even when Stephen was a young child. There was always something different about him, something I couldn't quite put my finger on. He was so intense, in everything he did. Obsessive, really – like he was with you.' He turned to Emma, who smiled weakly back. 'I'm just so sorry for all he put you through.'

'That was a long time ago.'

'Still, you don't forget those kinds of things in a hurry, do you?'

Emma shook her head.

'As soon as I found out what he was doing to you, I tried my best to reason with him, but he really believed that you were in love. I know it seems hard to understand, but he'd create alternative realities, and for him they were the truth. We took him to see specialists, psychiatrists, but it didn't really make any difference.'

'Like I said, it was a long time ago.'

'Yes.'

Wanting and not wanting to know in almost equal amounts, Emma asked the question she'd been dreading. 'How did Stephen die?'

'He committed suicide.'

A sickening stab hit Emma right in the stomach. He'd killed himself, and the date on the gravestone revealed it was shortly after she had moved to London – when reality had probably finally hit home that she didn't want to be with him.

'In the few weeks before he died,' Peter said, 'Stephen had been acting even more strangely than usual. I should have realised something was about to happen. He'd disappear for days at a time, and then just walk back in the house as if nothing had happened, like some kind of tomcat. Margaret was going out of her mind with worry, and he wouldn't even explain where he'd been. I got used to it, I suppose. I think I just tried not to think about it. But then, one time, he didn't come home for days.' Peter swallowed as his voice thickened. 'The police found him in a canal about three miles from here. He'd used a knife to cut himself and then jumped or fell into the water. Some people on a narrowboat found his body, hidden by some rushes.' He swallowed again. 'There wasn't much left of his face to identify him by. Foxes, scavengers, you know . . .' His voiced trailed off.

Emma had to take a deep breath. 'Do you think it was because of me?' she asked, painfully. 'Because I rejected him?'

Peter looked at her, hard. 'You're not to blame. If it hadn't been you, it would have been someone else.'

Emma nodded, grateful for his understanding. 'Did Stephen ever come to London to find me?'

'He may have done,' replied Peter, slowly. 'But I doubt it. He didn't really like being in unfamiliar places. That's why he always hung around outside those damn television studios – we used to take him there when he was younger, hoping to bump into some TV stars.'

'It's just that I found a photo of me in his bedroom, taken when I was in London.'

'Then I guess he did,' said Peter, slightly nonplussed. 'As I said, he went missing for days at a time, so he could have gone anywhere and we'd have been none the wiser.' He looked at Emma. 'I'm sorry you had to see his room, with those photos. I wanted to take all those things down, after . . . you know, but Margaret wouldn't hear of it. The place is like a shrine, and I haven't been in that room for years. I just can't stand it. And it's like that with the whole house now. That's why I had to get out.'

'What will happen to Margaret? Will she be okay?'

He shrugged. 'I hope so.'

'He didn't ask why we were looking for Stephen,' said Lizzy, as they began their drive back down to London.

'I'm glad,' Emma admitted. 'I felt bad enough, without him thinking that I suspected Stephen of attacking Richard.' *And making Dan disappear.*

'But it was a perfectly reasonable assumption.'

'I jumped to conclusions.'

'Anyone would have thought the same, especially after what Mrs Henderson said, with the number one fan thing.'

'He's been dead for four years, Lizzy. Lying in the ground – all that time when I thought I saw him in the street. I've been accusing him of things all this time.'

'You don't blame yourself, do you?'

'No, not really . . . oh, I don't know, I guess I do feel partly responsible. I can't help thinking that if I'd handled it differently, then maybe—'

'Don't,' Lizzy chastised. 'There was nothing you could have done. His father said it himself. They were his *family* and couldn't do anything to help him, so you wouldn't have been able to change anything.'

'Maybe,' Emma conceded.

'You're too hard on yourself, Emma. Bad things happen, and sometimes you can't do anything about it.'

'Bad things like what's happening with Dan and Richard?'

'It might all work out, Em.'

The journey home was torturous – there had been an accident on the M6 southbound, closing two lanes, and the traffic tailed back for twenty miles.

It took seven hours to get back to London.

Emma stopped by her flat, partly to pick up any phone messages but also in the vain hope that Dan might be there, all apologetic. But the apartment was dark, cold and empty.

There was only one message on the machine.

'Hi, Emma, it's Marie from Perfect Brides. I'm just calling to confirm the message your boyfriend left on our answer phone last night, about cancelling the wedding dress. If you can give me a call back as soon as possible, that would be great.'

24

It was Tuesday, and after a morning lazing around Lizzy's flat, Emma took an early-afternoon tube south of the river, alone. Lizzy had wanted to come with her, but she had to attend rehearsals, and no matter how much she joked about being indispensable, there would be limits to the director's patience.

The heat wave was continuing, and the temperature was again fierce. Despite being dressed in the necessary attire of short-sleeved top, skirt and sandals, Emma didn't feel in a summery mood. She reached the Perfect Brides shop and paused for a moment outside the decorative window, filled with mannequins sporting expensive dresses and large photographs of happy couples posing in typical English gardens. Her heart sank as she surveyed the shop front, thinking back to all the times she had visited previously, full of hopes and dreams. She took a deep breath and entered the shop.

'Hi,' she said, heading for the familiar face of Marie.

'Hi, Emma,' Marie said. 'I'm sorry about all this.'

Marie had worked in Perfect Brides for six years, and was quite an expert in dealing with distraught women coming to terms with an aborted marriage; when she had first started in the shop, she had had no idea how much of a counselling role she would have to play. She'd learnt from experience that it was important to curb the sympathy, for risk of upsetting the person too much. Nobody wanted a breakdown scenario.

'Would you like a cup of tea?' she asked. 'Or we have coffee—?'

'I'm okay.' Emma suddenly felt emotionally smothered by the sight of the wedding paraphernalia that met her at every turn.

'I'd just like to listen to the message and leave, to be honest. I can sort out anything else by phone, can't I?'

'Of course,' Marie said.

Things usually happened in the way they had done with Emma, with the potential groom backing out; the unusual part this time was that the potential groom himself had called them to tell them the news.

'The answering machine's in the back office,' Marie said. 'Just come around the counter and follow me.'

Emma waited as Marie stood over the office telephone, pressing various buttons. Her heart was racing with anticipation. She hadn't heard Dan's voice in days now, and she didn't know how she would react if it was indeed Dan who had left the message.

She couldn't deny that a part of her still refused to believe that it had been Dan who had cancelled the wedding dress.

'This should be it,' said Marie, pressing a button and stepping back from the machine.

'*Hello, it's Dan Carlton here. I was with Emma Holden.*'

Emma felt sick; it *was* Dan, although his voice sounded subtly different from usual – there seemed a hint of a quiver.

'*She asked me to call you, to cancel the wedding dress. We're not together any more. Sorry for the late notice. Thanks, bye.*'

The machine beeped off.

'That was the whole message?' Emma said.

'Sorry,' Marie said, 'that was all we got. That's why I thought it was best to give you a call and just confirm what Dan told us.'

'Thanks. I'm relieved, really – at least I know he's okay.'

Marie looked puzzled, but tried to hide her interest.

'Dan disappeared last Friday,' Emma explained. 'And that's the first I've heard of him since.'

'Oh, I'm so sorry.' Marie looked at her. 'He just left without saying anything?'

Emma nodded.

'That's awful,' said Marie, shocked out of her usual professionalism. 'Really awful.'

* * *

120

Emma held back the tears until she stepped out of the shop, then the floodgates opened and she ducked into an alleyway to hide her embarrassment. She wasn't used to showing weakness in public – she'd always had to be the strong one for the family – and she wasn't about to let herself down now.

She dried her eyes. Again she had been a fool, first putting her trust in someone who had let her down, and then refusing to believe the reality of the situation when it was clear to see.

She leant against the brick wall. Her first reaction was to call Lizzy, but she would be in the middle of rehearsals by now. Instead she called Will, but the call rang through to his voicemail. Lastly she called her dad.

'Oh, hi, Emma,' he said, sounding distracted. Emma could hear his girlfriend, Miranda, talking in the background, continuing the conversation that her call had obviously interrupted.

'I was wondering if we could have a chat,' Emma said, trying to block out the incessant chattering in the background.

'Sure, sure, how about you come around here in say, an hour or two?'

'That would be good, Dad.'

'Great, great. I'll get Miranda to rustle up something to eat.'

'We're having Clive and Vanessa over for dinner!' Emma heard Miranda protest, probably deliberately loud enough for her to hear.

'Just a second.' Her dad muffled the phone. A few seconds of silence followed, and Emma guessed he was moving into another room.

'Sorry about that,' he said in a whisper. 'I didn't want Miranda to hear what I was going to say.'

'Go on.' Emma was intrigued, and also happy that there were at least some things that were still sacrosanct between father and daughter.

'I'm glad you rang, Emma,' he said, 'because I've got something to tell you. Something I should have told you about some time ago.'

25

'Oh, hi,' Miranda said, feigning surprise as she opened the door and saw Emma standing there. 'Sorry, I'm just in the middle of preparing some food, so things are a bit disorganised in here at the moment.'

She was wearing an apron and her hands were speckled with flour. She still looked stunning. It had taken Emma a long time to get used to the fact that her dad was living with someone barely older than herself; in truth, she wasn't sure she would ever get used to the idea. Even though her mum was dead, and she wanted her dad to be happy, there would probably always be a part of her that resented Miranda.

'That's okay,' Emma said, as she followed Miranda into the house. It was still weird being in the family home she had grown up in and seeing another woman there, in charge of the household. It felt as if Miranda were trampling on Emma's memories.

They emerged into the open dining room and kitchen area to be greeted by an impressive spread of food.

'We're having some of my work colleagues over for dinner,' Miranda explained.

It looked like a banquet. From what her dad had told Emma, Miranda often cooked for work friends. She was a newly qualified consultant in paediatric medicine at St Thomas's Hospital.

'I'll go and get Edward,' Miranda said, heading towards the stairs. 'He's in the bedroom, I think.'

'It's okay,' Emma interrupted. 'I'll go up.'

It seemed petty, but this still felt like her house, and it always would. She didn't want to be treated like a guest.

'Emma,' her dad said, rubbing his eyes and rising from the

bed as he saw her standing at the doorway to the bedroom. 'I didn't hear you arrive.'

He got up from the bed and gave her an uncharacteristic hug.

'Miranda told me you were up here,' Emma said, warming to the embrace.

'How are you feeling?' He pulled back and examined her intently, his hands on both her shoulders.

'I've been better,' she admitted. 'Dan has called off the wedding.'

'*What?* You've heard from him?'

'Not exactly,' she said. 'He left a message on the answer phone at the bridal shop, cancelling the wedding dress.'

Edward looked shell-shocked. 'And you're sure it was him?'

'I heard the message myself.'

'Oh, I'm so sorry, Emma.'

Emma fought back the tears. 'At least I know now that he's okay.'

'Have you told the police?'

'The police? No.'

'I think you should,' he said. 'Emma, I know you'll still feel loyalty towards Dan, but if he had anything to do with what happened to Richard, then they need to know.'

'I know. I will call them, but just not yet.'

'I know it's difficult,' Edward said. He obviously realised that she was struggling to keep it together, and embraced her once again. 'I'm so sorry, Emma. I can't imagine how you must feel. You were so looking forward to the wedding.'

'I still can't quite take it all in.'

He looked at her and smiled kindly. 'C'mon, let's go for a walk.'

It was a beautiful evening, cooler than it had been for some time. They walked for a while, mostly in silence. It reminded Emma of a similar walk they had made some years before. Her dad had ended it by telling her that her mother was dying of cancer. She prayed now that the news her dad had for her this time wouldn't be so devastating.

They stopped on a bridge arching over the Thames, and watched as a team of rowers skimmed past below them. The sun reflected off the river, making it sparkle.

Emma decided to break the silence.

'I went to visit Stephen Myers yesterday,' she said, as the rowers disappeared into the distance.

'What?' Her dad was visibly shocked. 'Why would you go and visit him, after all he did to you?'

'I thought he might have had something to do with Dan disappearing.'

Edward went to speak, but, seemingly flabbergasted by the news, no words came out.

'So what happened?' he said at last.

'Stephen's dead,' she stated. 'They found him in a canal. It happened a few years ago.'

'Oh, right.'

'It was terrible, Dad,' she said. 'I met his mum, and she's got real problems because of what happened. The house she was living in, it was in such a state.'

'It must be difficult to deal with a death like that.' Her dad looked up at the sky. 'I can't imagine how I'd react if you or Will did that. As a parent, you're bound to wonder whether you could have done anything to stop it happening.'

'Pardon?'

He looked confused. 'I said, I can't imagine how I'd react if one of you did that – killed yourself.'

Emma looked at her dad hard. 'How do you know he killed himself?'

'What . . . well . . . you just said . . . they found him in a canal,' he said, sounding flustered.

'I said he was dead, I didn't say he killed himself.'

Her dad blew out his cheeks and gripped onto the bridge, as if for support. The colour had drained from his cheeks. 'I'm sorry, Emma.'

'You *knew*.' Emma shook her head. 'You knew Stephen was dead and you didn't tell me? All this time, you knew what had happened and you didn't say anything to me?'

Her father nodded.

'Do you know how many times in the past few years I thought I saw Stephen Myers following me? I used to lie awake at night, wondering whether he was outside the flat, pointing that damn camera up towards the window. If I'd known . . .'

'I'm really sorry, Emma, but we thought it would be for the best. We didn't want to bring up old memories – we were worried about how you might react.'

'*We?* Who else knew about this?'

'Just three of us – myself, Will and Stuart.'

She couldn't believe what she was hearing. 'This just gets better! Three of the people I trusted the most kept that from me!'

'Like I said, Emma, we just didn't see the point in telling you about it. You were getting on with your life in London, getting over him. He'd haunted you enough while he was alive. I didn't want him to haunt you when he was dead, too.'

'How did you find out? How did you know what happened?'

'Well . . . Will and Stuart came to me, and told me that they'd seen Stephen hanging around outside your apartment in London, shortly after you moved down here. I know you thought that he didn't follow you down here, but he did. They'd warned him off, and he swore that he wouldn't come back again, but we wanted to make sure. So we kept an eye on him.'

'You kept an eye on him? How?'

'We paid for someone to keep a watch on him.'

'A private detective?'

'Yes. I know it sounds crazy, but it was the only way we could be sure that he'd really stay away. A few weeks after we employed the guy I got a call from him, saying that Stephen had been found dead.'

'You said you'd never keep me in the dark again,' Emma said. 'Not after what happened with Mum.'

'Oh, Emma, that's completely different,' her dad protested. 'We just wanted to protect you.'

'You wanted to protect me from Mum's illness.'

'That's not fair,' Edward said, his eyes suddenly filling up. 'It was your mother who promised me not to tell you both. She didn't want you to worry.'

'But I wanted to worry!' Emma suddenly found herself shouting. 'She was dying, Dad. I should have been worrying. Not going off on holidays enjoying myself.'

'I'm sorry, that's all I can say. But, please believe me, I didn't do any of this to hurt you, or your brother.'

'What other secrets are you protecting me from?'

'What?' Her dad seemed taken aback by the question.

'You said on the phone you had something to tell me. Something you should have told me before.'

'I . . . I can't,' he said, turning away. 'It's not the right time now.'

'Tell me, Dad,' Emma said, pulling at his arm. 'If you mean what you say, then tell me whatever it is you were going to tell me.'

'It shouldn't be happening like this,' he said, turning back to her. The strain was etched across his face like carvings on rock.

'Tell me.'

'It's about Miranda and me,' he said. 'We're expecting a baby.'

26

'He's called you, hasn't he?' Emma said, as Will opened the door to his flat.

'You'd better come in,' he said, turning and leading her into the living room. 'I've been waiting for you to arrive. Take a seat.'

'I was going to come straight round,' said Emma, sitting down, 'but then I decided to go and see Richard.'

'You're really angry with me, aren't you? Em, I'm so sorry, really.'

'I'm not angry,' Emma said. 'I was, but seeing Richard lying there – well, it helped me to put things into perspective. I just sat there, watching him, and suddenly, for now at least, my worries don't seem that important.'

'How is he?'

'No change.'

'Right . . .' Will looked off into the middle distance for a moment. 'I'm glad you're not angry, Em, although I wouldn't blame you if you were. I've really let you down.'

'I'm not angry any more, Will, but I *am* disappointed. Of all people, I would have thought that you would be the last person to keep something like that from me. I mean, Stephen Myers had died and you didn't tell me. After all we've gone through with Mum and Dad. We promised there would be no secrets.'

'I know. I hate keeping secrets from you, Em. You've got to believe me.'

Emma thought fleetingly about the secret she was now keeping from Will – that their father was having a baby with Miranda. She was four months pregnant. *How had she not noticed?* Edward had sworn her to secrecy until he could find the right moment to break the news himself. 'Well, it's over now,' she said. 'Stephen's dead, and Dan has called the wedding off.'

'I'm sorry, Em. I thought it was going to be different this time, with Dan. I really didn't expect this.'

'Me neither. But with Richard lying in hospital, fighting for his life, it just doesn't seem the right time to be dwelling on it.'

'Have you tried to call Dan again?'

'There's still no answer. I want to know what happened to Richard, and why. I still can't believe Dan would hurt him.'

'I find it hard to believe, too,' Will agreed. 'So what are you going to do now?'

'Cancel the wedding arrangements, I guess. I need to contact the church, the reception venue, the caterers, and the people bringing the flowers. I'm wondering if Lizzy would do all that.'

'She's a good friend,' Will said.

'So are you. I don't know what I'd do without either of you in the next few months. You'll probably be sick of me by the end of it.'

Will looked down and bit his lower lip.

'What's the matter?' asked Emma, recognising her brother's body language as a sign that something was wrong.

'I'm sorry, Em.' He rubbed a hand savagely over his eyes. 'I'm going away.'

'Away?'

He nodded. 'I have to. I'm afraid if I stay around here, I might do something really stupid.'

'I don't understand. You can't just go away, with everything that's happening . . .'

'I've not been straight with you, Em. I haven't even been straight with myself until recently. I've got problems, big problems.'

'Problems?'

'I've been feeling really depressed,' he revealed. 'And I started drinking. The doctor gave me some tablets for the depression, but it's not stopped the drinking.'

'What? How long has this been going on?'

'A few months now. Em – I'm sorry, but I've decided that I need to get away. I've been in touch with Christopher, and he said I can go over to be with him for a while. My flight's booked for Thursday.'

'You're going the day after tomorrow? To Canada?'

Will nodded.

'I can't believe I didn't notice that things were that bad, Will,' Emma said. 'You're my brother, I *should* have noticed.'

'I hid it well,' he replied. 'Don't blame yourself.'

Will watched from the window as Emma crossed the road below. Sipping from a glass of whisky, he let the waves of self-loathing wash over him. He had taken a coward's way out, and he knew it. But this was about self-preservation. At least if he could get away and get his head together, then there was a chance that when he returned everything could get back to normal.

Maybe then he could start making up for all those lies.

Still, he felt enormous guilt and shame. He was leaving Emma when she needed him most. But at least now he was convinced that his earlier suspicions had been wrong, and that Emma's life was not in danger from that man, or the dark secret that he himself had held for all these years.

27

Early on Wednesday morning, while Lizzy was out again at rehearsals, Emma travelled over to her own flat and called them all herself: the church, the florist, the car hire firm, the photographer – the list went on. She felt oddly distanced from the whole thing, as if she were just a secretary cancelling her boss's meetings.

And it was that easy. Two years of planning was undone in less than thirty minutes.

She finished the last call, then placed the contact list into the wedding box and closed the lid. It felt symbolic: that the part of her life she had shared with Dan had ended. She felt like throwing the box out of the window, and imagined all the magazine cuttings and lists floating down onto the traffic below like confetti.

How had she got it so wrong, again? With Stuart, and now Dan. Both men with whom she had thought she would spend the rest of her life. But both had bailed out on the final approach, without warning.

What was she doing wrong?

And now her relationships with the two other men in her life had also received a jolt. Will was running off to another continent, depressed and on the verge of alcoholism; her dad was fathering a child with a woman barely older than she was.

Lizzy was right: men did act weird.

Instead of throwing the wedding box out of the window, she took it into the bedroom and slid it under the bed.

After leaving Will's flat, she had decided that the next day she would face her fears head-on and return to visit her apartment.

She had to go back there alone eventually, she had reasoned, so it might as well be then.

She lay down on the bedcovers, staring at the ceiling. Then she forced herself to get up from the bed and looked around, remembering the missing photographs of her and Dan. *If he had wanted to end it, why the hell had he taken those photos?* It didn't really make sense. And then, of course, there was the unexplained attack on Richard.

Just thinking of Dan's possible guilt made her head throb.

Instead, she changed into her training outfit of comfortable jogging bottoms and a vest top, before retrieving the punch bag and boxing gloves from the storage cupboard. It had been some time since she had used it, but she soon got back into the swing of things, punching and kicking the bag so hard that occasionally it flew back into the wardrobe behind. Then she went for a run, easing her way down Marylebone High Street before picking up the pace towards Euston Road.

Dodging and weaving through the noisy tourists and serious-faced business people, she crossed the main road and entered Regent's Park. The few days' absence of serious training and the heat were taking its toll on her body, but it felt good. She ran all the way to Primrose Hill, stopping at the top to admire the sun-drenched view across the London skyline.

She wondered if Dan was among that urban mass, and what he was doing. Had he already found someone else? Was he sitting in a coffee house somewhere, sharing a drink with a beautiful woman?

It really didn't sound like Dan at all.

She looked around the hill and suddenly wondered why she had chosen this place to come to. It was full of happy, smiling couples – some playing with their children, others just enjoying each other's company.

And there was a man with a camera.

Pointing it right at her.

'What the hell do you think you're doing?' Emma shouted, jogging over to the man.

He had brought the camera down. 'It's okay, I'm not paparazzi,' he said, holding his hands up. 'I was just taking one photo, that's all. You *are* Emma Holden, aren't you?'

'I might be,' Emma said, 'but what the hell are you doing taking a photo of me in the first place?'

'I'm sorry. People don't usually mind. I come here most days, to spot some movie stars and take their picture. I don't sell them or anything; I just do it as a hobby. Got a snap of Madonna the other day . . . although she's not that special any more, now she's a local. Tom Cruise was round here yesterday! He's in London for the premiere of his new film. I spotted him at the photo exhibition that's running at the National Portrait Gallery – Rock Royalty. He even gave me an autograph. It's an amazing exhibition by the way. They have stunning, previously unseen images of the Stones, the Beatles, Elvis. I've been there nearly every day since it opened last week, and I'll be there most days until it closes next weekend. There's so much to see. And the images are worth looking at again and again. Each time you see something different in them.'

'Sounds good.' As Emma watched him explain, she realised that he was quite young, maybe early twenties.

'Yes, it's been a great week. Tom Cruise, and now I've met you!'

'I'm surprised you recognised me,' she said.

'You're joking! I used to watch *Up My Street* every day. Once I was off school with glandular fever for about three months, and it's all I used to watch. When I got better and went back to school, I got my mum to record it for me so I could watch it when I got home. Never missed an episode for about two years. I'm not saying it was the greatest programme' – he looked at her quickly, embarrassed – 'sorry . . . what I meant is that it was a bit budget, wasn't it? Not like an *EastEnders* or *Coronation Street*. The walls used to wobble. I guessed they must have been saving money on the set so that they could pay you guys loads of money.'

'I wish,' Emma said, softening. She felt bad about over-reacting – he seemed harmless enough. 'You'd be surprised how little money you get doing a show like that. Apart from the guy who played Miles. He was on a fair bit.'

'You're kidding. Miles Macadam? That guy's acting was more wooden than a matchstick factory.'

Emma laughed.

'I'm surprised you weren't on good money,' he said. 'Is that why you left?'

'Not really. I just wanted to try something different – come down to London and try some stage acting.'

'Cool. So what have you done, then?'

'You ask a lot of questions,' she said, smiling.

'I'm practising,' he said. 'I want to be a journalist. So, come on then, what have you done since leaving the show? And it'd better be good – I was gutted when you left. Thought you were the best character in that show by a mile.'

'Thanks,' said Emma, blushing.

'Don't mention it.'

'Well, I've done quite a few stage shows. And I auditioned for a movie recently.'

'Wow. Emma Holden on the big screen. So when's the movie out?'

'Oh, I didn't go for the second reading. Couldn't make it.'

'That's a shame,' he said. 'I'm sure it'll come right.'

'Thanks, you're very kind.'

'So, can I keep the photo?' He smiled. 'You don't want to destroy the film or stamp on my camera, or punch me on the nose?'

'You don't use digital?'

'I have a digital camera too, but sometimes, like today, I use my old film camera because I like the anticipation of waiting to see whether the shot was good or not.'

'I can understand that. Don't worry, I won't make you destroy the film.'

'Cool,' he said, holding out his hand. 'My name's Eric, but you can call me your number one fan.'

133

28

'He said that?' asked Lizzy.

Emma nodded. 'And then he gave me his mobile number.' They were sitting backstage at the Lyceum Theatre, wedged between various props and clothes, tucked away where no one would bother them. Emma had come over and had caught the final few minutes of rehearsals of the musical Lizzy was going to be starring in, before they had taken a break.

Lizzy grimaced. 'Why did he give you his number?'

'I don't know. He didn't say. He just handed it to me.'

'You didn't give him your number, did you?'

'No, of course not.'

'Good. Maybe the phrase was just a coincidence?' Lizzy offered.

'Oh, I'm sure it was,' Emma replied. 'But just for him to say that, well, it freaked me out a bit. I was already on edge, really, after he took the photo.'

'Sounds like another weirdo. You didn't encourage him, or anything? You don't want another stalker.'

Emma thought back, slightly guiltily, on how she had laughed at his joke and allowed herself to be flattered. 'No, I didn't – well, not really. But he didn't seem like a weirdo. He was funny. And I'm sure it was just a coincidence that he saw me there. I'd only jogged up there at the last minute, so he wasn't following me. You think I should just have blanked him?'

'No, not really – it's not your style, Em. You're far too nice. And you shouldn't let bad experiences in the past change you for the worse.'

'You're right.'

'But surely he must be a little crazy to have watched *Up My Street* every day,' Lizzy added. 'I mean, it was a terrible show, wasn't it?'

'Yes, I guess it was,' Emma said, with a smile.

'Those swaying sets were a classic.' Lizzy laughed. 'And when that character got mauled by the bear that escaped from the zoo? You could so tell it was just a man in a suit – you could see the zip running up its back!'

'I forget how bad it was.' Emma also laughed.

Lizzy looked at her. 'It's good to see you smile again, it really is. I know it's not going to be easy for the next few months – maybe longer – but I'm going to help get you through this.'

'Thanks. I don't know what I'd do without you, Lizzy.'

'Ah, don't mention it. That's what friends are for – it's just part of my job description.' She glanced over her shoulder. 'We'll be getting the call to go back any minute. The boss doesn't like us to get too comfortable.'

'I thought you were fantastic up there,' Emma enthused. 'Absolutely brilliant.'

'Well, thank you.' Lizzy smiled. 'I try my best.'

'Seriously, Lizzy, you'll be great. You'll wow the crowd with your—'

'Ample cleavage?'

'Well, I was going to say your voice, but now that you mention it, that outfit is quite revealing! Isn't this supposed to be a family show?'

'Most families will be up in the gods,' Lizzy said. 'From that distance, they'd need binoculars to see anything. Actually, there might be binoculars available up there . . . just for the dads . . . I can't remember.'

'I know it sounds horrible,' Emma said, 'but that leading lady having to pull out might just be the big break you needed.'

'You're right,' Lizzy replied. 'I like Jessica, and I wish she hadn't had to drop the show, but it did work out well for me. That's if I can remember all my lines. It's much harder than I imagined.'

'You'll be fine. I didn't notice any fluffed lines when I was watching.'

'That's because I hide it well. I'm a professional,' joked Lizzy. 'Unfortunately, I can't hide it well enough from the director, and he gave me a bit of a roasting earlier. Said if I didn't get my act together, I'd be lucky to be singing in the chorus line.'

'Ouch.'

'Ouch indeed.'

'Is that my fault? You know, dragging you off to Stephen's parents, and getting in your way at home?'

'Don't be silly. Anyway, we're supposed to be thinking about the future.'

'Yes,' Emma said, 'you're right.'

Just then the call went out for cast members to return.

'Better go.' Lizzy jumped to her feet. 'And pray I can remember all those lines this time. You can stay and watch for as long as you want.'

'Thanks.'

Lizzy went to move away, then stopped. 'Oh, yeah. Do you fancy going out tonight? A few of the cast are going off to a salsa club in town. I wasn't sure if I was going, but I'll come if you will.'

'I'm not sure.'

'C'mon,' Lizzy encouraged, 'it'll do you good. You don't want to be hanging around the flat, just thinking about things.'

'It's just that I was thinking of spending the night with Will. I don't know how long he's going to be away for, and I don't like the thought of leaving him alone on his last night in the country, especially the way he's feeling right now. I feel terrible already for not noticing he was suffering so much.'

'See if he wants to come along,' Lizzy suggested. 'The more the merrier.'

'Okay,' Emma said. 'If he says yes, count me in.'

Emma sat at the back of the theatre, hundreds of empty seats ahead of and above her. This coming Saturday, when Lizzy débuted in the musical, all those seats would be filled. The musical was sold out for its first few weeks from advance bookings, and the press was already talking about it as the possible saviour of the West End. This really was Lizzy's big break. And she deserved it. She had worked so hard to get to this point.

Emma watched her friend belting out one of the show's closing numbers, a cast of dozens moving around her with military precision. Even without the full set and costumes, it was impressive.

Lizzy was just coming to the end of the song when Emma's mobile shrilled, seeming to echo all around the theatre.

'Oh, God!' Emma scrabbled in her pocket and, just before she switched the phone off, noted that it was reading an unknown number. She moved out of her seat, face flushed, and hurried up the aisle, not waiting to hear any chastisement. Fortunately, it seemed as if the rehearsal was carrying on uninterrupted.

She had just got to the main foyer when the mobile rang out again. It was the same number as before.

'Hello?' Emma said.

'Emma!' blasted a familiar voice, nearly bursting her eardrum with enthusiasm. 'It's Guy here, Guy Roberts.'

Guy Roberts, the casting director. Emma nearly dropped the phone in shock.

'Oh, hi,' she said.

'Look,' he said. 'I won't beat around the bush. We had our second reading the other day, as you know. And I'm afraid to say that, although the people we had were very good, they just weren't right for the part. Do you know why?'

'No,' said Emma, her heart fluttering with anticipation.

'It's because no one came close to touching what you did in that first reading. When I saw you read I thought you were perfect for the part, and it was really unfortunate you couldn't make the second reading. I know you had your reasons.'

'I'm sorry, too.'

There was a pause.

'Emma, are you still interested in this movie – in this role?'

137

'Well, yes, I suppose so.'

'I want to see you,' he said, suddenly sounding extremely businesslike. 'Can you come over to my place, say, tomorrow, around lunchtime? We can discuss everything then.'

'Discuss everything?'

'Of course,' he said. 'If you're taking this part, then there's a lot to discuss. Your fee, for instance. Which, I can assure you, will be more money than you've ever earned in your life.'

29

'Shouldn't you be getting ready?' said Lizzy, watching as Emma sat on the sofa in Lizzy's flat, reading a book, her legs tucked under her body. 'We're meeting Will in half an hour.'

'Is it really that late?' Emma got up, still focused on the book.

'Yes, it is. What are you reading, anyway? Must be engrossing – you've been glued to it for an hour.'

'You don't want to know.' Emma closed the book.

Lizzy peered at its red cover. She'd assumed it was a novel but on closer inspection it looked like a notebook. 'I'm intrigued,' she said, grabbing the cover.

Emma released the book from her grasp and watched as Lizzy flicked through it.

'What the hell?' Lizzy looked up. 'This is Stephen Myers' journal?'

'I took it before we found out he had died,' Emma explained. 'It was in his room – Mrs Myers was so spaced out sitting on the bed, that I had the chance to grab it and stuff it into the waistband of my trousers. I know it was risky, but I thought it might give us some clues.'

'You shouldn't be reading it,' Lizzy said. 'It'll just upset you.'

'It's okay. I just wanted to try and understand him. I thought if I read this, then—'

'I don't think it's a good idea, Em,' Lizzy interrupted. 'You don't want to know what was going on inside his mind. I'm going to take this and throw it in the bin.'

'Okay,' Emma agreed, knowing that this made sense. 'Get rid of it.'

* * *

'He looks like he's having fun,' Lizzy said, as she and Emma watched Will salsa dancing with one of the girls from the musical.

They had been in the salsa club for over three hours, and with over two of those hours spent on the dance floor, it felt as if they'd burned off enough calories to last a lifetime.

'Yeah,' Emma said, watching as Will laughed and joked with the girl.

'You're not convinced?' Lizzy said.

'Not really. He looks like he's trying too hard. And he's had quite a lot to drink.'

'Do you think he'll be all right in Canada?'

'I hope so.'

'I don't understand it,' Lizzy said. 'He always seems so happy and carefree. I'd never guess that something was wrong.'

'I should have known,' Emma said. 'He's my brother.'

'But he hid it well.'

'He did.'

'And he didn't say that there was a reason for him being depressed?' Lizzy took a sip from her drink.

'No. And I didn't want to press him on it.'

'How do you think he would feel about your dad's news?'

'It would probably tip him over the edge,' Emma said. 'I couldn't tell him. Not yet, anyway.'

'I understand. And, anyway, it's your dad's responsibility. So have you decided yet about tomorrow?'

'Tomorrow?' Emma was still watching Will. *Is he getting unstable on his feet?*

'Yes, tomorrow!' Lizzy nudged her playfully. 'You know, Guy Roberts, famous casting director . . .'

Emma continued watching her brother. He was leaning against the girl. 'I'm not sure.'

'But you said you'd go.'

'I know, but now I'm not so sure.' Emma was still distracted by her brother.

'Go,' Lizzy demanded, 'or I'll never speak to you again, Emma Holden.'

'Okay,' Emma said, looking round at her friend with a smile. 'If you put it like that, Little Miss Bossy, I'll go.'

It was well into the early hours when Will staggered over towards Emma.

'I'm going.' He turned and headed off through the crowds, not waiting for her to reply.

'Wait,' shouted Emma, going after him. She caught up with him at the top of the stairs. 'Will,' she said, pulling at his shoulder. 'Hang on a minute.'

'Time for me to go,' he said, straining drunkenly against her grasp.

'I'll come with you.'

'Why?' he said, turning around. Up close, it was clear just how drunk he was. His eyes were bloodshot and his face was flushed.

'Because I want to,' she said. 'We can get a cab.'

'If you want.'

'Let me just tell Lizzy. Wait here until I get back.' She pointed at the spot where he was standing.

He nodded, his head seemingly loose at the neck.

When Emma got back, Will had gone. She dashed outside, wondering what might happen to him in that state, wandering around the West End. When the night air hit, she realised how much she, too, had drunk.

Will was wandering across the road, trying to flag down a cab.

'Will!' she shouted, dodging the traffic and sprinting up to him. She pulled him onto the pavement. He seemed amused by the attention, and completely unaware that he'd just been standing in the middle of the road. 'I'm going to get you home, now.'

'Okay,' slurred Will. 'Home sounds nice.'

It was tricky hailing a cab with one hand whilst holding onto her brother with the other; Emma didn't dare let go in case he ran out into the road, or fell and smacked his head on the concrete. Eventually she did succeed, and then managed to persuade the driver that Will was fit enough to travel back without vomiting.

Ten minutes later they got back to Will's flat. She struggled up the stairs, with Will maintaining the silence that had begun in the cab. She gave him a glass of water, and two paracetamol; his flight was leaving from Heathrow at ten the next morning, and he would need all the help he could get to avoid – or at least dampen – the hangover.

'Thanks,' he said, breaking his silence, slugging back the water and the tablets.

Emma watched as he lay down on the sofa and covered his face with his hands.

'Are you okay, Will?'

'I don't deserve you,' he said, his voice muffled against his hands. 'Not after what I've done.'

'What's the matter?'

'I just want to forget,' he said, before falling asleep.

30

'You didn't have to stay, you know,' said Will, looking up from the sofa and grimacing against the morning light streaming through the living room window.

Over in the small kitchen area, Emma poured a cup of tea, then popped a couple of rounds of bread into the toaster. 'I wanted to. It wasn't a problem.'

'I appreciate it.' Will attempted to sit up. 'Ouch.' He brought a hand to his head.

Emma brought over the tea. 'Hangover?'

'One mother of a hangover,' he complained, taking hold of the cup. 'Feels like someone's playing pinball inside my head.'

'I don't know about pinball. Last night you were playing Frogger with the traffic on Tottenham Court Road.'

'Oh, hell.' Will looked concerned and ashamed. 'Was I really?'

'Really.'

'And you saved me from certain death?'

'Most probably.'

'I don't deserve you,' he said, taking a sip of the tea before breaking out into a cough.

'That's what you said last night,' Emma replied.

He looked up sharply. 'What else did I say? I didn't say anything stupid, did I?'

'I think you were still feeling guilty about what happened with Stephen.'

'Oh, right.' He looked down into the tea.

'You really can't remember any of that running about in the road?'

'Can't remember anything. Apart from dancing.'

'You did do a lot of that.'

'It just gets worse. Shit, what time is it?' He scrambled for his watch.

'Seven o'clock,' Emma said. 'You want me to book a taxi?'

Will rose from the sofa. 'Already done it, yesterday. It's due to pick me up in half an hour.'

Twenty-five minutes later Will stood in the centre of the living room, holding a travel bag in each hand. It didn't look enough for a transatlantic trip.

'Well,' he said, 'here starts my big adventure.'

'Are you sure about this?' asked Emma. Will didn't cut a convincing figure, and she was certain it wasn't just the hangover that made him look so washed out.

'Sure as I'll ever be.' He gave a watery smile.

'Maybe you should stay here,' she suggested. 'Get some help, with us to support you.'

'No,' he said simply, the smile vanishing. 'I have to do this, Em. I need to get away.'

He was so fragile. Now she knew, she could see it in his demeanour. But surely the signs had been there all along. *How did I not notice this before?*

'Aren't you just running away from your problems?'

'Maybe I am,' he admitted. 'But it's something I want to do. I think it will help.'

'What will you do over there?'

'I've always wanted to see the major sights – you know, Niagara Falls, go up the CN Tower, maybe go to the Canadian Rockies and see some bears.'

Emma watched as he enthused about Canada and, for a moment, he actually looked happy and excited. Maybe it was what he needed.

'And will your friend Christopher be around?' she asked.

'He said he could take a week off. But he's got some other friends I can hang around with, too. Don't worry about me, Em. I'll be fine.'

144

'Good,' Emma said. 'I'm glad. I just want you to be happy, Will.'

'I'll call you when I get to Canada,' said Will, his head sticking out of the taxi window.

'Make sure you do.'

'I hope everything is okay. I know it wasn't supposed to turn out like this.'

'I'm sure it'll be okay,' Emma replied. 'I've just got to get over it.'

'We'll both come through this, Em. When I get back, we can go out to celebrate our new start.'

Emma watched as the taxi drove off. She hoped that Will was right, and that he could somehow cure his demons so far from home. She hoped, too, that they would both be able to make a new start.

She checked her watch, then headed towards the tube. Hopefully she would catch Lizzy before she left for her rehearsals, and hopefully she would be fresh and reasonably awake, ready to give advice and support.

Because if she was going to meet Guy Roberts, she would need all the advice and support she could get.

Will sat back in the cab's seat and closed his eyes. His head was spinning slightly, and he prayed that he would keep his breakfast down on the way to the airport.

He opened his eyes and watched as London passed by. He didn't think he would miss it: at least, not at first, anyway.

As the taxi neared Heathrow he gazed skywards as aeroplanes flew overhead, transporting just some of the millions of passengers who left and arrived every year, each with their own mixture of hopes and dreams, disappointments and fears.

He wondered whether this really was the start of something new, something better.

His phone rang. And the realisation of who was calling crushed his optimism dead. 'What the hell do you want?' he said, grasping the phone tightly. 'You said it would be the last time . . . look, I told you, that's it, no more . . . I don't care what you do. Do whatever you like. Just leave me alone.'

He cut off the conversation and glanced at the driver. His eyes were fixed straight ahead, focusing on the road, apparently oblivious to what had just happened. Will considered apologising for the tone of the call, but then realised that the cabbie had probably heard much worse than that in his career.

Instead, Will turned off his phone and stuffed it into his bag, hoping that what he had just said, and the way he had said it, wouldn't prove to be his undoing.

31

Emma's new start began that afternoon, in a particularly exclusive part of Notting Hill. She'd rarely been to that part of London before, and had certainly never gone there to visit anyone. You had to be seriously wealthy to live in such a place – seriously wealthy, like Guy Roberts.

She reached his door and rang the bell, the sound of birdsong all around her in the leafy street, thinking back to the advice Lizzy had given her about keeping calm and maintaining control. But as she waited for someone to answer, she felt anything but relaxed. This was unlike anything she had ever done in the past.

She remembered the night she'd found out that she'd got the part in *Up My Street* – she had gone out to a nightclub with friends, and spent much of the night on the dance floor, trying to come to terms with the fantastic news. But this was taking things to a whole new level. The man who was – presumably – waiting inside to speak to her was a world-renowned casting director who had mixed with some of the world's biggest movie stars.

She took a deep breath as the door started to open.

'Emma, it's so great to see you,' said Guy Roberts, taking her hand and shaking it vigorously. 'C'mon in.'

Guy was only in his mid-forties, but his hair, which was cut short and worn messily, was prematurely white. His left ear sported a silver stud earring. He cut a distinctive, and not unattractive, figure.

She followed him down a hallway and into the living room area. The house was as nice inside as out, decked out like a

Hollywood mansion. Framed posters of movies adorned the walls, and a piano stood in one corner of the room.

'Take a seat,' he said. 'Can I get you a drink? Tea, coffee, something a little stronger?'

Emma sat down. 'Tea would be great.'

'Very wise,' he said, smiling. 'I always like to keep a clear head whilst doing business. Unless of course I go out to discuss terms with agents – then the more you drink, the better. I'll just be a second; I'd already boiled the kettle.' He disappeared around the corner. 'You can take a look at the paperwork, if you like,' he shouted from the next room.

Emma took a look at the papers that were lying upside down on the table in front of her.

On top of them was a cast list for the movie.

And her name was on it.

'You can close your mouth if you like,' joked Guy, as he came through with two cups of tea. 'I know it was a little presumptuous of me, but I was working on my laptop last night with the cast list on the screen, and that one gap was just so painful, I couldn't help myself.'

'I don't know what to say,' Emma admitted, looking down the list of people.

'I'm pretty pleased with the cast. You like the look of it?'

'Of course.'

It was an impressive list. Most of those playing the lead characters were already established movie actors, with three or four films under their belts. The leading man, Colin Farley, had been in a couple of Hollywood hits, albeit in supporting rather than leading roles.

'And how does it feel to see your name alongside theirs?'

'Good,' she acknowledged. 'It feels good.'

'Well, that's what I wanted to hear. So let's get down to business.' Guy reached down behind him and pulled out another piece of paper. 'This,' he said, sliding the paper across the glass table, 'is how much we would be offering you.'

Emma took one look at the details and had to put a hand

across her mouth just to stop herself from swearing out loud.

'I said we could offer you money you'd only dreamt of!' Guy smiled.

'But I don't deserve this,' she said.

He laughed. 'Oh, Emma, if only all the actors I work with were as honest as you.'

'But this would be my first movie, I don't have any experience . . .'

'Why do you think I do this job, Emma?'

'I . . . I don't know.'

'Well, it's certainly not for the money any more – I could easily afford to retire. The reason I do this, what gets me up in the morning to cast for new films, is because I love breaking new talent. It gives me a real buzz to identify someone with untapped potential: someone I think can make it right to the top. Someone like you, Emma.'

Emma smiled, embarrassed.

'The minute I watched you in that first reading, I knew that I wanted you to be in this film. That's why I was so disappointed when you called saying that you were pulling out.'

'I don't know what to say,' Emma replied, struggling to contain her excitement.

'Just say yes.'

'I'd have to consult my agent before making a final decision. She's on holiday at the moment.'

'Of course, of course,' Guy said. 'But that's just dealing with the formalities. So, is it a yes, or a no?'

The urge to reply was irresistible. 'Yes.'

'That's terrific,' he said, clapping his hands together. 'I can liaise with your agent on the exact terms. You know, Emma, I really believe you have a bright future in the business. You have something. Something all those other girls don't have. There's more to you.' He looked at her. 'I hear that you used to be a karate champion.'

'How did you know that?' asked Emma, surprised that he knew this aspect of her past.

'Ah . . . we casting directors have our ways and means.' He tapped his nose, without elaborating further.

'What else do you know about me? Nothing bad, I hope?'

'Well, that would be telling.' He winked at her. 'So, Emma, what's your diary looking like in the next couple of days?'

'Er, pretty empty,' she said, thinking quite irrationally that maybe he knew somehow about the wedding, and its subsequent cancellation.

'Perfect. Because tomorrow we've got a very special night planned. We've hired a boat on the Thames, for a party. All the cast are invited so you can get to know each other. There'll also be other people there – Dominic Fox, the director, and the producer, Craig Turner, plus the scriptwriters, and me, of course. I promise it'll be a great night.'

'Sounds good,' Emma said, a little breathlessly.

'You can make it then?'

'Yeah, sure, wouldn't miss it for anything.' Emma was aware that she was beginning to beam.

'Fantastic. You know, this is just the beginning, Emma. The money is just the half of it. Soon you'll be walking down the red carpet at the London premiere, mixing with the stars. This is the big time. You've got your big chance, and I've got my perfect leading lady. We should really be drinking champagne!'

Without asking, Guy went off and returned with two filled champagne glasses. He handed one to Emma. 'Here you go.'

'Thank you,' Emma said.

Guy clinked glasses. 'Cheers! To the beginning of a very exciting time.'

'Cheers,' she replied, somewhat distractedly. Emma took a sip, and then peered down into the liquid. 'I was wondering . . .' she said. 'When you first contacted me, you said someone had recommended me to you. Who was it?'

'Can't say,' he replied, making an apologetic face.

'Why?'

'They asked me to keep their name secret.'

'I don't understand.'

'It's not that unusual. I have a lot of contacts that I work with, and sometimes they just like their anonymity. It's nothing to get too hung up about. If it's about thanking him, then I'll pass it on for you.'

'So it's a him, then?'

'Yes,' he admitted. 'But honestly, I can't say any more.'

'I just don't understand why he doesn't want me to know who he is.' She was convinced that there was more to it, and that it was worth pursuing.

'Please, Emma, it's really not that big a deal.' But she saw something in his eyes that told her otherwise.

'I want to know,' she said. 'Otherwise I'm afraid I can't take the part in the film.'

Guy looked stunned at the threat. 'Emma. You're blowing this out of all proportion.'

'Then you won't tell me?'

'I'm sorry.' He held up his hands. 'I promised.'

Emma stood up. 'Then I'll be going.'

Emma closed the door behind her and walked down towards the gate. She couldn't believe what she had just done.

She'd thrown away possibly the one and only big chance she'd ever have to really make it as an actress.

And what for? For a stupid matter of principle. What did it matter, really, that the person who was kind enough to recommend her for the part wanted to remain anonymous? They must have had their reasons. But, added to all the other secrets of the past week, it was the final straw. Why did everyone have to be so cagey?

She had just reached the tube when her phone rang.

'I'll give you one thing, Emma,' Guy said. 'You're certainly strong-willed.'

'I'm sorry, Guy. I know it sounds silly, but—'

'It's okay. I admire your guts. So you're really prepared to lose this great chance over this?'

'Yes.'

'Okay then, I'll tell you, if that's the only way I can get you in this film.' He sighed. 'It was your ex-boyfriend, Stuart Harris.'

32

That Thursday evening, at Lizzy's flat, Emma recounted the conversation with Guy Roberts, the revelation about Stuart Harris, and her intention to meet with him. 'I don't think meeting up is a good idea,' Lizzy said. 'You might end up getting hurt again. You know what he did to you last time.'

'But that was years ago. A lot of things have happened since then.'

'Why would you even want to see him again?' Lizzy questioned. 'He just dumped you without any explanation. Why invite him back into your life like that?'

'I know what you mean, Lizzy, and I do agree with what you're saying . . .'

'I sense a big "but" here.'

'Well, it's just that he's the one who has invited himself back into my life. He's the one who recommended me to Guy Roberts. I just want to find out why he did it.'

'You want to thank him?'

'No,' Emma replied. 'But I can't just leave it like that, knowing that he went a long way to getting me that dream job, but not really knowing why.'

'You think he's got an ulterior motive?' Suddenly Lizzy looked more interested, despite herself. 'You don't think he might want to get back with you?'

'I'm sure that's not the reason. If he wanted that, he wouldn't have made Guy Roberts promise not to tell me he had been involved.'

'You wouldn't be interested in getting back with him, though, would you?'

'No way. He really hurt me – there's no way.'

'Did you still love him when he left?'

'Yes,' Emma admitted. 'But I don't now.'

Lizzy blew out her cheeks. 'Well, I still don't like it. I don't like it at all. I think you should steer well clear of the guy. Just get on with this great film opportunity.' She looked speculatively at Emma. 'You can't be in the right mental state to go meeting ex-boyfriends.'

'Maybe it's just what I need.'

'What do you mean?'

'Well, I never got an explanation of why Stuart left me. Okay, I assume it was because he couldn't settle in London, and that maybe he was jealous I was finding work when he couldn't. But I never found out for sure. He didn't tell me where he was going, and I never called him. So I was just dumped, without knowing what went wrong.' Emma brushed a hand over her eyes. 'And now it's happened again, with Dan. I thought we were in love, and then he just disappears. I know it's more complicated, with Richard and everything, but essentially the same thing has happened to me again. I'm not able to ask Dan why he left, but I have now got a chance to ask Stuart.'

'But Em, Stuart isn't Dan,' Lizzy counselled. 'You're not going to find out why Dan left by talking to Stuart.'

'I know, but maybe he could tell me something.'

'Come here,' Lizzy said, putting her arms around Emma. 'You're a wonderful person, Em. Don't you dare start thinking that this is your fault. I won't let you.'

'I'm sorry.' Emma spoke into her shoulder. 'I have to meet him. I can't take this part until I do – it wouldn't feel right. But I promise I won't start raking over old ground.'

Lizzy squeezed her tightly. 'Whatever you do, Em, I'll support you one hundred per cent.'

The next day, one week after Dan's disappearance the previous Friday, Emma took an early tube, resting her head against the window and stifling yawns. She had had a restless night, her mind buzzing with thoughts of whether she should meet Stuart. Could it be a potential disaster? After all, Lizzy was right; she wasn't in the best frame of mind for meeting ex-partners. And it seemed especially unwise, under the circumstances, to meet someone in whom she had invested so much love in the past. She would have given the same advice as Lizzy if she had been in her position: steer clear. But she would also have offered her the same support her good friend had offered her, irrespective of what she decided.

Guy Roberts had reluctantly given her Stuart's telephone number and home address. Stuart was living just south of the river. Emma thought it ironic that the man who she thought had hated London so much had chosen to stay in the capital after their break-up.

Maybe there *had* been something else wrong in their relationship.

She was surprised when she reached the address. She hadn't really known what to expect, but this stained concrete tower block certainly wasn't it. It was the kind of place that, under normal circumstances, she wouldn't have dreamt of going into. She hadn't asked Guy what Stuart was doing these days, but it couldn't have been that much if this was the best he could get.

She pressed the buzzer for his flat and waited. She had decided not to call him, and instead just turn up. If he was in, fine; if not, then maybe that would be a sign that she should leave well alone.

'Hello?' a voice said, unmistakably Stuart's.

It brought the memories flooding back, although they felt somehow distant, as if she were remembering someone else's life, or was watching it up on the big screen.

'Hi, Stuart,' she said, her voice cracking with nerves.

There was silence.

'Sally, is that you?' he said.

'It's Emma,' she said, wondering if Sally was his girlfriend. 'Emma Holden.'

More silence.

'I'll be straight down,' he said.

33

'It's just a temporary place,' he said, gesturing towards the tower block. 'Mostly it's student accommodation, but it'll do for now.'

Emma took in the sight of Stuart Harris. He had changed quite a bit in the years since she had last seen him. He'd lost some weight, and cut his hair short. He was still, however, essentially the man she had first fallen in love with.

She felt both guilty and weak with the knowledge that her heart was fluttering and that she was still very much attracted to him, even after all that he had done.

'It looks okay,' she said.

'I'm hoping to move soon,' he said. 'It can get a bit noisy. You know what students are like.' He smiled nervously as he met Emma's gaze. 'Er, I thought we could go to the café down the road,' he suggested, looking away. 'They do a good breakfast, and I haven't eaten yet.'

'Sounds okay,' Emma said.

It was weird sitting across from Stuart in the café: like stepping back in time. Emma watched as he sipped his coffee and then dived into the greasy full English breakfast that had just arrived; the café smelled strongly of fried food.

Emma glanced around. It wasn't the type of place Stuart ever used to visit. He'd always liked to eat at expensive places, but this was pretty rundown. The chairs and tables were made out of brown moulded plastic, bolted to the floor, and wire mesh covered the window, indicating that this was probably an area that required some protection against break-ins. And the place was virtually empty, apart from a rather scruffy-looking guy who was reading the newspaper in the far corner. Emma averted her gaze as the guy looked up from his paper.

'Sure you don't want some toast?' Stuart also looked up.

'I'm fine.'

He nodded and went back to eating. Emma watched him, feeling frustrated at the lack of conversation. She didn't want to just sit there as if everything were okay; she wanted to talk, about a lot of things.

'You haven't asked why I came to see you,' she ventured. 'Or how I knew where you live.'

'Guy told you,' replied Stuart, chomping on a mouthful of food before washing it down with a swig of coffee. 'He called me last night.'

'So you were expecting me?'

He shrugged. 'I wondered whether you would come. Although I wasn't sure.'

'How do you know Guy?'

'He didn't tell you?'

'No, he said you would explain.'

Stuart smiled. 'He likes to build the suspense. I met him at an audition, for a supporting role in a movie that he was casting. You heard of *Dark Room*?'

'Of course. I saw it at the cinema.' The British-made psychological suspense thriller had been a big hit in the UK. Emma and Dan had both really enjoyed it.

'I didn't think I had a hope in hell, but I actually got down to the final three,' he said. 'Good, but not good enough. Afterwards, I got talking to Guy and we became good friends. He's a great bloke. Not like some of the people in this industry.'

'"This industry"?'

'The movies. There are some real bastards out there. It's hard to know who to trust sometimes. But Guy's different. To be honest, sometimes I think he feels sorry for me.'

'Why?'

He smiled sadly. 'Well, he's the big-shot, successful casting director, and I'm the struggling actor, taking bit parts just to pay the bills.'

'I'm sure it's not like that.'

'Maybe, maybe not,' Stuart said. 'But it's telling that he hasn't cast me in anything yet. He says the right part will come along, but, you know . . . Not that I'm friends with him for that reason, of course.'

'You recommended me for the part in the movie,' Emma stated.

'I've suggested quite a few people to him in the past,' Stuart said. 'People I've worked with. He jokes that I'm his unofficial scout.' He took another mouthful of food.

'But why me?'

He paused for a moment before he swallowed. 'Because I thought you'd be perfect for the part.'

'Oh, come on,' Emma said, trying to rein in her rising anger. 'You haven't seen me for years, Stuart. How could you possibly know whether I'd be any good for that part? I could have given up acting, for all you knew. I could've been working on the checkout at Marks and Spencer.'

'I knew you were still acting,' Stuart said. 'And I knew you were good; even better than you used to be.'

'How?'

'I've been to see several of your shows,' he admitted, mopping up the last of his breakfast with a remaining piece of fried bread.

'Why?' she said, taking in the revelation. 'Why would you do that?'

He put down his knife and fork. 'Because I care about you, Em. I was interested to see how everything was going in your life.'

Emma stared at him. 'You walked out on me. You never called, didn't leave a forwarding address, never said goodbye. It's not exactly something I'd do to someone I cared about.'

Stuart smiled tightly and dabbed his mouth with the napkin. 'I deserve that,' he said, folding the napkin and placing it across his plate, just as he always used to.

★ ★ ★

'Is Sally your girlfriend?' asked Emma, sitting next to Stuart, as they looked across the park. She had meant to leave straight after the meal, but part of her had wanted to stay and talk to Stuart. So when he had suggested taking a walk, she had found herself accepting.

'Sally, yes,' he said, looking somewhat uncomfortable. 'Although I'm not sure it's really that serious. How about you? Are you in a relationship?'

Emma told him everything.

'My God,' he said, as she finished the tale. 'I'm so sorry, Em.'

Emma shrugged. 'Lizzy's been a great help. It's made it much easier. I think I'd have completely lost it without her support.'

'She sounds like a great friend. Those are the types of friends that don't come around too often.'

'She's great,' Emma said. 'A total star.'

'Make sure you hang on to her.'

'Don't worry,' she replied. 'I intend to.'

'I'd invite you up,' he said, as they arrived back at the tower block, 'but I'm in a rush. I'm supposed to be meeting someone in an hour, and I have to get to the other side of town. Sorry.'

'That's all right,' Emma said.

'Well, I guess I'll see you around.' He took a couple of slow steps backwards. 'Best of luck with the movie – you are going to take the part, aren't you?'

'Yes,' she said.

He beamed. 'That's great. I'm glad I recommended you.'

'I just want to know one thing. Why the secrecy? Why ask Guy to keep your name secret from me?'

'Because I didn't want to intrude,' he said. 'I didn't want this.'

'This?'

'Me and you, like this. I didn't want it.'

Emma looked away.

'I don't mean that I didn't want to see you,' he said quickly. 'Just the opposite, really.'

'I don't get it.'

'What I'm saying is . . . oh, God, I promised this wasn't going to happen,' he said, seemingly to himself. 'What I'm trying to say is that I really regret walking out on you the way I did. It wasn't a good time, and my head was all over the place. You wouldn't believe the state I was in.'

'You're saying you regret walking out without saying anything?'

'No, not just that,' he replied. 'I regret walking out, full stop. I regret leaving you, throwing everything we had down the drain.'

'It's too late, Stuart.'

'I know. And that's why I didn't want to talk to you again like this. I still love you, Em. But I know I can't have you back.'

34

Emma emerged into the living room wearing the black dress she had bought just a few days before Dan's disappearance. 'How do I look?'

'Stunning,' Lizzy said, looking her up and down. 'You're gonna wow those movie people,' she added. 'They won't know what's hit them.'

'Hope so.' Emma flattened an imaginary crease in the material. 'But I'm so nervous. They're all going to be there – the director, producer, the whole cast. What if they meet me and wonder why on earth I got chosen for the part?'

'Don't be daft. Guy Roberts wanted you, so he picked you. End of.'

'I guess. It's just that, you know, with Guy knowing Stuart, it just makes me wonder.'

'What are you going to do about Stuart?'

'I'm trying to forget about him. I've decided that I don't want to see him again.'

'I think that's for the best. I know it's up to you, but it doesn't sound like what you need right now.' Lizzy nodded her encouragement.

'I just wish he hadn't got involved in this, though. I feel like I owe him.'

'Don't worry about who it was that recommended you for the part,' Lizzy said. 'That isn't important. Okay, it gave you the foot in the door, but if you didn't have what it takes, you'd never have got this chance. Remember – contacts might give you the opportunity, but talent lets you take advantage of it.'

'Wow, Lizzy, I'm impressed.' Emma smiled. 'Have you been reading one of those motivational self-help books?'

Lizzy stuck out her tongue at her and went back to reading her stage notes.

'But, seriously,' Emma said. 'Thanks.'

Lizzy looked up and smiled. 'You're welcome. Hey, this is your big night, Em. It's finally happening.'

'I know,' Emma said, laughing, not quite able to believe it.

Lizzy grinned. 'It's so good to see you happy.'

'I do feel better than I have in a long while. I'm not saying that I feel particularly good, but at least something nice is happening amongst all the bad things.'

'That's great. Because I want you to be in your best frame of mind for my début performance tomorrow night.' Lizzy held up the stage notes. 'I want detailed feedback from you.'

'Of course,' Emma said.

'Only positive feedback, obviously,' Lizzy deadpanned.

'Naturally. Because I'm sure it'll be perfect, anyway.'

'Miracles do happen, I suppose.'

'I just wish a miracle would happen to Richard.' Suddenly, Emma felt guilty that they were laughing and joking while Richard was lying unconscious in a hospital bed, fighting for his life. She'd visited him almost daily since his admission, and although his condition was stable, there was as yet no sign of an improvement.

'Yes, so do I,' Lizzy said seriously. 'Do you think he'll ever wake up?'

'I hope so,' Emma said. 'But I don't know.'

Emma couldn't believe it when she saw the boat. She'd expected something like a canal barge, but it resembled a mini ocean cruise liner, all lit up like a floating Christmas tree. The other shock was the photographers on the quayside. There were only six of them, but that was six more than she'd expected.

As she got closer, they turned around and pointed their

cameras in her direction, flashing away, too close to her. Emma wondered whether they even knew who she was.

'Emma, is it true about your fiancé?' a man shouted from her right-hand side. He moved into view, blocking her path to the boat. 'Justin Marshall from the *London Daily News*. Can you confirm that the police want to speak to him?'

Emma didn't say anything, looking longingly at the people watching from the upper decks of the boat. She realised that the photographers were all bearing down on her now, and for a moment she thought she recognised one of them as being Eric, the man she had met in the park. She ducked past the reporter who had questioned her, but he gave chase.

'They think he might have tried to kill his brother—?'

'Leave me alone,' she said. The flash bulbs were blinding, and she wanted to push them all away.

Then, suddenly, she felt a strong hand on her back.

'It's okay,' the man said. 'Security.'

Emma nodded.

'Get back,' the man demanded to the press, 'otherwise you'll have no more access tonight. Back!' He swatted away a camera lens. 'Parasites,' he muttered under his breath, loud enough for Emma to hear.

'You're okay now,' he said, leading her up the gangway, before turning back to face the reporters and photographers.

Breathless and shaken, Emma made her way up onto the deck of the boat.

'Emma, I'm so sorry about that,' said Guy Roberts, handing her a glass of champagne, and then looking down towards the press. 'If I'd known that was going to happen, I'd have set the dogs on them.'

'It just took me by surprise, that's all,' admitted Emma, feeling quite breathless and giddy. 'I didn't think anyone would be interested in me.'

'Oh, how modest you are, Emma,' he said, putting an arm around her bare shoulders. 'The British press love their bright young things, especially when they're as attractive and talented as you. I had a feeling they'd bitc on this one.'

'Bite?' Emma queried.

'We sent out a press release,' he said. 'You were the main feature.'

'Oh, right,' Emma said. Now it made sense – the reporter had obviously been digging around for information following the press release, and had found out about Dan and Richard. *But does Guy and everyone else on the boat know about it, too?*

'Don't look so worried,' said Guy. 'I know it's a bit shocking at first, but you'll get used to it. One day you'll be walking down the road with the press two inches from your face, and you'll have got so used to it that you won't even notice.'

'I don't think I'll ever get used to that.'

'You know, once, when I was dating a movie star – I won't say her name because it makes me feel queasy – I went to take a shower and found a reporter hiding in the cubicle.'

'Really?'

'Honest truth. And do you know what I did?'

Emma shook her head.

'I turned on the shower,' he said, laughing. 'You should have seen his face. C'mon.' He led her through the crowds. 'There are lots of people who are dying to meet you.'

The inside of the boat was even more spectacular than the outside. Chandeliers hung over the main entertainment area, which was carpeted and headed by a low stage. Waiters and waitresses weaved in and out of the fashionably dressed guests, offering plates of nibbles and glasses of champagne. The luxury was like nothing Emma had ever experienced before. She would have felt lost if it weren't for Guy, who introduced her expertly to many of the guests. She met Craig Turner and Dominic Fox, the producer and director, both of whom said that they had heard a lot about her. Then she spoke to Colin Farley, the leading man, conscious that she was blushing. He seemed lovely, and said he was looking forward to working with her.

Everything was going great – she had even forgotten about the incident with the reporter. And then she saw him.

He was turned away from her, chatting in a group of four, but she recognised his profile instantly. As if on cue he turned around. He seemed genuinely surprised to see her, although he had to have known she would be on board.

'Em,' said Stuart as he came over. 'It's good to see you again.'

35

'I'll go if you want,' Stuart said. 'I wasn't planning to come, but Guy called me up at the last minute.'

'It's okay, Stuart,' Emma said, trying to banish thoughts of how attractive he looked in his black tie suit. 'You shouldn't have to leave because of me.'

'Okay, but I'll leave you alone if you like – let you talk to someone else.'

Emma looked around at the crowds. 'Guy has already introduced me to loads of people.'

'Always the perfect host.' Stuart took a nervous sip from his drink as, nearby, the pianist started up. 'No expense spared for this party,' he commented. 'That guy has played piano for the Queen, and lots of movie stars. And you're one of the stars now. What does it feel like?'

'Weird,' Emma admitted. 'I'm not sure I like it, either. I got cornered by a group of photographers before.'

'That's not good. Were you okay?'

'Security stepped in,' Emma said, thinking back to what the reporter had asked her.

'Thank goodness. You want to go outside?' Stuart ventured. 'Should be quite a view out there – we'll be sailing past the London Eye in a few minutes.'

'Okay. It's getting a bit stuffy in here, anyway.'

As they got out on deck, Emma realised they were indeed just approaching the London Eye. Right on cue.

'Told you it would be great view,' said Stuart, as they looked out across the city from the side of the boat.

Emma looked up towards the top of the wheel, seeing

children in the pods waving at the boat. She waved back, and so did Stuart.

'You remember the day we went on that thing?' he asked.

'How could I forget? I don't think I've ever seen anyone as scared in my life. I thought you were going to jump out.'

'I told you I didn't like heights.'

'I still don't know why you agreed to it.'

'Because you wouldn't have gone on it otherwise, and I knew you wanted to try it out.'

Emma looked across at him, and he smiled. She managed not to smile back.

'This is really weird,' she said, turning back to look across to the far bank of the Thames. 'You and me, talking about old times.'

'I know,' Stuart admitted. 'I never thought we'd talk again.'

They let that statement hang in the air for a few seconds.

'You really hurt me,' Emma said, not looking at him.

'I can imagine.'

'No,' she said, this time turning to look at Stuart. 'You *really* hurt me. In those weeks and months after you left, I thought I was going to have a breakdown. I cried non-stop for days. It was really scary – I was losing control.'

'I'm so sorry, Em.'

'I don't know why I'm even giving you the satisfaction of letting you know this.'

'I don't take any satisfaction from it at all,' he replied quietly. 'I know it was my choice to walk out, and I've only got myself to blame, but I suffered too. You don't know how much I suffered because of my mistake.'

'It did make me stronger,' she said. 'I think that's why I haven't lost it now that Dan has left. I don't know if that's a good thing, though. I should be really upset. I was supposed to be getting married this weekend.'

'You're just protecting yourself. And you're getting on with your life.'

'Oh, I don't know.' Emma shrugged. 'I'm wondering whether

all this movie business is just a distraction – my way of blocking out everything that's happened.'

'Is that such a bad thing? Maybe it will help.'

'Maybe.'

'Look, Em, I'm sorry for just coming out with what I said earlier today. I imagine it was the last thing you needed. I didn't plan to say it.'

'It's not the right time.'

'I understand.'

'Having a good time?' said Guy, suddenly appearing at Emma's shoulder.

'Great,' Stuart said.

'Emma?' Guy asked.

'It's really nice.'

'Only nice?' He grimaced. 'I can see I'm going to have to try harder with you. Only the very best for Emma Holden.'

Emma and Stuart laughed along with Guy, although Emma did wonder whether he was joking or not.

'How are you getting home?' Stuart said, as they stood at the end of the gangway.

The boat had just moored and most people were in the process of disembarking. Emma was glad to have returned to dry land, and she was even gladder to see that there were no press people waiting for her.

'I'll catch the tube,' she said, gesturing in the direction of the station.

'I'll walk you,' he offered.

'No, it's okay.'

'No, really—'

'I'll be fine, honestly. It was good to chat.'

'Maybe we could keep in touch? Here's my number if you want it.' He handed her a card. 'If you don't call, I'll understand.'

'Goodbye, Stuart,' Emma said, taking the card.

She turned and walked away, not quite knowing why she had

been so adamant in refusing Stuart's offer of walking her to the station. Maybe she was too proud to have him do her any kind of favour.

She moved through the tourists, who were still out at that late hour, heading for Waterloo Station. She was around the back of the station when her mobile registered a text message.

Although she wanted to wait until she was safely inside the station, she couldn't resist reading the message.

As she read it, a chill ran through her – an icy wind whipping up from behind and slithering down her back.

It was from Dan.

Why do you hurt the one you love?

She read the message again. Then she hurried into the station, heading for the tube entrance, her mind buzzing with thoughts about what he had meant by that strange message. Suddenly, she stopped and pressed the shortcut key to Dan's number, expecting the call to be diverted, as it had on all the other occasions.

But it started ringing.

She held the phone close to her ear, breathing hard, waiting for the pick-up.

It came on the sixth ring.

'Hello?'

'Dad?' Emma said, completely dumbfounded. 'I don't understand.'

36

Lizzy was fast asleep by the time Emma returned from the party, so she waited until morning before updating her on what had happened. 'Dad found it below the letterbox,' Emma said to Lizzy, trying to eat a piece of toast, but without much appetite. She yawned. The worry about the phone incident, with the cryptic text message, had not only affected her appetite, but had also resulted in a disturbed night's sleep. 'Dan must have posted it through. Miranda heard it ringing and called Dad. He picked it up.'

'But why?' Lizzy asked. 'It doesn't make sense. Why would he post his mobile phone through your dad's letterbox?'

Emma shrugged.

'And that text message. It's so strange, Em. Not just what he said, but the fact that he must have sent it whilst he was standing outside your dad's house. Do you think Dan's okay? Mentally, I mean? You hear about people suddenly having some kind of breakdown, then walking out and spending the rest of their lives wandering around, hanging around bus stations.'

'Don't,' Emma said, not wanting to think about Dan suffering like that. 'Anyway, he seemed okay when he cancelled the wedding dress.'

'You did say his voice was a little strange.'

'Yes, but not that strange. I just want to know what he meant by that message. Does he think I hurt him? *Have* I hurt him?'

'Not unless you've had an affair that you're not telling me about.'

Emma pondered some more.

'Could the police do anything with the phone?' asked Lizzy.

'What do you mean?'

'I don't know . . . check who he's called since he went missing? He might also have some text messages saved in there, too.'

'Good idea,' Emma said, 'I hadn't thought of that. I'll check it when I go round to Dad's this afternoon.'

'I meant give it to the police, really.'

'I don't think so.'

'You really don't like the police, do you?'

'I don't feel comfortable with them,' Emma said. 'Maybe it goes back to what happened with Stephen. The way Detective Gasnier questioned me, it just reminded me of how the police were back then when I had concerns – a bit dismissive. Anyway, even if they did take a look at the phone, they'd have to ask me about the contact list. I'm saving them the bother.'

'Your call,' Lizzy said, holding up her hands. 'You already know I don't think much of Gasnier. So, are you looking forward to lunch at your dad's?'

'Not particularly,' Emma admitted. 'He's probably going to go mad when I tell him I've met Stuart. He really hated him for walking out on me – made me promise that I'd never take him back.'

'You're going to tell him?'

'I think so.'

'Will you see him again? Stuart, I mean?'

'I don't think so,' Emma said, thinking back to the contact card he had given her, and the way she had just walked away.

'You don't sound so sure any more,' Lizzy noted. 'You're not still in love with him, are you?'

'No way, *no* way.'

'Okay,' Lizzy said. 'I'm convinced.'

But she didn't sound convinced, and Emma knew it.

'The other reason I'm not particularly looking forward to the meal,' Emma continued, changing the subject, 'is because Miranda's going to be there, and I'm not sure I can take all the talk about the new baby.'

'Your new half-brother or sister.'

'I know.' Emma grimaced. 'Don't get me wrong; I'm happy for Dad if he's happy. But I can't help thinking that it could be too much for him. It's a long time since he had a small baby.'

'Are you sure you're not just a little bit jealous? I mean, it would be understandable.'

'Jealous of a baby?'

'Jealous of his new family.'

Just hearing the phrase stopped Emma in her tracks – maybe Lizzy had got it dead right.

'Maybe,' she admitted.

'How do you feel about Miranda now?'

'I don't know, really. My instinct is still not to like her very much.'

'Why?'

'I don't know – because she's taken my mum's place,' Emma admitted. 'And because she makes me feel . . . jealous?'

'Maybe you should give Miranda a chance? Your dad's going to need all the support he can get, and it'll be so much better for him if you two are getting along. And Will, when he gets back.'

'Maybe you're right,' Emma conceded. 'Anyway, enough about me. How are your nerves for tonight's big opening performance?'

'Shot. Why do you think I'm throwing all my energies into solving your problems? It's a classic distraction technique.'

'You'll be fantastic,' Emma said. 'I can't wait to see the finished piece.'

'These shows never get finished,' Lizzy said. 'It might be the opening night tonight, but we'll be tweaking things right up to curtain call. Today is going to be a long day.'

'For both of us. I'll see you at the theatre.'

'Will there be anything else?' said the newsagent, an ageing Asian man with a patchy white beard.

'No, that's it, thanks,' she said, picking up the newspaper. It wasn't until she'd seen the *London Daily News* placard that she had remembered about the newspaper reporter from the previous night. With all the events that had followed – Stuart's reappearance, Dan's text message, and the mystery of why he had posted the phone through her dad's letterbox – she had forgotten all about it.

The newsagent handed over her change and smiled. 'I don't understand why people read that newspaper.'

'I know,' Emma said, feeling embarrassed for buying it. 'It's for research.'

'Good luck with the research,' he said. 'Have a nice day.'

'You too.'

She stopped outside the newsagents, leant against some roadside railings and opened up the paper.

Her worst-case scenario was in the gossip column. The story was there, covering half of page seven.

Secret torment of movie beauty.
Fiancé hunted by police.
Brother attacked and in coma.

'Emma's devastated by what's happened,' said a family friend.

'No one suspected a thing,' said another.

But no matter how bad the feature-length article was, it was the accompanying photos that made the most impact on her.

One was of her in her jogging trousers. It must have been one of the photos taken by Eric, the guy she had chatted with. She had swallowed his lies about not selling photos to newspapers. How naïve and stupid was she? Would she never learn?

But it was the second photo that really shocked her to the core.

It was a photo she knew well. It was the one of Dan and her in Rome – the photo that until last week had been on top of their television.

37

'Have you seen it?' Emma thrust the newspaper into her dad's hand as soon as he opened the front door. He looked at the front headlines, his brow knotted, clearly confused as to what he should be looking at. 'Page seven,' Emma directed. 'The story on page seven is about me and Dan.'

'What?' he said, aghast. He turned through the pages. 'I don't understand,' he said, scanning the article. 'Who gave them this photo, of you and Dan?'

'It was the one missing from our living room,' Emma explained.

'But then how did it get here?'

'Dan must have given it to them. I don't like to think that he would, but there were no other copies of that photograph.'

'And these quotes,' he said, visibly disgusted. 'Who are these quotes from?'

'I don't know,' Emma admitted. 'They might have just made them up.'

'How did you know to look for this? You don't buy this paper.'

'There was a reporter at the boat, asking me about Dan.'

'Why didn't you mention it when we spoke last night?'

Emma shrugged.

'What's up?' said Miranda, appearing at Edward's shoulder. 'Hey, that's you.' She looked up at Emma, then back down at the paper. 'Oh my God,' she said, as she read the article. 'Emma, that's terrible.'

'Let's get inside,' Edward said. He led them into the living room, shaking his head. 'I can't believe how I misjudged Dan. I never would have thought he'd do something like this. Take a seat.' He gestured to the sofa, unthinkingly. 'The meal's nearly ready. I mean,' he continued, sitting down himself, 'what the hell is going on inside that head of his? As if it wasn't bad enough running off shortly before you were supposed to be getting married, he goes and does this.' He slapped the offending photo, his anger rising.

Miranda stood behind him, twirling the hairs on the back of his head through her fingers. Even though Emma now knew about the pregnancy, it was still difficult to tell that Miranda was expecting a baby. It wasn't just the way she wore her clothes – the bump was small and inconspicuous. 'Try and stay calm, Edward. You know what the doctor said.'

Emma's ears pricked up. 'Doctor?' she said. 'You've been to the doctor?'

He waved away her concern. 'It's nothing. He just said I should make sure I try and stay relaxed, that's all.'

Emma looked at Miranda and caught a flicker in her eyes that told her it wasn't quite that simple. But she wouldn't push it any further, not for now.

'Don't talk to any other reporters,' he advised.

'I won't.'

'And if Dan tries to contact you again, tell me.'

'Okay.'

'Right,' he said, tearing the newspaper in two. 'Let that be an end to it.'

'Have you heard from Will?' Edward said, tucking into his salad as the three of them were sitting around the dining table.

'No,' Emma said. 'Have you?'

He shook his head.

'I never realised Will was so bad,' she said. 'I thought he was fine.'

'He'll be okay. He just needs a break.'

'When are you going to tell him about the baby?'

'As soon as he gets back. I hope that he'll be happy about it. Not at first, maybe, but eventually. Are you happy about it, Em?'

'Yes, of course,' said Emma, glancing at Miranda and smiling. 'Of course – it's great news.'

'You never were a very good liar,' said Edward sadly, pushing his plate away. 'I need to get some air.'

'Dad, wait . . .' Emma pleaded.

But he walked out of the room.

'I'm really sorry,' she said, looking across to Miranda.

'It's okay. It isn't just you – he's been tetchy for the past week or so. Better just to let him go and cool off.'

'I really am happy for you both,' Emma said.

'You don't have to be. I wouldn't blame you if you hated my guts, like Will obviously does. I've taken your mum's place. I know I wouldn't like it if the situation were reversed.'

Emma sat back in her chair and looked at her. 'Okay, I admit it was hard. It still is. But it's not personal, Miranda. I actually think you're very nice.' Emma was sure if she said it enough, it would eventually become true. 'It just takes time, that's all. And Will – he'll come around, too. It's just that Mum dying hurt him more than anyone.'

Miranda nodded. 'I didn't plan to fall in love with your dad, you know. I don't have some kind of fetish for older men. It just happened. My parents still think I'm crazy for being with someone not much younger than they are. But you don't choose who you fall in love with – you just go along with the ride and see where it takes you. Sometimes it works, sometimes it doesn't.'

'Like me and Dan,' Emma reflected. 'And me and Stuart.'

'If there's anything I can do to help—'

'I'd like to look at the phone,' Emma said. 'Dan's phone.'

'Sure, I'll go and get it.' Miranda rose from the table.

'Miranda,' Emma said. 'I am sorry for the way I've behaved towards you.'

Miranda smiled and went to get the phone. With that short exchange, years of cold hostility had melted away. At least some good was coming out of this situation.

'Here it is,' she said, coming back and handing the phone to

Emma. 'It isn't locked, so you should be able to go through all the messages.'

Emma scrolled through the menus to bring up the list of previously called numbers. Dan hadn't made many calls, but one number caught her eye.

'Found anything interesting?' Miranda enquired, as she watched Emma staring intently at the mobile screen.

'It's your number.' Emma looked up, stunned. 'He phoned here.'

'Dan?' Miranda said. 'He often calls, checking if you're around when he can't get hold of you on your mobile. He's done it a few times when I've been here.'

'No, he called here after he disappeared.'

'Are you sure?' Miranda looked confused.

'I'm sure,' Emma said. She turned the screen towards Miranda. 'Look, the phone lists all the calls in order. Your number comes before the number here, which is for the wedding shop. Dan called there on Monday evening. So it means he rang here this week.'

38

'I'm sorry about blowing up like that,' Edward said, as he came back into the living room. 'I'm just a little touchy at the moment.' He looked at Emma and then Miranda, who were both sitting on the sofa, stone-faced. 'What's happened?' he asked, his face deflating. 'Is it Richard?'

Emma shook her head.

'Then what?'

'Emma found our number on Dan's call list,' Miranda explained.

'Is that important? I mean, he's called here loads of times.'

'He called here this week,' Emma said. 'But Miranda says that she hasn't spoken to him.'

'And you think I have? You think I'd speak to Dan and not tell you about it, with all that you're going through?'

'I just need to ask.'

'I haven't spoken to him,' said Edward, his voice cracking with emotion. 'I promise I haven't.'

'I believe you,' Emma said, wanting to retract her accusation and saddened by the hurt expression on her father's face.

'I would never do anything to hurt you, Em,' he said. 'I know things haven't been easy for us, but I always want the best for you and Will.'

'Okay,' Emma said. 'Let's just try to keep calm.'

'Dan must have called when no one was home,' Miranda offered.

'It doesn't make sense,' Emma said. 'Why doesn't he just call *me*?'

'And I don't know why he would have called us,' said Edward, still sounding like someone on the defensive. 'Just like I don't know why he put that phone through the letterbox. Nothing about this makes sense, Emma.'

'I met up with Stuart the other day,' Emma said suddenly.

'Pardon?' said Edward. 'You spoke to . . . ?'

'Stuart,' Emma repeated. 'Stuart Harris.'

'What?' Edward's face flushed crimson. 'I . . . I don't understand. Why would you want to speak to him, after all that happened? After what that man did to you?' He stared at her. 'This wasn't just something to get back at Dan, was it?'

'No, of course not,' Emma protested. 'I wouldn't do that. It wasn't planned.' Now she was feeling defensive herself.

'Then why?'

'I found out that he'd recommended me for the role in the film.'

'He recommended you?'

'The casting director told me, so I wanted to speak to Stuart to ask him why.'

'And you met up with him?'

She nodded.

Her father shook his head. 'So, what did he say?'

'Not much. He said that he recommended me for the part because he knew I would be good in the role. He said it wasn't a way to get me back – he didn't even want me to know that he'd recommended me.'

'And you believed him?'

'I think so.'

Edward turned his head slightly, rubbing his face as if trying to wash away images of Emma and Stuart meeting again.

'Dad,' Emma said, 'I'm okay. It was fine.'

When he looked back at her, the sight was shocking. Although it was impossible, he seemed to have aged ten years in those few seconds of contemplation. Her father looked drained, defeated and broken.

'Promise me that you'll never see him again,' he said softly. 'Just that one time – never again.'

Emma paused.

'Emma. You might have forgotten what that man did to you, but I haven't. And I won't let him just walk back into your life, when you're already feeling so vulnerable, and risk it happening again. I won't allow it.'

'I have met him again,' Emma admitted.

Edward closed his eyes and breathed in deeply. He stood up and walked towards the room's bay window, holding onto the window ledge as if needing support.

'It was at the casting party last night,' Emma explained. 'I didn't know he would be there.'

'Will you see him again?' said Edward, still looking out of the window.

'I . . . I don't know.'

'For God's sake, Emma!' he shouted, turning around. 'Haven't you had enough of being messed around?'

Emma flinched. Her father never lost his cool.

'Edward.' Miranda stood up and moved to intercept him as he approached Emma. She placed a hand on his chest. 'Please, calm down. We can all discuss this calmly over a cup of tea.'

'I don't want a bloody cup of tea,' he bawled, straight into her face. 'I want my daughter to stop ruining her life.'

This time Miranda was the one to flinch.

Suddenly Edward's face contorted with pain and he thrust a hand to his chest.

'Edward!' Miranda said, wrapping an arm around his back.

'I'm okay,' he said, letting Miranda sit him down on one of the straight-backed chairs. 'Just get my spray. It's in my coat, in the hall.'

'Spray?' Emma said. 'What's the matter? Why do you need spray?'

'Angina,' he said, grimacing.

'But why—'

'He didn't want to worry you,' Miranda said, reading Emma's mind as she came back into the room. She handed Edward a small spray canister.

Emma bit her tongue as she watched Edward spray into his mouth and breathe deeply.

'The doctor diagnosed it six months ago,' Miranda said. 'Edward was getting chest pains when we were out walking. They did some tests and found he had angina, but it's manageable with the spray. As long as he doesn't get too worked up.'

'I'm fine,' Edward said, noticing Emma's worried expression. 'And I know I should have told you about it. I'm sorry.'

'At least I know now.'

'I'm sorry for shouting, too. But I meant what I said. I want you to stay away from that man. He'll only end up hurting you again.'

An hour after she left, Edward was still shaking. He paced around the upstairs study before sitting on a chair and staring at the wall.

What a mess.

He got up and moved over to the phone. He could hear Miranda clearing up downstairs, so it was safe to talk without fear of being overheard.

He dialled the number, wondering if he was over-reacting. But something told him that he wasn't.

'Hi, it's me. I know you didn't want to be disturbed, but something has happened – something I need to talk to you about.'

39

'Hi, Emma, it's me.'

'Stuart?' Emma said, as she negotiated the busy main road, later on Saturday afternoon. 'How did you—?'

'Guy gave me your number,' he said, pre-empting her question. 'I hope you don't mind. It's just that I've got some news that I wanted you to know about.'

'Go on.' Emma slowed to a stop on the pavement, fearing what was to come.

'I had a phone call earlier, from a journalist, wanting to know about you.'

'I don't believe it,' Emma said, shocked at the continued intrusion into her privacy. 'You didn't tell him anything, did you?'

'No, of course not. I told him I had no comment.'

'Good,' she said, moving to the edge of the pavement. 'That's good. Did he say where he was from?'

'The *London Daily News*.'

'They've already done a piece on me! It's in today's paper!'

'I know,' he replied. 'I saw it. Who gave them the photo of you and Dan?'

'I don't know.'

'You think it might have been Dan himself?'

'I really don't know. How did the journalist know to contact you? We haven't seen each other for years.'

'No idea,' he said. 'I suppose they have their methods.'

'It's just so weird to have people snooping about,' said Emma, as a businessman hurried past, deep in conversation on his mobile. 'I don't like it.'

'I'm sure it will all blow over,' he comforted. 'I wouldn't want you to be put off going for the film role by the press attention. Tomorrow they'll have another story, and that will be the end of it.'

'I hope so. It was a shock to see the photos, but it won't put me off.'

'I'm glad. You really deserve your success, Emma. I always knew you had what it takes to really make something of yourself. Someone with your talent was always going to do well – you just needed that lucky break.'

'Thanks.' Emma felt embarrassed and uncomfortable with the flattery.

'I had a really good night last night,' he said. 'It was great to chat to you properly, after all these years of wanting to explain what a fool I'd made of myself.'

'I had a good time, too.'

'I'm glad. I didn't want me being there to spoil your night.'

'No, it was good, honestly.'

'I was wondering,' Stuart began. 'There's this new play that's just started – it's had really good reviews. Tragic love story, I think. I wondered if you'd like to come and watch it with me next week? Otherwise I'll just be going on my own.'

'What about your girlfriend?' asked Emma, searching for an excuse to decline the offer.

'She's not really into the theatre,' he said, his disappointed tone betraying the fact that he had taken the hint.

'Look, Stuart,' Emma said. 'I really appreciate you asking, but I don't think it's such a good idea. Not just now.'

'I understand. I shouldn't have asked.'

Emma felt sorry for him. 'No, not at all. It was nice of you to ask. But I just can't think about anything else at the moment, not with everything that's going on. Please don't take offence.'

'Honestly, I won't. And, I promise, if any more press people call, I'll tell them to take a running jump.'

'I didn't take the photo,' said Eric, looking at the newspaper that Emma had bought on the way to the park – a replacement for the one her father had torn up. She'd called him on the mobile number that he'd given her when they'd met, being careful to call from a payphone so as to maintain her privacy.

'It must have been you,' Emma accused. 'This was taken on the day I spoke to you – the day you were taking my photograph.'

'But this isn't one of my photos,' Eric countered, pointing at the image. 'I only took your photograph up close. This was taken from a distance, with a zoom lens.'

'Why should I believe you?'

'Because it's the truth – and I already told you, I don't sell my photos to newspapers. I never have and I never will,' he said, with passion. 'Someone must have been watching you from a distance. It's nothing to do with me.'

'Are you sure it was taken from a distance?'

'Positive. Look, I know more about photography than most people. It was definitely taken from a long way away. I can tell from the image quality.'

Emma looked across the park, as if the person might still be there, watching with the long-range camera. Of course she couldn't see anyone. She turned back to Eric.

'Were you at the casting party last night?'

'No, I wasn't. Why?'

'I thought I saw you there.'

'Must have been my clone,' Eric joked. 'I was tucked up in front of the television. You can ask my mum if you like.'

'I'm sorry, Eric, for accusing you. It's just that when I saw that photograph, I thought it had to be you who'd taken it.'

'I can understand that,' he said. 'It must be awful being splashed all over the newspapers like that.'

'It is,' she admitted.

As Emma walked towards her flat, she couldn't shake the feeling that someone might be watching her – maybe the same someone who had taken her photo for the newspaper. She hurried there as quickly as she could without actually breaking into a run.

Occasionally, she glanced around, but she didn't spot any photographers. Then again, she reasoned, they were probably very good at keeping out of sight.

There were a few letters waiting for her back at the flat. She could tell from looking at most of them that they were junk mail, but one letter stood out. It was in a standard white envelope, with her address typed across the front. As she tore it open, she hoped it was from Dan.

It was. But within seconds of starting to read the typed message, she wished it hadn't been from him.

'No,' she said, shaking her head in disbelief, tears splashing down onto the paper. 'She wouldn't do that to me ... she *wouldn't.*'

40

'We were starting to wonder if you'd forgotten,' joked Sarah, as Emma entered the theatre lobby.

'Sorry, got delayed. Couldn't decide what to wear.' Emma met the group of girls with a smile and a 'What can you do?' shrug. But the smile was an effort.

It was hard not to think back to the hen party: the last time that they had been together. How things had changed. And as if that wouldn't have been bad enough, she was still reeling from the revelations contained in Dan's letter.

'You just missed Lizzy,' Sarah said. 'She popped out to say hello – she's invited us to some nightclub after the performance. Supposedly they've hired out the whole place. Should be a wicked night out.'

'Sounds great,' Emma said.

'And Lizzy's got herself a secret admirer,' Sarah continued.

'Really?'

Sarah nodded. 'Someone sent her a massive bouquet of flowers, wishing her luck for tonight's opening night.'

'She didn't say who it was from?' Emma asked.

'Unfortunately not,' Sarah lamented. 'We were hoping that you might have some idea – you being her best friend and all.'

'Haven't got a clue. She hasn't mentioned anyone to me.'

'Pity,' Sarah replied. 'We'll have to try and drag the truth out of her. Call me suspicious, but I'm sure she does know who sent those flowers. I just got the feeling that she knew more than she was letting on. Maybe I'm wrong.'

'Maybe,' Emma mused, thinking about what she was going to have to do.

'We'd better get to our seats,' interrupted Isabel, another one of the gang, poking her head around from the front of the group. She was holding a gigantic bag of chocolates. 'The show'll be starting any minute.'

Emma watched in the darkness as Lizzy gave the performance of her life. There was no denying that she was fantastic: the singing, the acting and the overall look were all flawless. After all those hours of stressing over the script, everything had come right. And, despite what Emma had just learnt, she still felt pleased for her best friend.

But, as the cast returned to the stage for the last time, taking their final bow, she feared that it wouldn't be long before the night would take a very different turn.

'Emma!' Lizzy shouted, rushing up to her friend and embracing her in a full-body hug. 'What did you think?' She stepped back but still held on to both of Emma's hands.

'I thought you were fantastic.' Emma smiled. 'Absolutely fantastic. The audience loved it.'

'Really?' Lizzy's eyes filled with tears and she broke out into a wide smile. 'You don't know how much that means to me. That's why I wanted to speak with you now, before I see the others. I don't mind what anyone else thinks, as long as you liked it.'

Shortly after the end of the show, as the group had been waiting in the theatre foyer, a message had come through from Lizzy inviting Emma backstage, to her dressing room.

'Well, I did,' Emma said, noticing the bouquet of flowers in the corner of the room.

'Someone sent them to me,' Lizzy explained, noticing Emma glance at the flowers. 'They look really expensive, as well.'

'You don't know who sent them?' Emma asked.

'No.'

'No note?'

'There is a note.' Lizzy moved towards the flowers and picked up a small piece of card. 'But all it says is "Good Luck".' She handed it to Emma. 'Doesn't give away very much.'

But it did.

'What's the matter?' said Lizzy, concerned, as Emma stared at the note. 'You think you know who they're from?'

'I went back to the flat this afternoon,' Emma said. 'There was a letter from Dan.'

'Really? You should have told me. I wouldn't have minded being interrupted.'

Emma closed her eyes briefly, searching for the right words. 'The letter was about you,' she said, looking away.

'What?' Lizzy said. 'I don't understand. Why would it be about me?'

'Promise you'll be honest with me,' Emma said, turning to face her friend. 'No matter what, promise you'll tell me the truth about this.'

Lizzy looked at Emma in concern. 'Em, I don't understand what you're on about. Just tell me what's going on, please.'

'Dan said that you two have been having an affair,' Emma said.

'What?' Lizzy said, aghast. 'But that's *rubbish*! I'd never do that, Em. Never! Why would he say something like that?'

'So it's not true,' Emma said, her voice faltering with emotion.

'It's complete bullshit,' Lizzy said, her face reddening. 'What else did he say?'

'He said that you'd been having a relationship for a few months,' Emma said. 'And that Richard and he fought because Richard found out about it and was threatening to tell me the truth.'

'He's lying,' Lizzy protested. 'Em, I don't know why he's saying this, but it's not true. I wouldn't do it to you. You know how much you mean to me! I can't believe he'd say that.'

Emma looked down again at the note. 'This note, with the flowers. It was written by Dan. It's his handwriting.'

Lizzy was speechless.

'He said in the letter that you would try to deny it. He says he's got proof that you two were having a relationship,' Emma stated.

'He can't have,' Lizzy countered, 'because it's not true. You do believe me, don't you? You can't think I'd do that to you?'

'I want to believe you. But I don't know if I can.'

Their eyes met, tears glistening.

'Please believe me,' Lizzy begged.

'I don't know what to believe any more,' Emma admitted. 'One of the two people I trusted the most is lying, and I've got to decide who.'

Lizzy nodded slowly. 'Maybe you'd better go,' she said sadly, 'while you decide.'

Emma turned and walked out of the dressing room. As she slipped out of the theatre and weaved her way through the Saturday night-time revellers of central London, she had never felt so alone.

But the problem was, she wasn't alone at all.

41

Nurse Mary Donahue had been keeping her eye on the visitor in the private room for some time now. He had seemed harmless enough at first, but when she'd gone in to check on Richard Carlton, something had felt wrong. It was as if she'd just interrupted a conversation – an argument, even. The man had been sitting, looming over Richard, just staring. And he was still doing that, a good thirty minutes later.

There was a time when Mary Donahue would never have thought the worst of anyone in a hospital, but it was different now. Things had changed the night a drugged-up patient had attacked her with a used syringe.

'Everything okay?' Mary asked now, entering the private room again but being careful to wedge the door open. She hoped that her question sounded relaxed, even if she wasn't.

The man didn't react. It was as if he were the one in a coma.

'Everything okay?' She tried again, this time her voice faltering.

'Oh, fine, fine,' he said, returning to life and seemingly shocked to notice her standing at the door. He straightened himself up and blinked a couple of times, rubbing his face.

'Would you like a drink?' she asked. 'I can do you a tea or coffee. Might not taste that great, but it's wet.'

Her smile wasn't returned.

'I'm okay,' he said, looking anything but.

'Are you a relative?'

'No,' he said. 'Friend of the family.'

'It's difficult, isn't it,' she observed, looking at Richard and then back at the unnamed man, 'knowing how to deal with someone in a coma.'

'Yes,' he agreed. 'Will he recover?'

'Impossible to tell, really,' she admitted. 'But there's always hope. Some people do make a complete recovery.'

'Will he remember everything?'

'Coma survivors often have some form of memory loss,' she said, being careful not to get the man's hopes up by referring directly to Richard's case.

The man turned back to look at Richard. Mary stole a glance at him, and it was then that she noticed that he was grasping something in his right hand. It looked like a piece of plastic – a cord, maybe. Her body stiffened as the man's attention shot back to her, noticing where she had been looking. His fist tightened around whatever it was he was holding.

'I'd better go,' he said, getting to his feet abruptly and striding out of the room, brushing past her.

Mary stood aside and let him go, unchallenged; she was in no position to do anything else – the man had towered above her slight frame. But she could do something now.

She moved out of the room and watched as the man disappeared through the double doors at the end of the corridor. Then she hurried over to the nursing station and picked up the phone.

'Hello, security? Nurse Donahue here, Ward 23. You wanted me to let you know if anything suspicious happened up here with Richard Carlton . . .'

Emma longed to go to the hospital to see Richard, but visiting hours had long since ended. Instead, she headed to her flat.

She needed to sort things out with Lizzy, but tonight wasn't the night to do it; maybe she should sleep here, let the dust settle and take stock in the morning.

She closed the door behind her and went around the apartment, flicking on all of the lights. It wasn't environmentally friendly, but it made her feel a bit better – a little safer. Then she ran a bath and made a cup of tea. Lizzy would be out at the nightclub with the rest of the cast, but she called her home phone, and left a message explaining that she would be staying the night in her own flat.

The intercom buzzed shortly after she had slipped into the bath. She remained there, her desire to soak in the warm water outweighing her desire to find out who it was. She closed her eyes and dipped her nose towards the water line.

Then the intercom buzzed again, and again, becoming more insistent. So much so that Emma began to worry about who it was. And whether they were in trouble.

Could it be Dan? Or Lizzy?

She climbed out of the bath, wrapped a towel around herself and pattered out into the hallway, leaving a trail of wet footprints in her wake. A chill whipped around her bare shoulders and legs as she reached the intercom. It buzzed again just before she could press the button to speak.

'Hello? Who is it?'

She waited, but there was no answer.

Again, the buzz – this time slightly longer than before.

'Hello?' she said again.

Silence.

'Look, if this is someone just messing around you can just go to . . .'

'Help me,' a weak, barely audible voice interrupted.

'*Dan?*' Emma shouted. 'Is that you?'

'Help me,' the voice repeated in its deathly whisper.

'Dan?'

'Quickly,' the voice said.

Emma raced into the bedroom, dropping her towel and throwing on her jogging bottoms and T-shirt, which were hung over the chair. She headed for the door, squashing her feet into her trainers. As she rushed down the stairs she had to check herself for fear of falling.

When she got to the entrance hall she slowed to a stop, taking the opportunity to look through the outside door, hoping to make out Dan's silhouette. But no one was there.

Emma stepped towards the door, breathing heavily, and

grasped the handle. Not knowing whether she was doing the right thing, she opened the door and stepped outside.

Flash!

'What—?' Emma exclaimed, shielding her eyes from the bright light.

Flash! Flash!

She squinted and saw a figure at the bottom of the steps, pointing a camera at her. The person was wearing a balaclava.

Flash!

'What the hell—?' Emma said, taking a step towards the individual.

The person turned and ran.

Instinctively, she gave chase. She pursued the silhouette down Marylebone High Street, keeping her target in sight, as they darted down one street after another, until they emerged onto Baker Street. But the figure gave her the slip by running straight across a road junction, narrowly avoiding a double-decker and a 4x4.

Emma watched, breathless with adrenalin as they disappeared into the night. She took a moment, then turned and headed back to the flat – there was no point in chasing them any further.

As she walked back, she tried to take in what had just happened. She was shocked and upset, and couldn't begin to believe the lengths journalists would go to, just to get a picture.

By the time she reached the apartment she was thoroughly unnerved. If this sort of undesired attention was the price of success, then she didn't want any of it. She ran up the stairs, locked the door and went into the living room, collapsing onto the sofa, her head spinning. She really needed someone to talk to – Lizzy, or Will.

Emma was woken by a knock on the door. At first, dazed by tiredness, she thought it might have just been part of a dream. But as she staggered across the room and moved towards the door, there was another knock.

Was it the photographer, coming back to get a closer shot? Or was it something more sinister?

But how had they got in? Had she not closed the main door properly?

Instead of asking who it was, giving them time to react, she crept towards the door. With her heart seemingly trying to punch its way out of her chest, she slowly brought her eye up to the spy-hole.

42

'You all right?' asked Stuart, as Emma entered the kitchen that Sunday morning. He examined her eyes, looking for an explanation as to why she had been crying.

'Today was supposed to be my wedding day,' Emma stated, taking a seat at the breakfast table.

She'd let Stuart stay the night on the sofa after his late-night visit. Having someone familiar in the flat eased her anxieties, especially now that the paparazzi were calling at her door. She had worried that asking him to stay might give him the wrong impression, and he certainly wouldn't have been her first choice of overnight guest, but he was there and willing. They'd watched some TV and then, when he'd mentioned calling for a cab, she'd asked him to stay.

'Oh,' he said, looking towards his feet for inspiration. 'Emma, I'm really sorry.'

'So am I.' She looked at the spread Stuart had prepared for breakfast – a pot of tea, toast, croissants, yoghurt and cereals. 'Where did all this come from?'

'Waitrose,' he answered, placing a bowl of strawberries on the tabletop and then taking a seat. 'I tried to make breakfast with what you had in the fridge, but there's only so much you can do with a half-eaten jar of beetroot.'

He smiled and Emma smiled back. That was the first flash of his trademark humour that she had once loved so much. And even though it was misplaced at this present time, it was still some comfort.

'Tuck in,' he said.

She just looked at the table.

Stuart grimaced. 'Please say you've got an appetite. Otherwise I'll have to eat the lot myself.'

'I'll try,' she said, picking up a croissant and placing it on her plate.

'That's better.'

'Did someone phone this morning?' asked Emma, buttering the croissant. 'I thought I heard the phone ring before I got up.'

'Wrong number,' Stuart replied, biting into a piece of toast. 'Some guy wanting to speak to someone called Debbie.'

'Right.'

'What are your plans for today?'

'I haven't got any.'

'You shouldn't be alone,' Stuart advised. 'This was supposed to be the greatest day of your life. It's bound to be difficult, and you'll need support.'

'Don't,' Emma said. 'I don't want charity.'

'What are you thinking about Dan's letter? Do you believe Lizzy?'

'I want to. But I want to believe Dan, too.'

'It's difficult. Either your best friend is lying or your fiancé is lying.'

Emma put a hand to her face.

'I'm sorry,' Stuart said.

'It's not your fault,' Emma replied, standing up from the table and walking over to the window. 'I just can't get my head around what the letter said. I can't believe that Lizzy would do that to me. Not if she's the person I've always thought she is. But then I still can't believe Dan would have done this, either.'

'Sometimes people let us down. Even those we love and trust the most. When it comes down to it, humans are pretty weak creatures.'

'I've been thinking. Maybe there is another explanation.'

'Go on,' Stuart said.

'Maybe Dan didn't write the letter. After all, it's typed, so it could be from anyone.'

'Like who?'

'I don't know,' she admitted. 'Anyone. The story was splashed all over the papers yesterday. Maybe someone decided to write the letter as a prank.'

'Some prank,' Stuart said. 'They would have to be really sick.'

'But it's possible. Maybe the press wrote it themselves, just to make a better story.'

'Are you sure you're not just kidding yourself? I mean, I can understand that you don't want to believe what it said—'

'But you know from last night the lengths they're prepared to go to,' interrupted Emma. 'They made me think that someone was in trouble down there, just to get a few photographs. It really scared me, Stuart.'

'I know. And when we find out who took them, they're going to regret it, believe me.'

'I doubt we'll discover who did it.'

'Oh, we will,' Stuart said confidently. 'And I know where we'll find our answer.'

'It doesn't make sense,' Stuart said, putting yet another newspaper back on the rack in the local newsagents. 'Why would they go to the bother of taking your photo and then not publish it? I was sure this was going to work.'

'I'm not sure,' Emma said, as she finished looking through the paper she was holding, 'but I have one idea.'

'Go on,' Stuart said.

'I met someone a few days ago, on Primrose Hill. He took my photo.'

Stuart looked worried.

'He seemed pretty harmless,' Emma said, knowing just what Stuart was thinking. 'It's not the same as last time.'

Stuart was unconvinced. 'Really?'

'Honestly, he's not another Stephen Myers,' she protested.

'But you still think he might have been hanging around outside your apartment, wearing a balaclava and pretending to need help?'

Stuart's tone of voice made Emma nod. 'Maybe you're right,' she acknowledged. 'Maybe I'm just being naïve.'

'Tell me more about him.'

'I don't really know much. Apart from he's probably in his early twenties, and he hangs around Primrose Hill taking pictures of celebrities. He was also a big fan of *Up My Street.*'

'For God's sake, Em,' Stuart said, in an aggressive tone that shocked her. 'How could you get involved with someone like that again?'

'Probably the same way I got involved with another man who just upped and ran out on me,' Emma shot back.

Her anger flaring, she turned and walked out of the shop. She didn't bother to look back and check if Stuart was following. How dare he just walk back into her life and start judging her like that?

'Emma,' Stuart said, catching up with her a few metres down the street. He moved around in front of her. 'Please, let me apologise.'

Emma stopped.

'I'm sorry for saying that back there,' he said. 'It's just I don't want to see you making the same mistake again.'

'You think Stephen Myers was my mistake?' she snapped. 'You think it was my fault?'

'No, of course not. I didn't mean it like that. Look, we're both stressing out about this. Let's just go and get a coffee, and relax a little.'

'Okay. I'm sorry too,' she said, softening. 'You were right – today is going to be difficult.'

They had just left the coffee shop when Emma spotted Eric.

He was on the other side of the road, a camera around his neck. But at that particular moment his attention was elsewhere, giving her the time she needed.

'Emma!' Stuart shouted, as she darted across the road. 'What's the matter?'

Emma reached Eric before he had time to react, grabbing the back of his collar using one of her much-practised karate moves.

'Hey,' he said, flailing around like a fish on a hook. 'Get off me!'

'What are you doing here?' Emma demanded, keeping her grip from behind. A couple of pedestrians gave her alarmed glances as they walked by, but for the most part people dismissed the altercation as just another everyday London occurrence.

'I . . . I . . . was—' Eric stuttered.

'Is this him?' Stuart said, catching up.

Emma nodded.

'What the hell are you doing?' Stuart said to Eric, who now looked genuinely scared. 'Were you following us?'

Eric shook his head.

'You're lying,' Stuart said. 'Was it you at Emma's apartment last night?'

'I don't know what you're talking about,' Eric protested. 'Please, just let me go.'

'Not before I take this,' Stuart said, yanking the camera from around his neck.

'Hey, give it back to me,' Eric shouted, trying to grab it. 'That's worth a lot of money. Be careful with it.'

Emma glared at Stuart, who was fiddling with the camera. 'Stuart.'

'It's okay,' he said, clicking the shutter until the camera began automatically rewinding the film. When it had finished, he opened up the back and pulled out the cartridge. 'Got it. Here you go.' He handed the camera back to Eric.

'Let me go,' Eric moaned.

Emma released him, and only then realised he was crying. She was shocked and embarrassed.

'If I ever catch you following her again, I swear I'll kill you,' Stuart said, jabbing a finger at Eric.

Eric just turned and ran.

'You open them,' Emma said, as they entered the photographers to collect the set of prints they'd handed in for one-hour processing.

'You sure?' Stuart replied.

'If you wouldn't mind.'

They gave their details and the cashier handed over the photographs. Stuart waited until he was outside to open them. Emma watched as he shuffled through them, his face not revealing any emotion.

'Are the photos there?' Emma asked. 'Of last night?'

'I think we'd better call the police,' Stuart replied. 'Right now.'

43

'Afraid of flying?' the woman asked, turning to look at the young man sitting to her left. She looked to be in her sixties and had a friendly smile.

'Is it that obvious?' Will answered.

'It's the way you're gripping the arm rest,' she said, nodding towards his white knuckles. 'Like you're hanging on for dear life.'

'I'm usually okay,' he said, smiling ruefully, trying but failing to loosen his grip. 'Didn't have any problems on the way out. Now, though, I just can't stop thinking about being so far up. I feel as though if I stop concentrating on the plane being up here, we'll just crash. I know it sounds really stupid,' he added, embarrassed.

'It's not stupid,' she said. 'My husband had a terrible fear of flying. Didn't bother him for a while – he just didn't fly anywhere. Then my son emigrated to Canada, and he had no choice but to fly.'

'So how did he get over it?'

'I bought him one of those self-help books. It said that the fear comes from a loss of control – the person wants to be in control, but ultimately they can't control anything, apart from how they react to the situation. So the first step is to accept that you're not in control of things. You don't have to focus on the engines, or the wings, or how high the plane is. Just sit back and let the pilot get on with flying the plane.'

'Sounds sensible,' Will said, considering that piece of advice. He turned his head and ventured a look out of the window, peering down at the Atlantic Ocean. But, again, his mind tried to single-handedly keep the plane from crashing down into the water. He closed his eyes in an attempt to calm himself.

'The other trick is to use a distraction tactic,' the woman said, noticing Will's continued discomfort. 'Did you notice that when you were talking to me, you started to relax a little?'

'Not really. But I'm willing to try anything.'

'Good. We'll talk some more. So was this your first time visiting Canada?'

'Yeah.' Will turned away from the window. 'Always wanted to visit the place. My friend lives in Toronto and he's been asking me to come over for a while.'

'And did you have a good time?'

'It was good while it lasted. In the end, I was only there for a few days.'

'Why's that?'

'Oh, I need to sort something out at home.'

'That's a shame – to go all that way just for a few days.'

'Couldn't be helped. I really do need to get back.'

'Must be important.'

'It is,' he replied. 'So, why did you go to Canada? To see your son?'

'Okay,' she said, knowing full well that he'd just slammed the door on that part of the conversation, 'we'll talk about me for a while. I was over to see my new granddaughter.'

'That's nice.'

'It was very nice. She's beautiful. Alex – that's my son – has such a wonderful family now. I just wish my husband was alive to see it.'

'I'm sorry about that,' Will said.

'That's okay,' she said, smiling. 'Anyway – he might not be around to see any more, but I can still feel his love. I love him now as much as I ever did, and I know that he loves me back.'

'It must be great,' Will said, 'to feel so close to someone, even though they're gone.'

'Isn't it the same for all those who we love? Just because they're not here in front of us doesn't mean they're gone.'

'I wish I believed that,' he lamented. 'My mum died a few years ago. But I don't feel like you do. She's dead and that's that.'

'What about the people you love that are still alive?'

'I don't really get on with my dad,' Will admitted, 'but I do love my sister – she's the person I love the most. We've always been really close.'

'Well, that's good,' the woman said. 'Isn't it?' she added, noticing Will's solemn expression.

'Oh, yes, of course,' he said. 'It's just that, well, I don't know whether . . . I have to tell her something, and I think that after I do, everything will change.' He stopped, suddenly feeling that if he carried on talking he might start to cry.

'It's okay,' she said. 'You don't need to tell me anything.'

He turned to look out of the window again and tried to wipe away a tear as subtly as possible. He hoped he wouldn't crack up in this flying tin can, where there was no chance of escape. 'I'm fine,' he said.

'Maybe it would help to talk about it?' the woman suggested.

He shook his head. 'You wouldn't want to know.'

'Maybe I do,' she replied. 'Look, if you're embarrassed about whatever it is, don't be. Once we get off this plane, you'll never see me again.'

Will looked around, not quite believing that he was even considering telling a stranger his secret. But the woman was right – they wouldn't meet again. And he needed to tell someone – to release all the built-up pressure that had been boiling away for years. She didn't even know his name, and he wouldn't have to give her the full details. He noted that the passengers in the seats in front and behind were wearing headphones as they watched the in-flight movies; the man on the other side of the woman was asleep. They wouldn't be overheard.

'Okay,' he said. 'I'll tell you.'

44

Emma and Stuart watched as Detective Inspector Gasnier leafed through the set of photographs as if he were reviewing his dealt hand during a poker game.

'And you had no idea that these photos were being taken?' he asked, paying particular attention to a photograph of Emma at her apartment window.

'No,' Emma replied. 'Well, except for the couple of photos he took up on Primrose Hill.'

Gasnier maintained his poker face. He then placed the photographs on the table and took a seat across from them, next to DS Davies.

'So, who did you say this man was?' he asked.

'His name's Eric,' Emma said.

'But no surname?'

'No,' Emma replied, angered that he had asked that question twice in less than five minutes. 'I have his mobile number, but I don't know where he lives. He said he always hangs around up on Primrose Hill.'

'How did you get these photographs?'

'We took them from him,' Stuart interjected. 'I took them.'

'Forcibly?'

'I didn't hurt him,' Stuart clarified. 'I just wanted to get the film.'

'Did you,' Gasnier mused, rather ominously.

'We thought that he could have been the person from last night,' Emma said.

'But none of these photos match the ones taken last night?' Gasnier asked.

Emma shook her head. 'No.'

'Emma,' he said. 'I appreciate that this is a really bad time right now. And I know that you're looking for answers to a lot of things – just like we are. But this just isn't on. You can't take the law into your own hands like that. If you think you can do a better job than us, then sign up to join the Met.' He chuckled, mirthlessly. 'God knows we're always after new recruits.'

Emma kept silent.

'You want to clear Dan's name. I understand that,' he continued. 'But, at the moment, we haven't found any evidence to suggest that anyone but your fiancé attacked Richard Carlton. We might be wrong, but as yet that's the situation. These photos might be proof that you've got an admirer – even a stalker – but they don't link this Eric guy with anything else.'

'So you're not going to talk to him?' Emma said, feeling utterly deflated.

'I didn't say that,' Gasnier replied. 'I'd say that on this evidence he certainly deserves a talking-to. But it will just be a warning. In the meantime, if you do have anything else that may help the investigation, let us know.'

'Tell them about the letter,' Stuart said.

Emma wanted to clamp his mouth shut, but it was too late.

'Heavy night last night?' Caroline, one of the co-stars, asked Lizzy as they waited behind the wings, ready to enter the stage area during rehearsals – even though the show had started its run, due to the last-minute cast changes they were required to continue rehearsing between performances to make sure things ran as smoothly as possible. And, cruelly, this even meant coming in the day after the opening night to review how it had all gone. 'Sorry,' she added, looking apologetic, 'I couldn't help noticing that you look a bit peaky today – and your notes are a bit off-key.'

'It *was* a heavy night,' Lizzy said, 'but I didn't drink anything.'

'Oh, right,' Caroline replied, looking confused.

'I've got some stuff to deal with,' Lizzy explained, 'and I'm finding it hard to concentrate on anything until I sort things out.'

There was no doubt that rehearsals that day had been a disaster. Lizzy couldn't get the discussion with Emma – and the accusations – out of her mind. What she couldn't understand was why Dan would have penned that letter in the first place. What would he gain by doing so? It didn't make any sense.

Lizzy certainly didn't blame Emma for believing what the letter had said. But what did disappoint her was that Emma seemed to have just shut her out. The way she had just hung up on her that morning without saying a word – without letting her explain – had really hurt.

'I'm sorry, Em,' Stuart said, once the police had left the flat. 'But they had to know about it. You can't keep something like that from them – not when there's so much at stake.'

'I can't believe you just did that without discussing it with me first! How dare you?' Emma was incandescent, all her old doubts and fears about Stuart flooding back.

'I know you've got your loyalties, but if that letter was from Dan, then it's really important for the investigation.'

'It wasn't,' Emma replied. 'I know now that it wasn't from Dan. Lizzy wouldn't do that to me, and neither would Dan.'

'But that's the thing. You *don't* know. It's just what you want to believe.'

Emma turned away.

'It was my decision whether or not to tell the police about the letter,' she stated, 'not yours.'

'Okay, maybe I was out of order,' Stuart said, moving over to Emma, 'but I did it for you, Em. I hate to see you suffering like this. You deserve better. And I still hate myself for everything I put you through.'

Emma turned around, face to face with her one-time fiancé.

Stuart placed his hands gently around the tops of her shoulders and, for a second or two, they just looked at one another in silence, inches apart.

Then Stuart moved in for a kiss.

45

'No,' Emma said, pulling back from the kiss. She turned away and touched her lips. 'This isn't right.'

'Maybe it is right,' Stuart replied. 'Maybe this is what is supposed to happen.'

'It's not.'

'But why?'

'Because I love Dan.' Emma turned around again to face Stuart.

'You loved me,' Stuart said.

'I used to love you, but not any more.'

Stuart stood there silently, looking as if he'd just been slapped in the face.

'How can you still love him, after what he's done to you?' he said finally. 'How could you still love someone who could do all this – attack his own brother, run out just before his wedding, have an affair with your best friend?'

'Because I don't think he did,' Emma replied.

Stuart shook his head. 'You're too trusting. Just like . . .'

'Go on,' Emma said. 'Just like when? When I first met Stephen Myers?'

Stuart pursed his lips.

'Tell me what you were going to say,' Emma pressed.

'It doesn't matter.'

'You blame him for us splitting up, don't you?'

'It didn't help,' he admitted.

'No,' Emma said, shaking her head. 'We'd put that behind us – everything was going to be okay. It was you walking out on me that split us up, Stuart. You can't blame that one person for your actions.'

'Yes, I can!' he screamed suddenly, losing his cool completely. Emma stiffened.

'Sorry,' Stuart said, holding up his hands and breathing deeply to calm himself. 'Look, Emma, it's just this might be our one chance to put things right. We can start again. It's been good these past few days, you've got to admit that. Like old times.'

Emma took a step backwards. 'Is that what this was all about?'

'What?' Stuart replied. 'I don't understand.'

'All this help. Was this all just a way to try and get back together with me?'

'No,' he said defensively. 'You needed help. I thought you appreciated it.'

'I do. I really appreciate it. But, Stuart, you've got to understand that there's no chance of us getting back together. Even if Dan is guilty of all those things, it doesn't affect you and me. You've got to accept that what's gone is gone.'

'But I love you,' Stuart said.

'I'm sorry.'

He just stood there for a moment, gazing at her. 'I'd better go,' he said, turning to the door. 'I need time to think. You know, Em,' he said, pausing in the doorway, 'if you knew just how much I love you, you'd give us another try – I'm sure of it.'

Will screwed his eyes shut and tried to control his breathing. He hadn't seen the woman since she had left her seat, shortly after he had finished his confession. And that was ten minutes ago.

Maybe she was just queuing for the toilet.

He had to find out. He undid his seatbelt and squeezed past the other passenger, giving his apologies as he moved into the aisle. He was halfway to the toilets at the back of the plane when he saw the woman, sitting some ten or so rows behind her original position. She saw him too, and quickly averted her eyes. Panic rose in his chest.

Why had he told her? Why had he been so stupid?

'You okay, sir?' a steward asked.

'Fine, fine,' Will replied, realising he was gripping the back of someone's headrest. He let go and carried on past the steward.

What if she had told the cabin crew? At this moment, the police might be waiting at Heathrow, ready to board the plane when it landed.

Fortunately the toilet was free. He locked himself inside and sat down on the seat with his head in his hands. He remembered the advice the woman had given him about using distraction techniques to cure his fear of flying.

He had all the distraction he needed now.

Back at her flat, Emma waited a couple of hours before phoning Lizzy. Stuart had been right in one respect – she couldn't do this alone. Unfortunately, Lizzy's mobile was off, so she left a message, asking her to get in touch as soon as possible.

She then spent a good half-hour training on the punch bag, her phone standing upright on the window ledge, hoping that Lizzy would call back soon. Rehearsals would probably be finished by now. Emma hoped that she wasn't deliberately ignoring her calls, though after the accusations she had levelled against her, it would be understandable.

She had just showered and dressed when the intercom buzzer sounded. She froze in fear, after what had happened previously, but eventually forced herself to answer. It was a courier, with a package for her. She decided it was safer to meet him downstairs in the foyer, rather than invite him up.

'Miss Holden?' he asked, as she approached him. He was young, dressed in Lycra, wearing a sporty cycle helmet.

'Yeah, that's me,' Emma replied.

'Package for you,' he said, bringing out an envelope from the bag tucked by his side. 'Can you just sign here, please?' He handed over an electronic device.

Emma scrawled a signature on the touch screen and exchanged the device for the envelope.

'Cheers,' he said. 'Have a good day.'

'Excuse me,' Emma called, as he headed for the door. 'Can you tell me who it's from?'

'Sorry,' he said, 'I don't carry that information. But head office might be able to help.'

'Thanks,' said Emma, watching him leave.

She stared at the white envelope, then slid her finger under the flap and pulled out a wedding card.

Her first emotion was one of sadness. Someone hadn't heard the news and had sent a card in ignorance – maybe one of her distant relations who couldn't make the wedding itself. It was a lovely and obviously expensive card, beautifully decorated with 'Happy Wedding Day' emblazoned on the front.

But as she opened it, her stomach turned over.

The first thing she saw, tucked inside, was a photograph of her on the doorstep outside the apartment block, looking startled, illuminated against the dark background of the building behind.

Her hands shaking, she lifted up the photograph and read the short and sickening message on the card underneath. It was written in a shaking, child-like scrawl:

I have the one you love.

46

'Thank God you're here, Lizzy,' Emma said, as she opened the door to her friend.

'I came as soon as I got your message,' Lizzy replied, stepping into the flat. 'Look, Em, I don't know what's going on with that letter, but I swear it's all complete rubbish. I would never do something like that to you – you've got to believe me.'

'I do believe you,' Emma replied.

Lizzy looked both surprised and hugely relieved. 'Oh, you don't know how happy I am to hear that,' she said, visibly relaxing. 'I was so upset last night. I couldn't bear the thought of falling out with you for good, Em.'

'Me, neither,' Emma agreed.

'What I can't understand,' Lizzy said, 'is why Dan would say those things. I've always got on well with him – I thought. Why would he just lie like that?'

'I don't think Dan sent the letter.'

'What?'

'Look at this.' Emma pulled out the wedding card. 'This was delivered half an hour ago.'

Lizzy took the card, screwing her face up as she realised what it was. She looked up at Emma, as if for guidance.

'Open it,' Emma directed. 'Read what it says inside.'

Lizzy did as requested. 'My God, Em,' she said, putting a hand to her mouth and looking at her with wide eyes. 'What the hell is this?'

'Someone *must* have Dan,' Emma replied. 'This was in the envelope, too.' She handed her the photo.

Lizzy examined the photograph. 'When was this taken?'

'Last night,' Emma said. 'I didn't see who it was because he was wearing a balaclava. I chased after him, but he got away.'

'Bloody hell, Em, why didn't you call me sooner? If you'd called last night, I'd have come around straight away.'

'Stuart came round,' Emma said.

'You invited him?' Lizzy stared at her friend.

'No. But I did ask him to stay the night, on the sofa. I just needed the company. You understand that, don't you?'

'I suppose.' Lizzy nodded. 'Where's Stuart now?'

'I asked him to leave. He tried to kiss me this morning – said he wants us to make another go of it.'

'No,' Lizzy said in disbelief. 'How could he, while all this is going on?'

'He's not thinking straight. No matter how many times I tried to tell him there was no way back, he just wouldn't hear it.' Emma shook her head.

'Maybe he's just in love?' Lizzy ventured.

'Maybe,' Emma said.

'So you think that the person who wrote the letter about me and Dan is the same person who sent this?' Lizzy held up the card.

'Yes. And I think they attacked Richard, and they've been holding Dan ever since.'

'But who would want to do that? Where's the motive for kidnapping him?'

'Dan or Richard might have upset someone – I don't know,' Emma admitted. 'Maybe it's something to do with me.'

'Do you think the police will be able to find out who sent the card?'

'I don't see why not. It was delivered by a courier company, and I have their name. They should have the details of the sender.'

'Will they tell us that information?'

'Probably not, but surely they'll have to tell the police.'

'Hope you enjoyed the flight,' the air stewardess said as Will disembarked the plane. He forced a smile and then kept his head down, trying to blend in amongst the passengers as they made their way down the tunnel to passport control.

He felt a hell of a lot better once he got through immigration, but his anxiety increased again, by the conveyor belt during the long wait for the luggage. He'd noticed the woman standing on the far side, and he wondered whether it had been a deliberate ploy on her part to get as far away from him as possible. Maybe he was just being paranoid.

Finally his bag arrived. He reached out and turned to walk away.

Then he felt a tap on his shoulder.

'Excuse me.'

He froze on the spot before turning around slowly.

'I think you've got my bag,' an elderly gentleman said, almost apologetically. It took a second or two for his words to sink in. 'My name's on the tag, there,' he explained, pointing at the case.

Will looked down to see the label. He had taken someone else's bag.

'I'm really sorry,' he said, handing the bag back to the elderly man. 'It looks exactly the same as mine.'

'That's all right,' the man said. 'Easily done.'

Will's bag came a minute or so later; this time he made sure he had the right one.

He couldn't wait to get out of the airport, so he upped his pace towards customs. He had just reached the customs area when he felt another hand on his shoulder.

'Excuse me, sir.'

'It's okay,' he said, turning around. 'It's definitely my—'

'Are you William Holden?'

'Yes,' Will answered, facing up to the policeman. 'That's me.'

47

He returned to his flat, her words taunting him.

There's no chance of us getting back together.

She had meant every word of it, he realised that. It wasn't just what she had said, but the way she had said it. The look was so heartless, so devoid of love. Maybe it was what he deserved.

It made him feel so lonely.

'Hi, it's me,' he slurred into the phone receiver. 'I've had a bit to drink, yes. It's Em – she doesn't want me back. She never wants me back. And she still loves Dan. After everything I've done to try and change things, she still loves him – can you believe that? She still loves him, not me. What? Okay, maybe speak to you later.'

He placed the phone back on its holder and stumbled into the kitchen. Nobody wanted to be with him, or even speak to him. He had to accept that this was the end of the road. All those weeks and months of hoping that things would turn out all right . . . it was what had kept him going.

But she loved Dan, not him.

It was all over.

He opened one of the kitchen cupboards and took out several boxes of paracetamol, then poured himself a pint glass of water.

'It's good to see you, Will,' Edward said.

'You too,' Will replied, not sounding particularly convincing. He flopped down into the front passenger seat of the car and closed the door. 'And thanks for picking me up,' he said, as they drove out of the airport. 'You didn't have to.'

'I thought we could use the time to talk,' Edward answered, as he negotiated a roundabout.

'Sounds ominous,' Will replied, looking out of the window.

'We need to talk,' Edward said, 'about a lot of things.'

'Definitely ominous,' Will quipped.

'No, I'm serious. I know that things haven't been great between us since your mother died, but things are going to change. I've been thinking about it a lot – I don't want things to carry on the way they have been. I want us all to be . . .'

'A happy family?' Will offered.

'Please, Will.'

'Okay, I'm sorry.'

'Miranda's pregnant,' Edward blurted out. 'I've been waiting for the right time to tell you.'

'Right,' Will said, shaking his head and laughing to himself. 'Now you picking me up from the airport all makes sense.'

'I hoped you'd be happy for me. This could be our chance to start again . . . we could get to know each other better – all of us. It would mean so much to me.'

Will thought for a moment. 'Okay,' he said.

'You mean it?' Edward said, unable to hide his surprise.

'I've been doing a lot of thinking, too,' Will revealed. 'Life's too short. I'll try my best to make it work.'

'Will, that's fantastic.'

They spent the next few minutes driving in silence, heading for London: Edward revelling in the chance of reconciliation, Will musing on how his life would never be the same again after his confessions.

'How's Em?' Will asked eventually.

'I haven't seen her since calling you in Canada yesterday,' Edward admitted. 'I was afraid that if I did see her, I wouldn't be able to control myself. She might have suspected something.'

'Would that have been a bad thing?'

'Pardon?'

'Well, it would have saved me the bother of telling her myself. That way, I could have stayed on the other side of the world – probably not far away enough for Em, but it would have been a start.'

'Emma isn't going to find out about anything.'

Will was bemused. 'But when we spoke, I thought—'

'I've changed my mind,' interrupted Edward. 'We can't tell her about what you did. We can't tell anyone.'

'I want to tell her. I've decided I want to tell her.'

'No.'

'I told someone on the aeroplane,' Will confessed. 'I told them everything.'

'What?' Edward said, horrified. The car swerved slightly as he glanced across at Will. 'What the hell did you do that for?'

'I needed to tell someone. At first I was scared, wondering why I'd done it, thinking that she'd tell someone else and that I'd get into trouble. Then when I got off the plane, a policeman came up to me. I thought that was it, but all he wanted to do was give me back my passport – I'd dropped it on the floor.'

'Christ, have you lost all your reasoning, Will?' Edward hit the steering wheel with his fist in frustration. 'You do under-stand that you could go to jail for what you did?'

'Of course I do! But, back there, standing in front of that policeman, I realised that I didn't feel afraid – I was relieved. I realised that going to jail would probably be the only thing that would really set me free. And when he just gave me back my passport, I was actually disappointed.'

'You can't do this, Will,' Edward said. 'You can't.'

'I can handle it, Dad.'

'You're living in a fantasy world,' Edward snapped. 'Prison is a horrific experience. And when you do get out, do you think the guilt will have gone? You'll still feel the same, except that you'll have lost your sister forever. She'll never forgive you for what you did.'

'I've made my mind up. I'm prepared to take the chance. I have faith in Em.'

'And what about me?' Edward put a hand to his chest and rubbed it, unconsciously. 'Do you think I won't be dragged into this, too? I'm in this up to my neck, all because I wanted to help you, William. If you do tell Em, I'll lose her, too.'

'It's the only way. How else are we going to open her eyes to what that guy is really like? We need to get that man out of her life. And if me going to jail is what it takes for Em to be safe, then that's what I'm going to do.'

'Maybe there's another way.'

Will doubted it. 'Like what?'

'Under your seat,' Edward directed.

Will reached down and felt around beneath his seat. His fingers glanced over a cool metal object. 'No,' he said, instinctively recoiling from it. 'Whatever you've got planned, I'm not doing it.'

48

'So, what do you think?' asked DS Davies, his shirt damp with sweat from the incessant heat as they tramped down the stairs from Emma's flat.

'I think I'll reserve judgement,' Gasnier replied, 'until we speak to the couriers.'

'You think we'll find a name?'

'I'm sure we'll get a name, but I very much doubt it will be the name we're really after.'

'Do you think Dan Carlton might have sent the card himself? To put us off the scent?'

'What do you think?' Gasnier said, batting the question back. 'Do you think this is all part of a carefully laid plan by Dan Carlton?'

'Could be. But personally I doubt it.'

'Why?' Gasnier pressed.

'I don't know,' Davies said. 'Just a feeling I have.'

'A feeling? Is that it?'

Davies shrugged. 'It's all I've got to go on at the moment.'

'Indeed,' Gasnier said, unconvinced.

'Hopefully the couriers will shed some light on things.'

The couriers' office was located just south of the river, a few minutes from Waterloo Station. As Gasnier had expected, it was a small back-street operation – much like the hundred or so other firms in and around the city, plying their trade by making deliveries using motorcycle or pedal cycles. It was a dangerous business; accidents involving couriers were commonplace.

'You're the police?' asked the young girl behind the counter.

'Indeed we are,' Gasnier said. 'So, can we have the details of who sent the package?'

'I'll have to ask the manager,' she replied.

'You do that. And if there's a problem, we'd be delighted to talk with him.'

The girl hurried upstairs and was back within the minute. 'I'll need to see some ID. Then you can have the name. We log all our deliveries electronically,' she explained, as she tapped away on her keyboard. 'That way we can keep track of everything.'

'Lucky for us, eh,' Gasnier joked, mainly for DS Davies' benefit.

'It's a great system,' the girl said, missing the sarcasm. 'You said it went to who?'

'Holden. Emma Holden.'

'Emma Holden,' the girl repeated unthinkingly, all the while tapping away at the keys. 'Yes, here it is. The delivery was requested today and they paid by cash. Here's the name.' She turned the monitor around.

Gasnier's eyes narrowed. 'Well, that is interesting.'

'You can't be serious about this,' said Will, still horrified from the discovery of a gun beneath the passenger seat of his father's car.

'It's not loaded,' Edward replied. 'No one is going to get hurt.'

'Where the hell did you get it?'

Edward glanced across to him. 'One of my friends. He belongs to a shooting club.'

Will couldn't believe this was happening. 'What did you tell him you wanted the gun for?'

'He didn't ask. Just said to take care.'

Will shook his head. 'This is crazy, absolutely crazy. I think you've lost your mind.'

'Will, this whole situation is crazy,' Edward replied, signalling left at a junction. He pulled away when the road was clear. 'Compared to what has already happened, this might be the most sensible thing to do.'

'My God, just listen to yourself, will you? We're actually on the way to someone's home, about to threaten them with a gun. Does that sound sensible?'

'It's the best way. The only way.'

'No,' Will countered, 'it's not. I've already told you. And he might not even be there.'

'He is.'

'How do you know?'

'I've had someone watching the place, to make sure he's around.'

'Bloody hell, Dad. This is madness.'

'We'll just scare him a little,' said Edward, ignoring Will's protests. 'If he thinks we're really serious, then he'll take notice and leave Emma alone.'

'It won't work. I've tried it before.'

'This time will be different. This time we'll really scare him.'

'Hurt him, you mean?'

'Of course not. We've just got to make him believe that we mean what we say. Look, we both know that he's fragile. It shouldn't take much to break him.'

'I still think this is a bad idea,' said Will, as they reached the apartment block and came to a stop in a small parking area.

'Let's just get this over with,' Edward replied. 'Give me the gun,' he added, gesturing to the passenger-side footwell.

Shaking his head, Will reached under his seat again and pulled out the handgun, holding it gingerly between finger and thumb.

'Don't lift it up so people can see,' Edward rebuked, grabbing hold of the weapon. He tucked the gun into his waistband and covered it with his jumper, as if he'd done it a million times before.

'I really don't like this.'

'Come on,' said Edward, 'before I change my mind.'

Edward and Will had no difficulty getting into the block – someone had wedged the door open with a traffic cone.

Will followed his father up the stairs, hoping that by the time they reached the flat he would have had a change of heart, realising just how foolish this all was. He wanted to turn around and walk away, but he had already let down one family member – and his dad shouldn't be alone.

When they reached the flat, the door was ajar.

'Dad, are you sure?' Will grabbed Edward's arm as he reached to push the door open.

'I'm sure,' Edward said, although his voice was faltering and he touched his chest. 'Let's get this over with.'

As they entered the flat, the first thing that hit Will was the total silence. It was eerie, and he didn't like it one bit.

They moved down the entrance hall and turned to look in the living room. The room was empty, so they continued past the bathroom and then towards the kitchen.

'We know you're in here,' Edward said loudly, reaching for the gun and bringing it out from his trousers. Will hung back, but only a few feet. He glanced over his shoulder, paranoid.

They saw Stuart's legs first, sticking out from behind the kitchen table.

'My God,' Will said, pushing past Edward into the kitchen. He looked at Stuart lying motionless on the kitchen floor, then noticed the empty packets of paracetamol and the half-empty glass on the table. He looked back towards Edward, who was just staring, emotionless.

Will knelt down at Stuart's side. 'He's still alive,' he said, checking his pulse. 'Call an ambulance.'

Edward remained glued to the spot.

'He's dying,' Will said.

'Let's go,' Edward said. 'There's no reason for us to be here any more.'

49

'Thanks for this,' Emma said, as she and Lizzy left the apartment block. 'I couldn't just sit in there, waiting for something to happen.'

'That's okay,' Lizzy said, 'although I think it's unlikely that we'll be able to find Eric when the police couldn't. He obviously doesn't want to be contacted.' Gasnier had called them en route to the couriers to report that Eric wasn't answering his phone, and when Emma had then tried to call him, she'd had no luck either. 'Surely he wouldn't be hanging around the very place where you'd expect to find him?'

'Probably not,' Emma said, 'but I've got to try something.'

'What if Eric doesn't have anything to do with Dan's disappearance?'

'Then we've run out of suspects,' Emma said, taking care while crossing the road, as they headed north towards the park.

They walked on for a while in silence, and then Lizzy said, 'Did you notice a difference in attitude with the police officers?'

'Maybe.'

'I think they're starting to believe you.'

Emma stopped and turned to face her friend. 'I'm so sorry, Lizzy. I should have believed you about the letter.'

'It's okay. Let's just forget about it.'

'I can't. I should have listened to you.'

'Hey,' Lizzy said, putting an arm around her shoulder, 'don't beat yourself up over it. If the situation had been reversed, do you think I would have been any different?'

Emma shrugged.

'I'm surprised you can trust anyone at the moment,' Lizzy continued, as they started walking again. 'This whole situation must be really screwing with your mind. I'm just glad that you believe me now, and that you're letting me be here to help you through this.'

'Thanks, Lizzy.'

'It doesn't look like he's here,' Lizzy said.

They had been on Primrose Hill for half an hour now, wandering around, scanning the area for Eric. Emma had given Lizzy a full description of him.

'No,' Emma admitted, looking off to her right, hoping that she would catch a glimpse of Eric's face amongst the people standing there, admiring the view. 'It doesn't. I thought maybe if I came up here, we'd lure him out into the open.'

'You're using yourself as bait?' Lizzy said, horrified.

'I suppose so, yes.'

'Em, this isn't a good idea.' Lizzy took her arm and shook it gently. 'If Eric did have something to do with what happened to Richard and Dan, then you shouldn't really be playing games with him. You shouldn't put yourself in danger.'

'But he doesn't seem threatening.'

'That means nothing if he's really involved in all of this.'

'Anything's better than just imagining what's happening,' Emma replied. 'I just keep thinking of Dan – where he is, what's happening to him. If he's being kept somewhere, what are the conditions like? He's been gone for over a week now. Are they feeding him?'

'I know it's hard, but you can't think the worst. Everything will be okay.'

'No, Lizzy. Whoever attacked Richard has already shown that they're willing to kill . . . if we hadn't come back to the flat when we did, Richard wouldn't have survived. That's why we need to find Dan quickly, before something happens.'

'Hopefully the police will find something from the couriers. If they get a name, that could lead them straight to Dan.'

'I hope so. But I can't see it being that easy. Why would the person give their real name, knowing that it was likely the police would investigate where the letter came from?'

'So what do we do now?' Lizzy said, still scanning the sea of people for a man with a camera. 'Just wait here and hope Eric turns up?'

'I can't think what else to do. I just know that I need to find Eric, and ask him outright if he had anything to do with this. But if he's not here, then I don't know where else to look. I don't know where he lives – I don't even know his surname.'

'Where else would someone who likes photography visit?' Lizzy asked. 'Maybe he's got another favourite location.'

Emma thought for a moment. 'That's it! Lizzy, you're a star! I think I know where he might be.'

They found him at the Rock Royalty photo exhibition in the National Portrait Gallery, standing admiring a huge photograph of Elvis Presley. It was an early shot of 'the King' on stage, mid hip swivel, stage lights glaring. The image was full of energy.

'Are you sure about this?' Lizzy whispered, as they watched Eric from a distance.

Emma nodded. She couldn't believe her luck that he was here. Thank God she had remembered what he had told her up on Primrose Hill about his love of the exhibition.

Eric was so much in awe of the image that he didn't notice Emma walk up to him.

'Eric,' she said.

He spun around so fast that he lost his balance, staggering back a few drunken steps and narrowly missing an elderly woman who had also been admiring the photograph.

As he righted himself, Emma was shocked by his horrified expression. 'Eric, I just want to talk,' she said, stepping towards him.

But he shook his head and headed for the exit.

'Eric,' Emma said, catching up with him and grabbing hold of his arm. 'Please, I need to speak to you.'

'Get off me!' he shouted, shrugging her off.

His shout attracted the attention of the exhibition's security officer, who rose from his seat in the corner, so Emma let go of him.

'What are you going to do?' Lizzy said, as they watched Eric leave.

'Follow him,' Emma said, setting off in pursuit.

'Leave me alone,' Eric said wildly, crossing the road and jogging down the steps into Trafalgar Square.

Emma and Lizzy followed.

'Eric, the police are looking for you,' Emma shouted, drawing interest from groups of tourists. 'If you keep running, they'll just think you're guilty.'

That stopped him dead in his tracks. 'Guilty of what?' he said, his face a mixture of anguish and anger. 'I haven't done anything wrong.'

'The police just want to ask you some questions,' Emma said, deliberately softening her tone. 'That's all.'

'I'm sorry about the photos,' he said. 'It's just that . . . you're so photogenic. I didn't follow you for long – they were all taken on the same day. I know it looks like I'm some kind of stalker, but I'm not, really. Please, there's no need to threaten me any more. I won't go near you again, I promise.'

'I wouldn't threaten you, Eric.'

'But you got him to find me and threaten me,' he replied. 'You didn't need to do that.'

'Eric, I don't know what you're talking about. Who threatened you? Was it Stuart, the man who took your film?'

'I just want to forget about it.'

'Eric, just tell me who threatened you,' Emma demanded.

'Don't pretend you don't know. He said you'd asked him to tell me to stay away. If you wanted me to leave you alone, you should have just said. I'm not a stalker. I'm not.'

'I don't know what you're talking about,' Emma said. 'Honestly. Who spoke to you? *Was* it Stuart?'

'No, it wasn't him. Please, leave me alone.'

Emma watched dumbfounded as Eric stormed off across the square, breaking into a run and scattering the flocks of pigeons.

50

'We can't just leave him here,' Will said, looking down at Stuart, then across at his father. 'If we go, he'll die.'

'It's what he wants, Will,' Edward replied, his voice strangely emotionless.

'How can you say that?' Will protested. 'Dad, he's going to *die*.'

'Will, if we do save him, do you think he'll thank us for it?'

'I . . . I don't know. Maybe he did this on the spur of the moment – maybe he doesn't want to die. It might have been a cry for help.'

'Will, this man has no friends. He destroyed any chance for happiness when he did what he did.'

'No.' Will shook his head. 'I won't let him die.' He looked around the kitchen, then headed for the phone and picked up the receiver.

'Think about it, Will,' Edward said, coming quickly over and putting his hand on the telephone to cut the connection. 'If we call an ambulance, the police will end up getting involved. How will we explain this?' He held up the gun.

'I don't know. We can hide it.'

'And when they ask us why we're in his flat, what our relationship is with him – what are we going to say?'

'I – I don't know . . .' Will's voice trailed off.

'Exactly,' Edward said, 'you don't know. Will, no matter what we do, he's probably going to die anyway. Why should we throw everything away, trying to save a dead man? A man who has made your life hell? Why jeopardise everything for him?'

'Because I'd never be able to forgive myself, Dad. Haven't you got any conscience?'

'How dare you.' Edward suddenly snapped, rounding on his son. 'Everything I've done – everything I'm doing *now* – is to protect you. Do you think I really want to be here, in this flat, wondering what to do with him?' He jabbed a finger at Stuart's comatose form. 'I'm only here because of you.'

Will stared at the floor. 'I'm sorry if you resent helping me.'

'For God's sake,' Edward said, throwing his hands up in the air. 'Will, don't you see that this could be the end of your nightmare? All you have to do is walk away. You can leave this building and get on with your life. You just need to have the courage to do it.'

'No.' William seemed to reach a decision, lifting his chin and squaring up to his father. 'You go if you want to, but I can't just leave him to die.'

'Then you're a bigger fool than I ever imagined,' Edward spat, turning and walking out of the flat.

'Do you think Eric was telling the truth, about being threatened?' Lizzy asked, as they sat in Trafalgar Square.

'He looked like he was,' Emma said. 'But if he was telling the truth, then I don't see how that fits with everything else.'

'I know,' Lizzy said, pondering on the implications.

'I was thinking,' Emma said. 'Whoever has Dan must have written that letter, pretending to be him. The person who has Dan also accused you of having an affair with him. Why would they do that?'

'I don't know. I really don't.'

'But you know what this means,' said Emma, realisation suddenly dawning. 'Whoever has Dan knows us all. It's probably someone close to us, Lizzy.'

'What makes you think that?' Lizzy looked shocked at the suggestion.

'Well, they must be, otherwise how would they know about you, to include you in the letter?'

'Okay,' Lizzy said, not sounding as convinced. 'But if it is someone who knows all of us, then that narrows it down quite a lot. We'd be talking about someone really close, Em. And why would one of our friends kidnap Dan and attack Richard?'

'I don't know,' Emma said, trying to think.

'And why would they pretend to be Dan and say I was having an affair with him?'

'No idea.'

'Em,' Lizzy said, slowly. 'There could be another explanation.'

'Go on.'

'Maybe the person who sent the letters, and the person who threatened Eric, was Dan after all.'

Will replaced the receiver and moved across to Stuart, kneeling next to his head. 'Don't worry, Stuart, you're going to be okay. The ambulance is on its way.'

He felt completely useless, and just had to hope that the ambulance would arrive quickly. He thought back to how his dad had walked out. *How could he have done that?*

There was a knock on the outside door. No ambulance was *that* quick.

Will stood up slowly and poked his head out of the kitchen, looking down the corridor at the door.

Again a knock – maybe his dad had come back, having had a change of heart. He took a step out of the kitchen.

'Stuart Harris?' an unfamiliar voice bellowed.

Will froze on the spot.

'Stuart Harris – this is the police. We'd like a word.'

Hell, Will thought. What would it look like if the police found him in the flat with Stuart dying? Would they think he'd forced him to take those tablets, in some sort of attempt to murder him?

He ducked into the room opposite, which turned out to be Stuart's bedroom. He closed the door. His heart was pounding and his breath shallow. He stood in the middle of the room, listening for the police.

But no one else spoke.

Have they gone?

He waited for a few more minutes, taking a look around the room. Stuart had a computer set up in the corner, and Will was surprised to find it on – the screensaver was running. Intrigued as to what Stuart had been doing just before his suicide attempt, he slid into the chair and hit the space bar.

'What the hell—?' he breathed, as a sickening image appeared on the screen.

51

The photo had been taken up close. Dan's head was thrust back, his eyes bulging as if they were about to explode from his head, a gag visibly tight around his head – Will could make out marks on either side of Dan's mouth where the gag had rubbed his skin raw. He was tied to a chair – you could just make out its back, and what looked like rope around Dan's waist.

'My God.'

Will's first reaction was to switch the computer off, to get rid of the image, but then he wondered what else the computer might contain. As he was about to grasp the mouse, however, he suddenly thought of the police. They would be taking this computer as evidence. It was best if he left it alone.

He rose from the chair, unable to keep his eyes from the image of Dan. He had been in trouble, all this time. And it had been Stuart all along – just as he had first suspected.

If only he had summoned up the courage to tell Emma the truth at the outset.

He prayed it wasn't too late to save Dan.

That's when he began to search each room of the flat, just in case. But Dan wasn't there.

He moved into the kitchen, breathless and panicky. Stuart was still out on the floor.

'What the hell have you done?' Will shouted. 'What have you *done?*'

He looked towards the phone. The ambulance should be arriving soon. Then he remembered the police. They might not have gone yet. And the sooner they were told about this, the better chance Dan might have.

'I should have left you to die!' Will said, before rushing out of the room.

But as he said those words, heading for the door, he knew he didn't mean them. Whatever Stuart Harris had done, Will didn't want any more blood on his hands. He was glad he had called the ambulance – at least Stuart would face justice, and he would also be able to tell the police where Dan was. And if he was still alive.

How would he ever forgive himself if Dan were already dead? How would he face Emma?

Will emerged from the block and caught sight of a car, parked a hundred or so metres away. There were two suited men standing next to the vehicle, deep in discussion.

'Hey,' he shouted, trying to attract their attention.

Gasnier and Davies turned around.

'Are you the police?' Will asked, sliding to a stop in front of them and shielding his eyes from the sun.

'Who are you?' Gasnier asked, refusing to answer the original question.

'Will – Will Holden.'

'Emma Holden's brother?' Gasnier was unable to hide his surprise.

'Yes.'

'I'm DI Gasnier. This is my colleague, DS Davies.'

'Look,' Will said, 'you've got to come up to the flat. Stuart's in there – he's taken an overdose. And I've found something – about Dan.'

'Tell us here,' Gasnier demanded in a soft voice. 'We're not going anywhere until you explain everything.'

Just then they heard sirens, and an ambulance swerved in from the main road.

'You called them?' Gasnier said, looking back over his shoulder. Will nodded.

'Let's take a look at this then,' Gasnier said to Davies. 'And you, Mr Holden, can come with us – I've got some questions for you.'

* * *

'How long since you found him?' the paramedic asked Will as he knelt beside Stuart, carrying out various checks.

'About twenty minutes ago,' Will said, aware that Gasnier was looming over his shoulder, listening to every word.

'But you don't know how long he's been out?' the paramedic continued. 'How long ago it was that he took the tablets?'

'No,' Will said. 'I found him like this.'

'If you do know, it would be a really big help,' the paramedic pressed.

'I don't,' Will protested. 'I'm telling the truth.'

He might have just been paranoid, but it looked as if the guy didn't believe him – the way he turned away without further questions.

'We need to talk,' Gasnier said, almost whispering in his ear.

Will nodded, turning to face the detective.

'You said you called the ambulance twenty minutes ago,' Gasnier said, as they stepped out into the hallway.

Will nodded. He knew exactly where this was going. He noticed that the other officer had closed the door to Stuart's bedroom, obviously looking on his computer.

'And you remained in the flat after that time?'

'Yes.'

'Then you would have heard us knocking on the door ten or so minutes ago.'

Will remained silent. For all his good intentions, he was scared of what he had set in motion by alerting the police.

'You must have heard us knocking, Will,' Gasnier pressed.

'I didn't,' Will said, searching for a plausible explanation. 'I was just trying to make sure that Stuart was okay. I can't even remember what happened – I didn't hear the knocking.'

'And you're sure of that?' Gasnier said. 'You didn't hear us shouting "Police"?' He made imaginary quotation marks in the air with his fingers, which seemed to ridicule Will's absurd claim.

'No,' Will said. 'Please believe me.'

'You see, the thing is, Will,' Gasnier said, smiling ruefully, 'I don't believe you.'

'But why?'

'Because of this,' Gasnier said, gesturing at his jacket and trousers.

'I don't understand,' Will said, looking at Gasnier's clothes for some explanation.

'What car am I driving?' Gasnier said.

'I . . . I don't know,' Will admitted, still not understanding where the conversation was heading.

'A BMW,' Gasnier said, answering his own question. 'An unmarked BMW. DS Davies and I aren't in uniform. Yet you ran over to us, pretty damn certain that we were the police. How did you know that, Will? And please don't tell me that it's because we look like police officers – I don't want to hear that.'

'Okay, okay – I panicked,' Will finally admitted. 'When I heard you at the door, I just panicked. I thought that it would look bad – that you might think I had something to do with it.'

'Why did you come to Stuart's apartment, Will?' Gasnier asked.

'I came to . . . threaten him,' Will said. 'Look, I know this sounds really bad' – he realised he was gripping the back of his neck with both hands and quickly brought them down – 'and that's why I panicked. But I'd already called the ambulance by that stage. I wasn't going to leave him.'

'Why were you going to threaten him?'

'I wanted him to stay away from Emma. He really hurt her when he just walked out on her a few years ago, and I didn't want him to do it again. I didn't want him taking advantage of her when she was so upset about Dan.'

'Did you think he was responsible for Dan's disappearance?'

'No. But I know now that he was.'

Gasnier waited a few seconds in quiet contemplation.

'If there's something you're not telling me,' he said at last, 'something that could help us locate Dan, then you're better off telling me now.'

Just then the bedroom door opened, saving Will from having to answer.

'You'd better come and take a look at this,' DS Davies said, beckoning Gasnier.

Will made to follow him into the bedroom.

'Not you,' Gasnier said, placing a palm on his chest. 'You wait there, and pray that Stuart Harris pulls through.'

Will watched as the door closed. He turned around just as the paramedics carried Stuart past on a stretcher.

'Will he be okay?' Will said, following them out of the flat and onto the landing outside.

'Touch and go,' the paramedic answered, 'but we'll do our best.'

Will watched helplessly, praying that this affair hadn't claimed yet another victim.

52

'What's the matter?'

Miranda stood in the doorway to the study, waiting for Edward to turn around. But he didn't – he just continued to stare out of the window. He'd been holed up there for over half an hour now, having returned home without even announcing his arrival. Miranda was getting worried; maybe he was having second thoughts about the baby.

'Is it something to do with Will?' she ventured.

'You were listening to my conversation,' Edward said sadly.

'I . . . I didn't mean to,' Miranda said, edging into the room. 'I was coming to see if you were all right and I heard you talking, that's all. You called Will in Canada, didn't you?'

Edward turned around. Miranda was shocked at how sad and old he looked. She thought that maybe he had been crying, although she'd never seen him cry before.

'What did you hear?' he asked.

'Er, nothing really.'

'But you knew I was talking to Will.'

'Yes, but I didn't hear any details.'

'Couldn't hear any details,' he corrected. 'You tried to listen but couldn't hear.'

'No,' she denied. 'I wasn't listening on purpose, Edward. What is this, anyway? All this secrecy?'

'You don't want to know.'

'Edward, if this is going to work then we've got to trust each other. Love is about trust. You do love me, don't you?'

'I can't take this right now. I might go for a walk.'

'But you've only just got back in,' she said, her voice

softening into a more conciliatory tone. 'Can't we sit down and have a chat? You've been acting strangely for a few weeks now – I've noticed it. Maybe if you talked things through, then it might help.'

Edward just looked at her. 'How do you feel about the baby?' he said, gesturing towards Miranda's midriff.

'Feel? I don't understand. I'm happy about it, if that's what you mean. I hope you are, too.'

'I didn't mean like that. I mean, what are your feelings towards your child?'

'It's your child, too,' Miranda countered.

'I know.' Edward paused, gathering his thoughts. 'What I'm trying to say is, even though the baby hasn't even been born yet, even though you've never set eyes on it, you'd probably do anything for it, wouldn't you?'

'I hope so,' Miranda said. 'But I don't understand, Edward – what's this all about? Are you nervous about being a father again? I could understand if you were.'

'I don't think I've ever been a father,' Edward replied, sitting down on the edge of his desk.

'But you're a good father,' Miranda said, moving over to put an arm around him. 'I know you've had a few problems with Emma and Will, mostly because of me, but things seem to be improving now.'

'Don't you dare blame yourself,' Edward said, pulling away. 'It started before I met you. When their mother was first diagnosed, when she was dying, when my children needed me the most, I wasn't there for them. All I cared about was myself.'

'But you were upset, too.'

'I was selfish. And I haven't changed.'

'I don't think you're selfish.'

Edward turned to look at her. 'You know, Miranda, I don't think you know me at all.'

It had been worth the journey there – ten minutes of frantic motorcycling across the capital, dodging London buses and weaving through lanes of traffic. But that was why he loved this job – the adrenalin rush, the chase for the picture. He imagined hunters got the same buzz. They were both stalking prey, of sorts – one with a gun, the other with a telephoto lens. And, in many ways, the lens could be just as damaging.

'Hi,' he said into the mobile phone. 'I've got some fantastic shots here.'

The first shot had been of Will talking to the police – fortunately, he had parked some distance from the unmarked car.

Then he had got a few great ones of Stuart Harris being carried into the ambulance, including a fantastic close-up of his face.

The guy looked in a really bad way.

And, finally, when he thought things couldn't get any better, Will Holden had appeared at the front of the flats, kneeling down with his head in his hands.

It was pure soap opera.

'I don't know what's going on with all this,' he said, 'but Emma Holden's brother was at Stuart's flat . . . I've got shots of that, yes. Then the police arrived, followed by an ambulance . . . no idea . . . but from what I could see, it looked pretty serious to me.'

He looked over at the flats. Will was still sitting there, head in hands. If he'd thought about it for too long, he could have felt sorry for him. But there was no time for such emotion, not with so much money at stake.

'Yes,' he said, turning his attention away from Will. 'Should be able to get them to you quick sharp. More than enough time for the morning papers – they're going to love this.'

53

'So what are we going to do now?' Lizzy said to Emma, as they sat in Lizzy's flat, early Sunday evening. 'You tempted to go and look for Eric again?'

'I don't think it would do any good,' Emma replied. 'The state he was in, I don't think we'd learn anything new.'

'Probably right. I wonder whether the police have found out anything yet about who sent the envelope?'

'They must have found out something by now.' Spurred into action, Emma pulled out her mobile and searched for the number Gasnier had given her.

The call was answered on the second ring.

'Hello?' Gasnier's tone was clipped and impatient.

'Hi, it's Emma Holden here. I was wondering if you'd found out anything about who—'

'Now's not a good time,' he interrupted. 'We can talk later.'

'So you've found something?'

'Not now,' he said, sounding distracted. 'I'll be in touch.'

And with that the line went dead.

'What did he say?' Lizzy asked.

'That it wasn't a good time.'

'What's that supposed to mean?' Lizzy replied, pulling a face.

'I've no idea. But it sounds like something has happened. I could tell – he was distracted.'

'I suppose they'll tell us when they decide to,' Lizzy mused. 'But that just leaves us hanging around in the dark.'

'I feel completely helpless,' Emma admitted, stretching back on the sofa and looking up at the ceiling. 'And I don't like it.'

Then her mobile rang.

'Maybe it's the right time now,' said Lizzy with a smile, as Emma reached for the phone.

But the number wasn't Gasnier's.

'Hi, is that Emma?'

'Speaking.'

'It's Nurse Donahue here from the hospital. I've got some good news about Richard – he's woken up.'

'Try not to get your hopes up,' Lizzy said, as they stood in the lift taking them to the floor on which Richard's room was situated.

'I'm trying,' Emma said, 'but this could be the break we've been waiting for. Richard must have seen what happened to Dan. He must have seen who hit him. He'll be able to clear Dan's name.'

'I hope you're right,' Lizzy said.

They stepped out and headed down the corridor. Nurse Donahue met them at the entrance to the room, as if she had been waiting there on guard since her phone call.

'Take things slowly,' she warned. 'Richard's been unconscious now for over a week. He's bound to feel disorientated, and it's important not to push him. The doctors have said that he really shouldn't be having visitors, but I thought you ought to be able to have a quick word.'

'Thanks,' Emma said, as they walked towards Richard's room. 'Have you told the police that he's woken up?'

'Just. They said they wanted to know as soon as anything happened, and I dare say they want to be the first to see him. But I wanted Richard to see some friendly faces – he doesn't need an inquisition.'

'No,' Emma said, remembering Lizzy's note of caution.

They got to the room and, through the glass, Emma could see Richard sitting up, his eyes open. It was the best thing she had seen in weeks.

'I've brought a couple of people to see you,' Nurse Donahue said, entering the room, Emma and Lizzy following behind.

When Richard saw them he smiled, albeit uncomfortably.

'I'll leave you to it,' Nurse Donahue said, smiling at them and leaving the room.

'Thanks.' Emma turned to Richard. 'How are you?'

'Confused,' said Richard, trying another smile. 'I feel like I'm dreaming – not much is making sense at the moment.'

'Have the doctors told you anything?' Emma asked.

'They've explained some things,' he said, his face appearing somewhat vacant, 'but I can't say I've taken much of it in, really. I know I've been in a coma for over a week.'

'Can you remember what happened in our flat?' asked Emma, knowing that this sort of conversation wasn't what Nurse Donahue would have had in mind.

'The doctors told me I got hit on the head. But I can't remember anything, Em. I wish I could.'

Emma tried to hide her disappointment. She had pinned her hopes on Richard being able to remember something. 'So you don't remember if there was someone else in the flat, apart from you and Dan?'

'I can't. Em, I can't even remember going to your flat – or even why I was there.'

'Dan's stag night. You were going on his stag night.'

'Right,' he said, looking as though he was trawling through his mind for buried clues. 'The wedding – have you . . . ?'

Emma shook her head. 'Dan's been missing since that night,' she said, wondering whether she should be telling him this.

'What?' Richard's face creased with confusion. 'Dan's missing?'

'The police thought at first that he was the one who hit you.'

'Em,' Lizzy interjected, putting a warning hand on her arm.

Emma looked at Richard, who was staring blankly off to his left, and realised that she had gone too far. 'Don't worry, Richard,' she said. 'Everything's going to be okay.'

'I shouldn't have told him about Dan,' Emma lamented, as they sat outside the room on a couple of plastic chairs. 'Did you see his face? He was devastated.'

242

'You didn't plan to tell him,' Lizzy said. 'And he has to find out sometime.'

'But he didn't have to find out now.'

'Maybe he did. Look who's just arrived.'

Emma looked up to see Gasnier and Davies talking to Nurse Donahue. They turned, Gasnier spotting Emma instantly. He spoke a few words to Davies and they came over.

'Ms Holden,' he said.

Emma stood up – she didn't like him looming over her like that. Lizzy did likewise.

'Detective,' said Emma.

'You've already spoken to Richard?'

She nodded.

'Anything I might be interested in?'

'He can't remember anything.'

Gasnier nodded, as if that was what he had expected. 'I'm sorry about earlier. It really wasn't a good time to talk. I wasn't dismissing you – I don't play those kind of games.'

Emma was taken aback by the apology. 'That's okay.'

'I understand how frustrating all this is,' he said, glancing over to look at Richard's room.

'Are you going to speak to Richard now?'

'Yes. Although we don't expect him to be able to help, if what you and the medical staff say is correct.'

'Right.'

'We'll do our best not to upset him,' Gasnier promised, 'but we've got to do anything that can help us to find your fiancé.'

'So you do believe that Dan is in danger?'

'New evidence has come to light,' he replied. 'We need to discuss that in private.'

Emma and Lizzy followed Gasnier and Davies into a nearby side room.

'I have some news,' Gasnier said. His stony expression set alarm bells ringing. 'We believe that Dan is being held somewhere,' he continued, 'as we found evidence at Stuart Harris's flat that leads us to believe that he kidnapped him.'

'Stuart?' Emma said, completely taken aback. 'Are you sure?'

'There was a photo of Dan on Stuart's computer. I'm afraid it showed him tied up. We also found on it a copy of the letter sent to you, supposedly from Dan. Added to the fact that Stuart's name was recorded at the couriers.'

'But you didn't find Dan?'

'He wasn't being held at the flat,' Gasnier said. 'Our officers are searching the place for clues as to where he might be.'

'But what does Stuart say about it? Can't you make him tell you where Dan is?'

Gasnier paused and glanced down at the floor. Emma noticed that his hands were clasped, as if in prayer.

'I'm afraid we won't be able to ask Stuart anything,' Gasnier said finally. 'He died an hour ago. I'm sorry.'

54

'I find it so hard to believe Stuart is behind all of this,' Emma said, as they entered Lizzy's flat later that evening.

They'd returned shortly after being told the news of Stuart's death, deciding that there was little else they could do at the hospital. Richard needed to rest, and the police had things in hand. Emma had wanted to go and talk to Will, following Gasnier's revelation that he had been in Stuart's flat, but Lizzy had persuaded her it was best to wait until the morning. *What the hell had her brother been doing there? And why hadn't he told her that he had returned from Canada?*

'Attacking Richard and kidnapping Dan. I can't understand what Stuart was thinking of,' Emma continued, closing the door behind her. 'What did he think he could gain by doing this?'

'Maybe he wasn't thinking,' Lizzy offered, heading for the kitchen and filling the kettle. 'Maybe he was just doing whatever he thought it would take to win you back.'

'You're saying he did all this for *love*?'

'Maybe. Love is a pretty strong emotion – it can make people do strange things. Bad things. Just look at what Stephen Myers did to you. That was all supposedly for love.'

'It's not the kind of love that I recognise.'

'It's a warped version,' Lizzy said. 'Some of the worst things are done in the name of love.'

There was a pause. 'I'm the common factor here,' Emma commented.

'Don't be silly,' Lizzy chastised.

'Stephen Myers loved me and he died. Stuart loved me and now he's dead, too. We don't know if Dan is dead or alive . . .'

'I'm certain he's alive, Em. The police will find him soon, you'll see.'

'I hope you're right. It's just that I can't help thinking the worst. If Stuart did do all this to punish me, why would he keep Dan alive? What would he have to gain?'

'Dan must have been alive to make the call to the wedding shop, when he cancelled the dress. You heard his voice, so it was definitely him.'

'Yes,' Emma agreed. 'But maybe that was Stuart's plan all along – to force Dan to call them, and make it look like he was just running out on me. In his mind, it would have set things up perfectly for us meeting again – I thought Dan had left me, and then Stuart comes back into my life, wanting to get back together.'

'Sounds plausible.'

'But what really worries me,' Emma continued, 'is what happened after Dan made that call. We know Stuart wrote the letter that was supposed to be from Dan. And he must have been the one using Dan's mobile to text me.'

'The note on the flowers,' Lizzy said. 'You said it was in Dan's handwriting.'

'But even if Dan was forced to write that, there's been nothing since. So he could have murdered Dan at any time.'

'Do you really think Stuart would be capable of murder?'

'Who knows?' Emma said, her voice cracking. 'Maybe he killed himself because he couldn't face what he'd done.' She looked at Lizzy. 'Maybe leaving the image of Dan on the computer screen was his suicide note.'

First thing Monday morning, Emma travelled by bus to Camden, where Will lived in a one-bedroom rented flat. It was on the small side, but the rent was reasonable, the landlord and neighbours were friendly, and he could walk to work.

As she waited for Will to answer the door, she realised she really needed answers to the myriad questions that had kept her awake most of the night.

'Emma,' Will said, opening the door. 'You'd better come in.'

She followed him through into the living room. He was still in his sleepwear, even though it was half past ten.

'Want a drink?' he asked.

Emma looked over at the messy breakfast bar and shook her head.

'When did you get back from Canada?' she asked, not wanting to waste any more time.

'Yesterday,' he replied.

'You only went on Thursday,' she noted, deliberately not sitting down.

'Yes. I decided I was just running away – best to get back and face reality, like you said.'

'Why didn't you tell me you were back?'

He shrugged, and then moved over to the kitchen and began clearing the plates, sliding them noisily into the sink. Then he turned on a tap and squeezed in some washing-up liquid.

'You went to see Stuart,' Emma said.

Will turned the tap off but didn't turn around. 'The police told you,' he stated.

'Yes,' she answered. 'They also told me what they found at his flat.'

'I wanted to tell you last night,' he said, turning around to face her, 'but the police said they'd speak to you. I've been waiting for you to arrive ever since. Have they found out any more about where Dan is?'

'No. At least, they hadn't found anything last night.'

'And Stuart? Have they talked to him yet?'

'He died,' Emma said.

Will closed his eyes.

Will returned from the bathroom, his eyes red and puffy. 'Sorry,' he said, taking a seat next to Emma. 'It's just a shock. I thought he was going to be all right.'

'Will, why were you at Stuart's flat?'

'I wanted to warn him not to hurt you again. I was going to tell him to stay away from you.'

'Okay,' she said, waiting for more explanation.

'I wasn't going to hurt him,' he pleaded. 'Just warn him.'

'What I don't understand is, how did you know Stuart was back in contact with me?'

'Dad called me.'

'Right,' Emma said, thinking about that. It made sense, especially considering the way her dad had flown off the handle when he found out she'd met Stuart again. He must have called Will shortly after that conversation.

'I did it because I love you, Em,' said Will. 'I didn't want to see you hurt again.'

'How did you even know where he lived?'

'I found his address in the phone book.'

Emma could tell that he was lying. She knew him too well. 'What time did you arrive back in London?'

'Pardon?'

'When did your flight land?'

'Late in the afternoon.'

'You went straight to Stuart's from the airport.'

'No . . . yes,' he said. 'I wanted to get it over with. The sooner we spoke to Stuart, the sooner we could forget about it.'

'We?'

Will reddened.

'How did you get from the airport to Stuart's?' Emma looked narrowly at her brother.

'Taxi,' Will said.

'You're lying,' Emma responded. 'I know you, Will. I can tell. Please, don't lie to me now. You went to Stuart's flat with Dad.'

Will nodded reluctantly.

'But the police didn't say anything about Dad being there,' Emma pressed. 'They just mentioned you.'

'He left me. He did what he's always done – he could have stayed, but he chose to leave, because the only person he cares about is himself.'

248

'Unfortunately, I can believe that.'

Will lowered his head and gripped his hair. 'This is all such a mess,' he said, starting to sob. 'I'm sorry, Em.'

Richard could hear voices. First they were distant, spiralling around in the darkness like spectres. Then the volume increased, the clarity sharpened, and he could make out two voices: his own, and Dan's.

'You ready for tonight?'

'Ready as I'll ever be.'

'It's your last night of freedom – better make the most of it, Danny boy.'

The images came next – a strobe-effect sequence of flashes. He was in Dan's flat – kitchen, living room, bathroom, living room, kitchen, bathroom.

Then a doorbell rang.

'Can I help you?'

A figure loomed up in front of him.

Richard's eyes snapped open, his breathing was heavy, his sheets wet with sweat. Standing on the outside of the hospital room, looking in with his face pressed up against the glass, was a man. The man's eyes burned into him, and the sight chilled him to the bone.

He blinked and the figure was gone.

At first he thought the guy really had been standing there, but it must have been just a hangover from the dream. Things were still hazy, reality blurring with imagination. But one thing was clear; it was the man.

He was starting to remember.

55

'Am I glad to see you,' Richard said, as Emma walked into the hospital room.

'Nice to hear it,' Emma replied with a smile, sitting down in the chair next to the bed.

Richard looked better than he had last night, which wasn't difficult, but he still seemed groggy. 'Have the police been in touch?' he asked now, closing his eyes briefly as if he had just suffered a blast of pain.

'No,' Emma said. 'No news, I'm afraid.'

'Right.' Richard grimaced.

'Are you okay?' Emma rose from the chair. 'I can get a nurse.'

'It's fine. The doc said I would get some twinges from time to time. My body's way of telling me that it's still functioning.'

'I guess that's good news, then.'

'We could do with some good news,' Richard noted sadly. 'Em, I don't know how you've coped with everything that's happened.'

'I had no choice.'

Richard broke out into a series of gasping coughs.

'Are you sure you're all right?' Emma said, panic rising. She couldn't face losing someone else close to her.

Richard nodded. 'I'm starting to remember,' he announced, in between the trailing coughs. 'About that night.'

'Really?' Emma tried desperately not to get her hopes up.

'It's all pretty vague. But there was another person in your flat.'

'Stuart?'

Richard looked vague.

'Sorry,' she said, realising her error, 'you don't even know who Stuart is. He's an ex-boyfriend of mine, who the police think might have taken Dan and attacked you.'

'The police told me about him.'

'What else can you remember about that night?'

'I keep dreaming about it. It's like a nightmare. There are shapes and voices – I'm pretty sure there was a fight. But I don't know what it was about.'

'It's okay,' Emma said soothingly, noting Richard's anguished expression. 'You'll probably remember more things, given time.'

'But we haven't got time.'

Emma couldn't argue with that.

'This morning,' Richard said, 'when I woke up, I saw the man. He was staring at me through the window. I blinked and he was gone.'

'It was part of your dream?'

'I think so. I think it was just my imagination. But it seemed real.'

'Maybe it was one of the hospital staff?'

'No,' he said, shaking his head. 'It was him – I was really scared, Em.'

'What did he look like?'

'Quite old, middle-aged maybe. It's hard to say. Dark hair, I think. I don't know, Em. I'm sorry.'

'It's okay,' she said, wondering whether Richard was actually capable of remembering anything accurately. If the person in the flat had been middle-aged, then it would rule out Stuart.

'Do you think Dan is still alive?' Tears welled up in Richard's eyes. 'I don't know what I'd do if anything bad has happened to him. He's not just my brother, he's my best friend. I really love him, Em. I was looking forward to being his best man.'

'I know,' Emma said, bending forward and embracing him, whilst trying to hold back her own tears. 'We've just got to pray that he's okay.'

Edward waited until Miranda had left the house. He watched her from the window, before heading for the study. Even though there was no one else in the house, he closed the door behind him before taking the gun out of the desk drawer.

He stared at it as it lay there in the palm of his hand.

When the phone rang suddenly, he nearly dropped the gun in his panic. As he placed it back in the drawer and reached for the receiver, he noticed that his hands were shaking.

'Hi, Dad,' Will said, his voice solemn. 'Have you heard the news?'

'No,' Edward said, closing the drawer. 'I haven't heard anything.'

'Stuart's dead,' Will announced.

Edward had to stop himself from saying 'Good'. He satisfied himself with a smile. 'Maybe it's for the best,' he said.

'They still haven't found Dan,' Will said, ignoring the remark. Will had already brought Edward up to speed on what he had found on Stuart's computer. 'They don't even know if he's alive.'

'Right. Let's hope things turn out okay.'

'Things aren't okay.'

The line went dead.

Edward held on to the receiver, ruminating on what Stuart might have told Dan about the circumstances behind his detention. If the police did find Dan alive, it might not all be good news.

Lizzy was halfway through the matinée performance when she noticed the man in the audience. He was in an end seat, towards the middle of the stalls.

It was difficult to get a clear view of him – the audience was mostly in darkness, and she had to concentrate on performing – but from the stolen glances she was able to take, he looked familiar. She just couldn't place where she had seen him before.

The freaky thing was that whenever she did look over, he seemed to be focusing solely on her. It made her feel uncomfortable, and when she eventually saw him rise from the seat and head back up the aisle, towards an exit, she hoped he wouldn't come back.

He didn't return, but she was still unnerved as she returned to her dressing room after the performance. She was also annoyed that she couldn't remember who the man had reminded her of.

She spent most of the hurried journey back to her flat looking over her shoulder, trying to pick out the man in the crowds, but she didn't see him.

She was nearing the flat when she suddenly remembered who the man had resembled.

It couldn't be, could it?

She picked up her pace – there was something she needed to check. Then she would call Emma with the news.

56

Edward had just knocked back his second whisky when the doorbell rang. At first he let it go but, remembering that Miranda was out, he made his way to answer it.

'Hi, you must be Edward,' said the man at the door, holding out his hand and smiling. 'Is Miranda there?' He lowered his hand as Edward's hands remained clasped around the doorframe.

'She's out,' Edward replied, trying to think who this guy could be. He didn't look familiar.

'It's just that we'd arranged to meet.'

'Who are you?' Edward checked himself. 'I'm sorry, I don't mean to be rude. You're a friend of Miranda?'

'Uncle.' He smiled. 'She forgot to tell you I was coming?'

'She hasn't mentioned anything.'

'Same old Miranda, never was the best at remembering things. I imagine the pregnancy is playing havoc with her memory, too.'

'It is,' said Edward, relaxing a little. 'So you're her—?'

'Dad's brother.'

'Right,' Edward said.

Miranda had never spoken much of her family. It wasn't surprising, seeing as her parents had as good as disowned her for moving in with him.

'I'll give Miranda a call sometime,' said the man, backing away from the door. 'Let her know that I was here, will you?'

'Hang on,' Edward said. 'She'll be back in a minute – she's only gone to the shops. You can wait in here if you like.'

'Thanks.' The man smiled. 'That's very kind of you.'

He followed Edward through into the living room, and sat down without invitation.

'It's good to finally meet you,' the man said, leaning back into the sofa. 'Miranda has told me a lot about you.'

'She has?' Edward said, sitting down in a chair opposite.

'You seem surprised.'

'I am,' Edward admitted. 'I didn't realise she spoke to her family about me.'

'Oh, I know more about you than you'd imagine,' the man said, now glancing around the room in a way that immediately raised Edward's suspicions.

'You sure you don't want a drink?' Edward asked. 'I can do beer, wine, spirits—?'

'Better not,' replied the man, still looking around the room. 'I'm driving.'

'Miranda should be back any minute.' Edward looked at his watch. At least he hoped she would be back soon – he didn't think he could take much more of being in this guy's company.

'Sorry to hear about your recent troubles,' the man said, his attention suddenly switching back to Edward.

'Troubles?'

'It must be very hard for Emma.'

'What are you talking about?' Edward replied.

'Emma. It must be difficult dealing with all those troubles – her fiancé disappearing like that, just before they were due to get married.'

'Miranda told you about that, did she?'

'And now her ex-boyfriend has committed suicide, hasn't he – Stuart?' said the man, evading the question. 'Must be really hard for her to deal with.'

'How do you know about Stuart?'

'Haven't you seen today's newspapers?' said the man incredulously. 'The story is in a few of them.'

'Emma will be okay.' Edward wondered what exactly the newspapers had said and whether Emma had seen them herself. 'We'll look after her.'

'It's lucky she's got her family around her for support.' The man smiled strangely.

'What is it?' Edward asked, his anger growing. 'I fail to see what's so funny about all this. My daughter has been to hell and back this past week, and those scumbags in the media treat it like some form of cheap entertainment.'

'I know. I'm sorry.' Unbelievably, the man smiled again. 'I wasn't smiling at what Emma has been through. I was smiling at what *you* are going through, Edward.'

'What? I don't understand,' Edward said, facing the man out.

'You will,' he replied.

'What's that supposed to mean? Who the hell are you?'

'How's Will? I hear that he's not been very well recently.'

'Who are you?' Edward repeated.

'Think about it,' the man replied, tapping a finger to the side of his head. 'Think carefully, Edward.'

'You're not Miranda's uncle, are you?'

'No, I'm not. But I am looking forward to meeting her.'

Edward stood up. He had to get this man out of here before Miranda returned. 'Please leave.'

'I thought you might want to hear the rest of what I've got to say,' the man replied.

'I don't want to hear anything. Get out!' Edward shouted, pointing towards the door.

The man's lips curled into a cruel smile. 'Do you know how I felt when I heard that Stuart Harris was dead?' he asked, getting up.

'Go,' demanded Edward.

'I felt as though all this had been worth it.' The man moved so close to Edward's face that there was barely air between them. 'It felt good, really good. I couldn't believe my luck when I broke into the flat and found him dying on the floor. I was tempted to finish him off myself, just to make sure, but I wasn't there for that – I had a present to leave him on his computer. A photo gift. It's amazing how much you can learn from a photo, Edward. I learnt *so* much from what I saw recently. As soon as I saw them, I knew what I had to do.'

He smiled and Edward flinched. *What the hell is this guy talking about?*

'You know, it was fitting that Stuart Harris ended his own pitiful life. That's what you've turned me into, Edward – someone who delights in another person's death.'

'I don't know who you are. Please leave me and my family alone.'

'Soon,' the man said, heading for the exit.

Edward followed him to the door, longing to strike down hard on the back of his neck. But he simply opened the door and watched the man step out onto the driveway, where he then paused.

'Do you know what it's like to really hurt?' the man said, turning around and looking back at Edward. 'To hurt so much that it takes all your energy just to get out of bed in the morning?'

'Leave,' Edward said.

'This is your fault.'

'I don't even know you,' Edward insisted. 'I think you need to get help.'

The man laughed to himself, as if remembering a private joke. 'Soon you'll know what it's like to really hurt, to lose the one you love.'

Edward was chilled by the threat. 'What the hell is that supposed to mean?'

But the man didn't reply; he just turned and walked away.

Part Three

57

Emma stayed for another hour, watching Richard sleep. The answers to what had happened that night were locked up there in his head, but would he ever be able to retrieve them?

She had just left the hospital when her mobile rang.

'Emma, it's Guy Roberts here.'

'Hi,' Emma said, caught by surprise. All the business with the film seemed a world away.

'Can we meet?' he asked. 'I need to speak to you.'

'It's not really a good time,' Emma said. 'There's a lot going on. I can't really deal with anything at the moment.'

'I heard about Stuart. It's terrible news.'

'Yes. I'm sorry. I should have remembered that you were friends.'

'It's fine. Well, you know what I mean.'

'I think so.'

'I'd really like to talk. It's about what's happened. There's something that you need to know.'

'Thanks for coming over,' said Guy, as he ushered Emma inside. 'Come in, take a seat.'

Emma followed him through into the living room and sat down.

'Drink?' he asked.

'I'm okay,' Emma said.

'How are you doing?' Guy sat down opposite her. 'I know it's an awful time for you.'

'I'm dealing with it.'

'Still no news on your fiancé?'

'No. The police are looking, but I haven't heard anything yet.'

'It's terrible.'

'You said you wanted to tell me something. Is it about Stuart?'

Guy nodded, appearing to steel himself for the conversation to come. 'The police think Stuart had something to do with your fiancé disappearing, don't they?'

'Yes,' Emma said.

'He didn't,' Guy replied. 'I'm sure he didn't have anything to do with it.'

Emma looked at him. 'What makes you so sure?'

Guy looked down towards his right, in thought. 'Because I asked him, and he swore to me that he had nothing to do with it.'

'You asked him whether he had kidnapped Dan?' Emma said, shocked at the revelation. 'What made you even ask him? *When* did you ask him?'

'I asked him a week ago,' Guy admitted. 'I just wanted to be sure – to hear him say that he didn't have anything to do with it.'

'One week ago? That would be just after Dan disappeared.'

Guy nodded.

'I don't understand,' Emma said. 'Why would you even think of asking Stuart that question at that time?'

Guy blew out his cheeks and ran a hand through his hair. 'I'm afraid I've not been straight with you, Emma. I'm sorry – but hopefully I can start to make amends now.'

'What is it?' she pressed.

'I always knew that Stuart wanted you back. That day, when you asked who had recommended you for the part and I didn't want to tell you, it was an act. Stuart wanted me to tell you. He was hoping you would ask.'

Emma shook her head. 'So everything to do with the film role – the initial recommendation, the auditions, your compliments – was all just a way for Stuart to try and win me back?'

'Initially,' Guy admitted. 'I agreed to invite you to the audition as a favour for Stuart. And, I've got to admit, I thought that it would end there – I thought you'd do your piece, and that would be it. But once I saw you at the reading, well, you just blew me away; you were so dazzling, and from then on I really wanted you. I *genuinely* wanted you for the part. And I still do.'

'But Stuart still planned this, with your help.'

'Yes.'

Emma thought about that for a moment. 'What I don't understand is why you would have done the favour in the first place. Why did you even agree to invite me along to the audition?'

'Because I felt I owed him.'

'Owed him? What do you mean?'

'This is difficult,' Guy said. He paused, then continued. 'Stuart and I have been through a lot together. Did he tell you about how we met?'

'He said he auditioned for a part in a movie that you were casting, and you became friends.'

Guy smiled. 'Stuart was always good at improvisation.'

'So that was a lie?'

'Yes. We met at a support group. A group for those with mental health issues.'

'A few years ago, I was going through a really bad time,' Guy said now, clutching a glass of water. 'I was depressed – not for any particular reason, which I guess makes it all the more depressing. I'd been seeing a shrink for a while. He helped a bit, but I was getting pretty lonely. Then one day I saw a leaflet for a local mental health support group, so I thought, what the hell, what had I got to lose?'

'And Stuart was also in that group?' Emma asked.

'His psychiatrist recommended it to him,' Guy said.

'Psychiatrist?' Emma said wonderingly. 'I know things weren't right, that he was having a tough time mentally, but I never imagined he'd sought professional help. He never mentioned anything to me.' She shook her head. 'So that was how long ago?'

'Just under four years ago,' he replied.

'It must have been around the time he walked out on me.'

'It was,' he replied, surprising Emma with his certainty of that fact.

'How do you know that?' she asked.

'Because he spoke about you at the group,' he explained. 'He told us all how much he regretted walking out on you – how much he loved you.'

'Then why walk out?'

'He'd been forced to leave you.'

'Forced? By what?'

'He never told us the full details,' Guy replied. 'At the group, it was always made clear that we should never push people. As far as the group was concerned, Stuart had a right to tell as little or as much as he wanted. And, anyway, I expect most of the group was also keeping big secrets. I know I was.'

'You said you owed him something,' Emma said.

'We became friends,' Guy continued. 'He really helped me through a pretty bad time – a time when I considered suicide. If it hadn't been for Stuart, I really believe that I would be dead by now.'

'So he called in the favour, to try and get me back?'

'Yes. When I told him about the casting for the upcoming film, he begged me to contact you. He saw it as his chance to try to win you back, to get back into your life. I didn't think there was any harm in it, at least at first.'

'Did Stuart know I was getting married to someone else?'

'He didn't say anything about that.'

'But when you found out Dan had gone missing, you thought Stuart might have something to do with it?'

'I had suspicions, yes,' Guy said. 'I knew how much Stuart loved you, and I did wonder what lengths he might go to, to get you back.'

'So you asked him outright if he had anything to do with it?'

'Yes.'

'And what did he say?'

'He swore to me that he didn't do anything.'

'He must have been lying,' Emma said. 'The police found evidence at his flat – a photo of Dan.'

'I can't explain that,' Guy said. 'I can only say what I believe. And I believe that Stuart didn't have anything to do with your fiancé's disappearance.'

'Then why did he kill himself?'

'Because he had given up hope of getting you back. You told him that there was no chance, and it pushed him over the edge.'

'You're blaming me?'

'No, I'm not. I'm just saying that the hope Stuart had – that you two would get back together – was the only thing keeping him going. I'm just trying to explain.'

'I still don't understand how you can be so sure that Stuart wasn't involved,' Emma said. 'Just because he told you he didn't do it – he might have been afraid that you'd go to the police if he told you the truth.'

'He called me just before he died,' Guy revealed. 'And even then he still denied it – he had no reason to lie to me then.'

'He wrote a letter to me, pretending to be Dan. The police found it on his computer.'

'He did admit to that. He wanted you to think Dan didn't want you any more. But at that time, he still believed Dan had just run away.'

'But why say that Lizzy was involved? He said they'd had an affair.'

'To push you two apart. He wanted to be the shoulder to cry on – he saw Lizzy as competition for your attention.'

Emma took a deep breath. 'Okay, just say you're right and Stuart had nothing to do with what's happened to Dan,' she said, humouring him. 'Have you got any idea of who did?'

'I have a theory. But you're not going to like it.'

58

Edward spent some time sitting at the breakfast bar in the kitchen, trying desperately to think who the man was. But it was no good – he couldn't remember ever meeting him before, despite the man's insistence that he had somehow ruined his life. Half an hour later, he moved through to the living room – and that's when he saw the brown envelope on top of the coffee table.

It hadn't been there before, which meant only one thing.

Even though Miranda was still out, he retreated to the study to open it. As he did so, he felt a strange sense of foreboding. Peering inside, he pulled out a photocopied newspaper cutting.

He only needed to read the headline to understand who the man was.

He took a deep breath. There was something else in the envelope – a small piece of paper on which was written five words.

I know what really happened.

Edward closed his eyes.

Suddenly everything was making sense.

Soon you'll know what it's like to really hurt . . . to lose the one you love.

He had to do something, and quickly. He picked up the phone and dialled Will's number.

'Hello?'

'Will,' he said, trying to calm down. 'Thank God you're okay. Where are you?'

'In my flat, why?'

'You're not with Emma?'

'No. She was here a couple of hours ago, but then she went to the hospital to see Richard.'

'So you don't know where she is now?'

'No, I don't. I guess she might be at her flat, or maybe at Lizzy's. Are you okay? You sound out of breath.'

'Call her,' Edward said. 'Find out where she is. Then stay with her; make sure she's all right. Don't let her out of your sight.'

'What's the matter? You think she's in trouble?'

'Just go and make sure your sister is all right.'

'But I don't understand,' Will said. 'Stuart's dead. I thought you said this was all over now.'

'Just do what I say,' Edward demanded, his chest tightening. 'And hurry.'

'You think this all has something to do with Will?' Emma said.

'Yes,' Guy said. 'I know it's a shock, but I really do believe that your brother is involved. How, I don't know.'

'You're just saying that to protect Stuart's memory,' Emma accused. 'Why would Will be involved?'

'I'm not sure. And no, I'm not just saying this to protect Stuart. I wouldn't do that, Emma.'

'What proof have you got?'

'I haven't got any proof, as such,' Guy admitted. 'But it's just something Stuart told me once.'

'What?'

'That Will had something to do with you and him splitting up.'

'Stuart told you that?'

'In so many words. And if he split you two up, then maybe he did the same with you and Dan.'

'This is crazy,' Emma said, 'and I don't believe it for a second. Will wouldn't do that. Why would he want to split me and Dan up, or me and Stuart?'

Guy shrugged.

'I trust my brother, totally,' Emma added.

'You shouldn't ever trust anyone totally,' Guy countered. 'We all have secrets, Emma.'

267

'Will has nothing to do with this.'

'Will was the first to find Stuart,' Guy said. 'Why was he at Stuart's flat?'

'How did you know about that?'

'From the newspaper.'

'Newspaper?' Emma said. 'There was a story?'

'In here.' Guy brought out a newspaper from by the side of his chair and handed it to her. 'Page ten.'

Emma flicked to the page.

'He's somehow involved in all this,' Guy reiterated. 'Why else would he have been hanging around Stuart's flat?'

'How the hell did they get these photos?' Emma said, examining the photograph showing Stuart being carried into the ambulance. Another one showed Will sitting outside Stuart's flat, his head in his hands.

'Someone must have been following Stuart, or Will,' Guy suggested. 'They were waiting for the right photo, and they got it.'

'And I think I know who.'

'I wouldn't let it worry you. I know it sounds a cliché, but whoever he is, he's just doing his job. It might be unpleasant, but you're better off forgetting him and focusing on the more pressing issue – finding your fiancé. And I know you still don't want to hear it, but I truly believe that your brother holds the key to all this.'

Richard stirred from his drug-assisted sleep; it took him a few moments to realise that the phone by his bed was ringing. Using all his energy, he reached over and wedged the receiver between the pillow and his ear. His arm ached, as if he had just lifted a ton weight.

'Hello?' He tried to sit up as far as the equipment would allow; his voice came out croaky, like an old man's.

His question was met with silence.

'Hello?' he said again. 'Emma, is that you?'

'Richard.' It was a male voice.

268

'Yes. Is that you, Will?'

'You still can't remember, can you?' the voice said.

'I'm sorry, who is this?'

'I spared your life, Richard. I came to visit you, stood by your bed and could have ended it then – but I didn't. You should be thankful.'

'It's you, isn't it?' Richard glanced towards the far wall in the fear that the man would be there, talking to him through the glass. 'Where's Dan? What have you done with him?'

Silence.

'I'm starting to remember what happened,' Richard said. 'I can nearly see your face – soon I'll remember everything. And it will be better for you to give yourself up to the police now, before they come looking for you.'

'Not until it's over,' the man replied.

'Please, just stop this,' Richard pleaded. 'I don't know why you're doing this, but just stop it, now. Let Dan go.'

'It's too late for your brother.'

'No,' Richard said, shaking his head, starting to sob. 'No, please say he's okay. Tell me you've not hurt him! Please, tell me.'

'I'm sorry.'

'Why?' Richard screamed. 'Why?'

'Because I want you all to understand.' The man's voice suddenly cracked with emotion. 'I want you to understand how much it hurts. And I think you are starting to understand, aren't you, Richard?'

59

'Still no breakthrough?' Gasnier asked, as DS Davies sat down on the other side of the desk.

'They've been through Stuart Harris's flat top to bottom,' Davies replied, 'and we've had his computer searched thoroughly. Apart from that image and the letter he sent to Emma Holden pretending to be Dan, there's nothing else to indicate where Dan is, or what happened to him.'

Gasnier sucked on his bottom lip, tapping on the desk.

'They found something interesting,' Davies continued, 'although I can't see how it's relevant to the case.'

'Go on,' Gasnier said.

Davies brought out an envelope from a folder he was carrying and handed it to Gasnier. 'They found these photographs in his bedroom, hidden inside the mattress. He'd slit a hole in the base and slid them inside.'

Gasnier shuffled through the set of twenty prints. 'Any idea who the girl is?'

Davies shook his head.

'These aren't holiday snaps,' Gasnier noted. 'They're covert surveillance photos.'

'It does look like that,' Davies agreed. 'That's why I thought it would be worth showing them to you. Though I still can't see how they could be relevant to this case.'

'Who knows,' Gasnier said. 'But I think we should at least show these to Emma Holden.'

'Emma?' Will said. 'Where are you?'

'Just about to get the tube back to the flat,' Emma said.

'You're not with Lizzy?'

'No, I'm on my own. Lizzy had a matinée this afternoon and she's got the evening performance tonight. I've just been to see Guy Roberts. I've got an idea of how we might find out some more information about Dan – although it's probably a long shot.'

'Don't do anything until I get there,' Will insisted. 'Go back to the flat and stay there until I arrive. I might even get there before you.'

'What's up?'

'Nothing. I just don't think you should be on your own at the moment. Especially with the press following you around – I just saw the story in the newspaper.'

'That's where I got the idea.'

'What do you mean?'

'I'll explain everything when you come over.'

'You sure you want to do this?' Will said, back at Emma's flat, as Emma headed for the telephone. 'I mean, by contacting the press you might just encourage them to run more stories about you. They might try and dig even deeper into your private life.'

'They might' – Emma picked up the receiver – 'but then again, this guy might be the best witness we have. If he has been following us all around, Stuart included, then he might have seen something, or someone, that can help us find Dan.'

'Wouldn't he have said so, though?' Will suggested. 'If he'd seen anything suspicious, he would already have gone to the police.'

'Probably. Although he might have seen something that to him doesn't seem important, but actually could be really important.'

'Are you sure you're not just looking for someone to take your anger out on?' Will looked at his sister carefully. 'I mean, you said yourself that the guy really scared you the other night when he called on the intercom. You chased him for about half a mile.'

'If he can give us any clues that help us find Dan, then I don't mind what else he did,' Emma replied, punching in the number for the newspaper.

'Thanks,' Emma said, scribbling down the details on the pad next to the phone. 'You've been a great help.' She hung up.

'You got the name?' Will asked.

'Eventually,' Emma said. 'The photos in today's paper all came from the same person. He's a freelance photographer called David Sherborn.'

'Contact details?'

'Telephone number and address. I think it's better if we go and see him face to face. I don't want to scare him off by calling him cold.'

'Maybe he's watching us right now.' Will moved over to the window and looked down at the street.

'Don't,' Emma said. 'It gives me the creeps.'

'It's not the same as before, though,' Will said. 'This guy isn't crazy, like Stephen Myers. He's just doing his job.'

'That's what Guy Roberts said, but it's still stalking, whatever the motivation.'

'True,' agreed Will. 'And you still want to meet this man?'

'Yes. The way I see it, I haven't got a choice.'

'This is the house,' Emma said, standing in front of a pretty blue door.

They had travelled across London late on Monday afternoon, just over the river to Balham, in Wandsworth. The walk from Tooting Bec tube station, down the high street, had underlined the demographics of the area – wine bars and bistros lined the road, with a number of thriving independent shops. This was a place that had developed over recent years into a home for the professional middle classes. It was certainly a lovely location; the street itself wouldn't have been out of place in a rural setting, with its greenery and attractive houses.

'One last chance to change your mind,' Will said.

Emma knocked.

'Can I help?' A young, pretty woman answered. She was carrying a tiny baby over her shoulder and patted his back as she stood there, rocking gently.

'We're here to see David,' Emma said.

'You're a client?'

'Yes,' Emma lied.

'Hang on a minute,' she said, turning around and shouting upstairs. 'David, door for you.'

They heard a toilet flushing and then the sound of someone bounding down the stairs.

When David Sherborn appeared, Emma caught her breath.

It was Eric.

60

'I built this studio onto the back of the house, two years ago,' David Sherborn said, shepherding them around to the rear of the property. 'Thought that it would be nice to be able to work from home, but not be at home, if you know what I mean.'

Emma stepped inside onto the wooden flooring. The studio was nicely done, each wall decorated with stunning photographs, some of panoramic mountain views, and others black-and-white close-ups of faces. In the centre of the room was a stylish black leather sofa and a glass table, on which were several large photo albums. The room smelt of vanilla.

'Please, take a seat,' said David. 'Can I get you anything to drink?'

'I'm okay,' Emma said, sitting down.

'Me too,' Will said, taking a seat next to her.

David nodded, before pulling up a stool.

'This was always my dream,' he said, looking around the room. 'My dad bought me a camera when I was ten and, ever since, that's all I ever wanted to do. It's not a bad life, either. That photo over there,' he said, gesturing towards a photo of a desert landscape, drenched in red, 'was taken in Australia. I got paid to fly out there, working for the Australian Tourist Commission. They were trying to promote the country in the UK and wanted an English photographer.'

'It's beautiful,' Emma said, but then turned back to look at him. 'Eric' looked older now – he was dressed smartly, and was talking more eloquently and authoritatively. Despite his baby face, she now placed him at least six or seven years older than her original estimate. 'This is all a bit different from your more recent work.'

'Yes,' David said, looking distinctly uncomfortable. 'That Australian trip seems like a long time ago now. Things have changed since then.'

'You're now spying on people,' Emma said. 'And selling your photos to downmarket newspapers.'

'I am,' he said, looking her in the eye. 'That's exactly what I'm doing. I never dreamt that I ever would, but sometimes things don't turn out the way you planned, do they?'

'No. Sometimes they don't.'

'I fell into it, really,' David continued. 'My other work started drying up with the economic downturn, I was getting fewer and fewer commissions, and suddenly I was struggling to pay the mortgage on the house. I had also taken out a hefty loan to build this studio. Then, Helen, my wife, found out she was pregnant, and I knew that I had to do something. I met a guy at a conference and he suggested freelance celebrity photojournalism. It's not easy, but it can pay well if you get the right photo.'

Will snorted. 'Like the photo of Stuart being carried into an ambulance?'

David averted his gaze. 'I'm not particularly proud of some of the things I do.' He sighed. 'I know it sounds like a cop-out, but this is all for my family.'

'You pretended to be someone you're not,' Emma pressed. 'You lied to me, just to get photographs.'

'Yes,' he said.

'All that business about you being threatened to stay away from me, it was all a lie. When you were crying outside the gallery?'

'It was all an act. I played the part of Eric so that I could get close to you. I'm sorry.'

'You're just sorry you got found out.'

'Maybe,' he said. 'Maybe I'm just embarrassed about what I do. Not many people know that I do this – not even Helen. She thinks the money is still coming in from my preferred work.'

'I can't say I'm happy about what you've done,' Emma said, 'but that's not why we're here.' She looked closely at David. 'We were hoping you might be able to help.'

'Go on,' he said.

'You obviously know all about our situation. You know that Stuart died, and that they still haven't found my fiancé.'

'Yes. I know. I hope they find him, I really do.'

'But you've not just been following me,' Emma said. 'You must have been following Stuart too – otherwise you wouldn't have got those photographs outside his flat.'

'I was following him that day, yes,' David confirmed. 'But I swear I didn't realise he was going to do what he did.'

'Did you follow Stuart a lot?'

'On occasions. Mostly when he was with you, though.'

'Did you ever see him do anything suspicious?' Emma said. 'Did you ever see him go anywhere? Somewhere he might have been keeping Dan?'

David shook his head. 'I'm really sorry, Emma, but I didn't. If I had, I would have gone straight to the police. I'm not that much of a mercenary.'

'Anything?' Emma tried again. 'It could be something that seemed innocuous at the time, but might be significant. It could help us find Dan.'

'I saw nothing suspicious,' he reaffirmed. 'I'd love to help, I really would. At least then I might start feeling a little better about myself. I didn't want to get into this situation. I wish I'd never been asked to—'

He stopped dead and the silence hung in the air.

'You were *asked* to follow me and take those photos,' Emma stated. 'That's what you were about to say, isn't it? These weren't just speculative, freelance shots.'

He looked away.

'Who asked you to do this?' Emma pressed. 'Please, tell me. It could be important.'

'It isn't. It won't help you find your fiancé.'

'You don't know that,' said Emma, trying to control her anger and frustration.

'I can't tell you. Now I think you'd better go.'

'Tell me, or I'll tell your wife exactly how you earn your money.'

'It won't help you, knowing the name,' he insisted.

'I'll tell her,' Emma said again.

'She'll understand.' But he didn't sound completely convinced. 'She'll understand why I do what I do.'

'She probably will.'

David pressed his hands around his nose, closing his eyes. 'Okay. If I tell you, promise you won't tell my wife.'

'I promise.'

He hunched forward, playing with his bottom lip. 'Oh, sod it,' he said, taking a breath. 'Okay, I was commissioned to do this – to follow you and take pictures.'

'Go on,' Emma said.

'You know him,' he said. 'It was Guy Roberts.'

61

'Why did you do it?' Emma demanded, even as Guy barely had a chance to open the front door.

Guy looked at Emma, and then at Will, before walking back into the house, leaving the door ajar as an invitation.

They followed him through into the living room.

'I can understand why you're angry,' said Guy, who had obviously been pre-warned by David Sherborn. 'But just hear me out.'

'You paid that man to follow me, take photographs and sell them to the newspapers,' Emma said. 'You exploited this whole situation, for money. How much did you get for those photographs?'

'Nothing,' Guy replied. 'I didn't receive a single penny for any of them.'

'You expect me to believe that,' Emma snapped.

'You can believe whatever you want to believe, Emma,' Guy said, taking a more confrontational tone, 'but the only money paid for those photographs went straight to David Sherborn – not to me.'

'Then why? Why commission him to do it?'

'You really don't know much about the entertainment business, do you?' Guy smiled wryly.

'I don't understand,' Emma said.

'The movie business, Emma, is a fickle industry. In my career I've been involved in countless films – some successes, some failures. Often the films you think will do really well just don't. Sometimes it works like that.'

'I still don't see what this has got to do with anything.'

'What I'm trying to say is that making a movie is a risky business. As an actress or an actor, being involved in a commercial flop is, how should I say it . . . ? Undesirable. But they can just move on, put it down to a bad decision on their part. For the investors, though, it's more serious – a lot more serious. They have the financial risk.'

'I understand all that, but—'

'As an investor,' Guy interrupted, 'they want to see their movie generate interest. And I don't just mean interest when it opens to hopefully rave reviews – often it's too late by that stage. The big Hollywood studios trail their films up to a year in advance, with the stars doing chat shows all around the world to generate interest in the movie well before the release date.' He looked at Emma. 'The studios throw a lot of money at generating this interest. They can. But, people like us, making a movie on a much smaller budget, can't afford to do even a quarter as much as that. We have to be more, ah, *creative* in how we generate interest in our movie. Now are you beginning to understand?'

'There's no such thing as bad publicity,' Will said.

Guy smiled. 'Very true.'

'So it was all to publicise the movie,' Emma stated flatly. 'To generate interest in the film, even before we'd started shooting.'

'Yes,' Guy said, 'that's exactly it. And, I must say, the strategy was more effective than we hoped for.'

'We?' queried Emma.

'The investors, the director, the producer, me,' Guy expanded. 'Everyone is very happy at the way things have gone.'

Emma shook her head in disbelief. 'You exploited us all. My fiancé might be *dead*, Stuart *is* dead, and all you could think about was getting column inches in a newspaper?'

'Try to understand things from our perspective, Emma.'

'You're unbelievable.'

Guy nodded. 'This is the life you'd better get used to. If you want all the rewards that come with being a successful actor, then you'll have to accept that sacrifices have to be made.'

'When you found out Stuart was dead, were you really sorry?' Emma asked. 'Or did you just see it as another headline?'

'That's not fair,' said Guy, gesticulating. 'The last thing I wanted was for that to happen.'

'You said he called you just before he died,' Emma said. 'Did he ask for help? Did you ignore him and let him kill himself?'

'No,' Guy said forcefully. 'I told you that I didn't know he was going to do it.'

But Emma continued. 'And, this morning, when you told me that you thought Stuart hadn't taken Dan – is that just a way of keeping the story going? You make out that someone is still out there, needing to be caught, when all along Stuart did do it?'

'I truly believe that Stuart did not take your fiancé.'

'It suits your purpose,' Emma said accusingly.

'You'd better leave,' Guy said icily, 'before you say something that might jeopardise your big break.'

'Don't worry,' Emma replied, understanding the threat, 'I don't want anything else to do with your film. I've got more important things to think about.

'C'mon,' she said, turning to Will, who looked quite stunned, 'let's go.'

'You sure you did the right thing back there?' Will asked, as they walked back towards the tube.

'Yeah,' Emma replied. 'I'm sure.'

'But you've wanted to be in a film ever since I can remember.'

'I know. But I don't regret what I just did. Sometimes you have to do what you think is right, and to hell with the consequences.'

Will smiled. 'You know, Em,' he said, putting an arm around her, 'I really admire you. I wish I could be as brave.'

'Hey, you're here supporting me,' Emma said. 'You shouldn't put yourself down all the time.'

'Maybe.'

Emma's mobile rang just as they were about to enter the tube station – the number coming up as unknown. She doubled back, heading outside again with Will in tow. 'Hello?'

'Em, it's me, Richard.' His voice was shaking with emotion.

'Richard, what's the matter?' She glanced up at Will, who looked concerned.

'He called me,' Richard said. 'The man who took Dan called me.'

Emma listened as Richard relayed the details. 'Have you told the staff?'

'Yes,' he said. 'The police are coming.'

'Good. We'll be right over.'

'What's up?' asked Will, the second the call had ended.

'Richard said a man called him today, saying that he had taken Dan,' Emma explained.

'Hell,' Will said, taking in the news. 'Looks like Guy Roberts was right, and Stuart didn't do it after all.'

'Maybe Guy Roberts did it himself,' Emma said slowly.

'You really think he could have done?'

'Something about him isn't right,' she replied. 'Maybe he engineered this whole situation just to get the publicity he wanted.'

62

Later that evening, Emma and Will watched through the glass as Gasnier and Davies questioned Richard. They'd been waiting there for five minutes now, having been told by the nurse not to disturb them. It was frustrating, not knowing what was going on.

'You really think that the person who called Richard is responsible for all this?' Will asked.

'I don't know,' Emma admitted. 'I'll tell you after we speak to Richard.'

As if on cue there was movement in the room, and Gasnier swept out of the door, followed by Davies.

'Emma,' Gasnier said, flashing a smile. 'Good to see you.'

'I've been waiting for you to call,' Emma said, the words slipping out and sounding more accusatory than she had intended.

'I know,' Gasnier acknowledged, his voice hinting at regret. 'I was waiting until we knew something for definite, but I'm afraid, so far, we still have no clue as to your fiancé's whereabouts. Richard is still very confused at the moment and, as you know, there was nothing at Stuart's flat, or on his computer, apart from what we had found already, of course.'

'Don't you think that's strange?' Emma asked.

'Strange?'

'That you haven't found anything else linking Stuart with Dan?'

'I wouldn't be too quick to believe that someone else is responsible,' Gasnier said, reading her mind. 'The phone call might have been a dream.'

'Or it could have been a prank,' Davies chipped in.

'That's what you said about the other letter,' Emma countered.

'Yes, and it was from Stuart,' Gasnier said. 'I still believe that Stuart Harris was responsible. Emma, I know you want to believe that someone else has Dan – it increases the likelihood that he's still alive. But the evidence points to Stuart. Talk to Richard, and make your own mind up as to whether he really knows what he is talking about.' He saw that she still wasn't convinced. 'We're doing all we can – we've got a nationwide alert out to try and find Dan, as quickly as possible.'

'I have an idea of who might be responsible,' Emma said.

Gasnier looked only vaguely interested. 'Go on.'

Emma explained to them about Guy Roberts: how he had paid the photographer to follow her, and also how his relationship with Stuart had gone back several years.

'We'll talk to him,' Gasnier promised. 'But I very much doubt he has anything to do with it.'

Emma nodded – it was the best she could have got from this stubborn man.

'And before you talk to Richard,' Gasnier said, 'have a look at these.'

Emma examined the photographs that Gasnier presented, one by one. Each of them showed Stuart and the same girl kissing, holding hands across a table, his arm around her.

'Where did you find these?' Emma asked.

'Hidden in Stuart's flat,' Gasnier replied. 'Do you recognise the girl?'

'No,' Emma said, unable to take her eyes off the images. 'Why did you show me these? Do you think they're relevant?'

'Not really,' Gasnier said. 'We just wanted to be sure.'

'Someone took these without them knowing, didn't they?' Emma asked, looking up at Gasnier.

'Looks like it. Do you think they're recent?'

'No,' Emma said, with certainty. 'He's wearing the gold watch I gave him as a present. When he left me, he left the watch, too.'

'So what you're saying is,' Gasnier said slowly, 'these photos were taken when you two were still together?'

'Definitely.' Now it all made sense. He had left her for another woman.

'But you don't know who might have taken these photographs?' Gasnier enquired.

'No,' Emma replied. 'Unless . . .'

'Go on,' Gasnier encouraged.

'Unless it was Stephen Myers.'

'The police don't believe me,' Richard said, rolling his head from side to side on the pillow. 'They looked at me like I was delusional. You know, they even suggested I dreamt the telephone conversation. Can you believe that?' He laughed bitterly.

'Gasnier doesn't seem to give away much,' Emma said.

'He thought I was crazy. Maybe I am. Just before the police arrived I fell asleep and dreamt about the attack. But Dan was the one attacking me – he just kept screaming something, bawling right into my face. I can't remember what. I didn't tell the police about it. I would have just confirmed what they were already thinking.'

'It was just a dream,' said Emma soothingly.

'I wish this was all a dream,' Richard replied. 'I wish I would just wake up and it would all have been one bad dream.'

'So do I.'

'Don't take any notice of me,' he said, noticing her pained expression. 'Things will be okay.'

Emma reached out and held his hand. 'We've all got to stick together. Right, Will?'

'Oh, yeah, of course,' Will said, seeming somewhat distracted. 'Stick together.'

'I didn't imagine it, Emma,' Richard said. 'The guy *did* call me. He said he had done it. I think he's out there – you should be careful.'

'You okay?' Emma asked Will as he walked back over to her. She had been waiting at the entrance to the hospital in the semi-darkness while Will spoke to someone on his mobile, just out of hearing distance.

'Yeah, fine,' Will replied, slipping the phone back into his jeans pocket.

'It's just that you seemed a little subdued in the hospital.'

'I'm fine,' he reiterated. 'I just can't help thinking about what Richard said. If someone is still out there, then maybe we're all in danger.'

Emma's phone rang. 'Hello?' she said.

'Emma, it's Sarah here.'

'What's wrong?' Emma asked, immediately thinking the worst.

'It's probably nothing,' Sarah replied, 'but the show is due to start in less than half an hour and Lizzy hasn't turned up yet. We've called her mobile and home number, but there's no answer. I just wondered whether she was with you.'

63

'You're really worried, aren't you?' Will said, catching his breath as they ran along the pavement towards Lizzy's flat, having just got out of the taxi that had brought them the few miles across the city to north London.

'Something's happened,' Emma replied, dodging an elderly couple and picking up the pace. 'Lizzy wouldn't just disappear like that.'

They reached the apartments, sprinted up the stairs and got to Lizzy's door. As Emma banged on the door and rooted around in her bag to find the key Lizzy had given her, it all seemed horribly familiar.

'Lizzy?' she shouted, as they burst into the flat. 'Are you okay?'

They moved around the flat together, room by room.

The place was deserted.

'Something's happened,' Emma said again, pacing around the living room. 'I know it.'

'What are we going to do?' Will said, looking at her.

'I don't know.' Then Emma spotted the open book on top of the television. She moved over and picked it up.

'What is it?' Will said.

'Stephen Myers' journal,' Emma replied, looking in morbid fascination at Stephen's black scrawl. 'Lizzy told me she was going to throw it away.'

'Looks like she's been reading it,' Will said, at her shoulder.

'It does,' Emma agreed.

She read the open page, in which Stephen was rambling in his usual style, talking about how much he loved Emma, how much he looked forward to being with her. It was terrifying and sad at the same time.

'I don't think it's a good idea to read that,' Will advised.

'You're right,' she said. She went to close the book, and out fell the photograph – the one she had picked off Stephen's bedroom wall, proving that Stephen had been to London.

She bent down and picked it up, looking at herself crossing the road at Oxford Circus.

Suddenly realisation dawned.

'You okay?' Will said, moving up to her.

'Look,' she said, pointing at the photo. 'Look at the junction at Oxford Circus. I can't believe I didn't notice it before.'

Will peered at the image. 'Notice what?'

'The American-style countdown crossing, you can see it in the background. And the markings on the tarmac – so you can walk diagonally across the road, rather than having to cross twice.'

'I still don't follow, Em, sorry.'

'Stephen died four years ago,' Emma said. 'We saw on the gravestone. But these road changes were only introduced last year. The junction was completely redesigned, and the new crossing system was put in place. It means that this photograph must have been taken after Stephen Myers died.'

'Where are you going?' Miranda asked, as she stood at the doorway, watching Edward loading up the car.

'I just need to do something,' Edward said.

'But it's getting late,' Miranda replied. She pulled her dressing gown tighter around her body as a passer-by sneaked a surprised glance. 'Can't it wait until the morning?'

'It can't wait, no.' Edward reached through the driver's side and fiddled with something in the car.

'What's the matter? You're worrying me, Edward.'

'It's nothing. There's no need to worry.'

'But if it's nothing, why can't it wait until morning?'

'It just can't,' he stated.

'Please, don't go,' Miranda said, moving out onto the

driveway in her bare feet. Small, sharp stones dug into her soles, but she ignored the pain. 'Please don't go like this, without any explanation. I worry about you.'

Edward turned and moved towards her, placing a warm hand on each shoulder. 'You know I love you?' He looked deep into her eyes. 'I'd never want to do anything to hurt you.'

'You're not leaving me, are you?' Miranda asked. 'If you are, I'd rather you just admit it now.'

'I'm not leaving you,' he replied. 'I've let people down in the past, but I'm trying to change.'

'You've never let me down,' she said, embracing him.

Edward held her for a few seconds, taking in her scent, but he knew it was only wasting time and making things harder to face. 'I'd better go.' He kissed her on the cheek before pulling away. 'I'll be back in the morning.'

'You'll be gone overnight?' Miranda stared at him. 'But where are you going to stay?'

Edward got into the car and closed the door. He started up the engine, not answering her.

'Edward!' she shouted, knocking on the car window. 'Have you got your angina spray?'

Edward nodded, glancing in the rearview mirror. 'Don't worry about me,' he said through the glass, as he began to reverse the car out of the drive.

He backed out onto the main road, and then moved forward, slipping the car into second gear. He deliberately didn't look back to see if Miranda was there watching him.

Instead, he glanced across at the glove box, which contained the loaded gun.

He was going to finish this, once and for all.

Emma sat on the sofa in Lizzy's flat and stared at the photograph, searching for answers. She looked across at Will, who was kneading the sides of his head.

'I know it sounds crazy,' she began, 'but I've been thinking – maybe Stephen Myers isn't really dead.'

Will shook his head.

'What if the person they found in the canal wasn't him?' Emma tried. 'His dad said that they couldn't identify him visually.'

'They would have used dental records.'

'Maybe they didn't,' Emma countered. 'Maybe they just assumed that it was him, and didn't do the proper tests. I might have been right all along, and it's Stephen Myers that has been doing all this. Everything's pointed to him from the very beginning.'

Will blew out a deep breath, closing his eyes.

He started to cry.

'Will, what's the matter?' Shocked, Emma moved across to comfort him.

Will shook his head.

'What's up?' she said, placing a hand on his shoulder.

'I know he's dead,' he said, struggling to fight back his emotions. 'I saw him.'

'What do you mean?'

Will looked up, his face contorted with grief and regret and his eyes glazed with tears. This was the moment.

'Please forgive me, Em,' he pleaded. 'Don't hate me. Everything just got out of hand – if I'd had time to think, I wouldn't have gone along with it. But I thought I was doing the right thing.'

Emma looked at him. 'You're worrying me now, Will. What are you talking about?'

'Stuart. He killed – murdered – Stephen Myers.'

'What?' Emma said, horrified. 'But they said he committed suicide.'

'No,' Will countered, shaking his head. 'It was meant to look like a suicide, but it was murder. Stuart murdered him.'

'How do you know this?' Emma said, standing up, feeling the urge to move away from her brother. 'Please tell me you weren't involved.'

'I'm sorry, Em. I was involved. I helped him dispose of the body.'

64

'I don't understand,' Emma said, pacing backwards and forwards across the living room. 'This can't be true!'

'Why would I joke about something like this?' Will said, looking up at her through teary eyes. 'I've been carrying around this secret for years, Em, and it's been tearing me apart.'

'Then tell me everything,' Emma instructed, still not sitting down. 'From the beginning.'

'Well,' he began, struggling to find the words, 'you know how I told you that we had warned Stephen Myers off you – well, that was true. We knew he'd started coming down to London, watching you, taking photographs. Stuart and I tried to reason with him, and then things got a bit nastier. Stuart threatened him, saying that if he didn't leave you alone, something bad might happen.'

'Go on,' Emma said.

'Well, I didn't really agree with what Stuart had done, but it seemed to work – I thought Stephen had finally got the message. But then one night I was in my flat – I can still remember what I was watching on the TV – and I got a call from Stuart. He was really freaking out, saying that something had happened with Stephen and could I come around to your place straight away. So, unfortunately, I did.'

'And he'd . . .' Emma couldn't bring herself to say it.

'I got over to yours. You were out at work. Stuart answered the door – his face and shirt were dripping with sweat. He let me in and took me through to the living room, and Stephen was just lying there on the floor. Dead.'

Will's words didn't seem real. *Stuart was a murderer?* Emma struggled to find the words. 'Did . . . did he say how it happened?'

'He told me that Stephen had come around, forced himself into the flat and then pulled a knife on him. They fought, and as they were fighting, Stephen fell over onto the knife. I thought he was telling me the truth.'

'But he wasn't?'

'No,' he said. 'It wasn't true at all. Stuart Harris used me. I had a car, and he didn't. He just said what he needed to, so that I would help him dispose of the body. And I did. I was so stupid. We wrapped Stephen up in bed sheets, then took him down to my car and put him in the boot. Then we drove up to near Stephen's home. Stuart thought we could make it look like suicide. We found a really isolated stretch of canal and dropped him in, along with the knife.'

Emma looked out of the window at the lit streetlamps, taking some deep breaths.

Her brother was an accessory to murder.

'Say something, Em,' Will said.

'I don't know what to say,' she admitted finally. 'This is all so . . . oh, I don't know. So unbelievable.'

'I hate myself for what I did. I had to get rid of that car. I sold it the next week.'

Emma turned around to face him. 'To get rid of the evidence?'

'No,' he said, 'it wasn't that. I just couldn't bear to drive it any more, not after what I'd done, what had happened in there.'

'How could you have done it, Will? How could you?'

'I don't know,' he said. 'Everything happened so fast, but I guess at the time I was just trying to help. Stuart and you were going to get married, and I thought that him killing Stephen was just an accident. I was trying to help him out – I thought he was innocent.'

'But he wasn't innocent! You said that Stuart hadn't been telling you the truth about what happened with Stephen.'

'No, it didn't happen how he said.'

'How do you know?'

'Because one day, when I was round at yours, I found

something.' Will looked up at his sister. 'The set of photographs showing Stuart with that girl.'

'The photos the police just showed us?'

Will nodded. 'He found me looking at them and told me the truth. He'd started an affair with a girl he'd met at an audition – it had been going on for a couple of months. One day Stephen had come around, with the photographs, threatening that unless Stuart left you, he'd show you them.'

My God. 'So he killed him to stop me finding out about his affair?'

'Exactly,' Will confirmed. 'When he told me, I didn't know what to do. I was already panicking about what we'd done, but knowing the truth made it worse. I wanted to go to the police, but I was scared of what might happen to me.'

'But what I don't understand,' Emma said, 'is if Stuart was willing to kill Stephen just so we could be together, why would he then walk away?'

'He started losing it. I mean, really cracking up. At first I thought what he'd done hadn't affected him, but it had.'

'And I thought his behaviour, the depression, was about not getting work . . .'

'Eventually, I think he just decided that he needed to get away from anything that reminded him of what he had done, including you.'

'So why did he decide he wanted me back now? Why?' Emma's head was whirling.

Will shrugged. 'A few of months ago he called me,' he said. He started threatening to call the police and tell them everything that had happened. He said that he was prepared to take me down with him, unless I gave him money. So I did.'

'Will!' Emma said.

'I know. I know it was stupid. But I was frightened. I just wanted him to go away. He said he would, but he kept coming back, asking for more. Then he started talking about wanting to get back with you. And then Dan disappeared.'

'You thought it was Stuart from the start?'

'I . . . I wasn't sure,' Will replied, 'but, yes, I did wonder whether he had done something. I found something in your bathroom, on the floor next to Richard. A photograph.'

'A photograph?'

'One of the set taken by Stephen Myers. I found a photograph of Stuart and the girl, lying there.'

'And you didn't tell me?' said Emma, her anger rising. 'You found something like that and kept it to yourself?'

'Yes,' Will said, hanging his head. 'I'm sorry – I'm a coward, Em.'

Emma watched the steam rise from the kettle. She had retreated into the kitchen, needing to get some space from Will, and calm herself. She made two cups of tea and brought them through to the living room. Will was standing up, looking out of the window.

'Here you go,' Emma said, handing him one of the cups.

'Thanks,' he said, avoiding her gaze. 'Look, Em, I wouldn't blame you if you never wanted to talk to me again. I should have—'

'Don't,' Emma interrupted. 'We haven't got time. I've been thinking, and the important thing here is to consider whether what happened with Stephen helps to explain what's happening with Dan and Lizzy.'

Will nodded, collecting himself with a visible effort. 'The fact that there was a recent photograph of you in Stephen Myers' bedroom makes me think that it must have something to do with it.'

'I agree,' Emma said. 'And as it wasn't Stephen who took it, it must have been one of two other people – Stephen's mum or dad.'

'But what would they have against Dan?'

Emma nodded to herself. 'Maybe it's me they want to hurt.'

Will looked at her. 'But why?'

Emma opened her mouth to speak, then shut it again. She shook her head, exasperated. 'I don't know. Look, maybe it isn't them. We're clutching at straws really, aren't we? And while we're standing here, who knows what has happened to Lizzy.'

'I think we should go and see Dad,' Will announced.

'Why?'

'You'll just have to trust me. I know I haven't done anything to deserve it, but I think Dad might be able to help us find whoever is behind this.'

65

'Dad knows about all this, doesn't he?' Emma stated, as they neared their father's house. 'He knows about what happened with Stephen.'

'I told him, yes,' Will admitted.

'How long has he known?'

'Since the beginning. I needed someone to talk to about it, and he was the only person I could turn to.'

'And did he help?' Emma looked at Will's face. 'No, I didn't think so. So why do you think he might be able to help now?'

Will stopped the car just before they reached the house. 'He called me today,' he explained, 'and told me to make sure you were okay – to stick with you wherever you went. I think something happened, or he knows something, to make him react like that.'

'He didn't say anything else?'

'I know I should have pressed him,' Will said, 'but at the time I just had my mind focused on getting to you as quickly as possible. He sounded really worried about you.'

'That doesn't sound like Dad.'

'Don't be too hard on him, Em. He tries.'

'You've changed your tune.'

'If I can't forgive Dad for what he's done to us, then why should I expect you to try and forgive me?' Will said simply.

Emma nodded slowly. 'You're right,' she conceded.

They parked close by and walked on, reaching the entrance to the house.

'Looks like he's out,' Emma noted, looking down the empty drive.

'Miranda must be in,' Will replied. 'The bedroom light's on.'

They had to knock three times before Miranda came to answer the door. Her face was streaked with make-up.

'What's happened?' Emma asked.

'Edward's gone,' Miranda said, breaking into a series of sobs. 'I think he might have left me.'

Emma and Will waited impatiently in the living room while Miranda regained her composure.

'Did Dad say where he was going?' ventured Emma.

Miranda shook her head, dabbing her eyes with a tissue provided by Will. 'He wouldn't say where he was going. I asked him, but he just told me not to worry. You know how he is – he likes to keep things to himself. He didn't even take his mobile phone with him.'

'He didn't say when he'd be back?' Emma said.

'He said he'd see me tomorrow – he's staying somewhere overnight.'

'Going on a long journey,' Emma murmured to herself.

She looked across at Will, who had obviously heard her mutterings. 'Did he leave suddenly?' he asked Miranda.

'Very,' she replied. 'He didn't give any warning about going out, especially not going somewhere and staying overnight. I'd suggested that we watch a DVD tonight, relax in front of the TV, and he said he'd love to. Then the next thing I know, he's on his way out of the door.'

'Something happened,' Will said, too loudly.

'Is something wrong?' Miranda's face flooded with new anxiety. 'Is your father in trouble? Do you know something? If you do, please tell me.'

'Nothing's wrong,' lied Emma, flashing a reproving glance at Will. 'Not that we know of, anyway.'

Fortunately Miranda accepted the lie and calmed down.

'Do you mind if I just pop to the bathroom?' Emma asked.

'Of course not,' Miranda replied.

Emma got up and, from behind Miranda's shoulder, gestured to Will.

'I'll go and make us all a drink,' Will said. 'Tea with one?' he asked Miranda.

'Thanks, Will,' said Miranda, staring into space. 'You're both a big help.'

'What are you looking for?' Will asked, as Emma searched their father's study.

'I don't know,' Emma said. 'Anything that might help. Something must have prompted Dad to call you, and made him leave like that.'

They found the envelope in the bottom desk drawer, containing a newspaper cutting reporting Stephen's suicide.

Local loner discovered in canal.
Parents distraught.

Emma peered into the envelope and found the accompanying note.

'My God,' Will said, staring at the note. 'They know what really happened.'

'Dad's gone up there. I hope he doesn't do anything stupid.'

Will's mouth was suddenly bone dry. 'He has a gun.'

'What?' Emma stared at him, aghast.

'He borrowed it from a friend,' Will explained.

'We've got to get up there,' Emma announced, 'before this gets any worse.'

66

'Do you think Miranda will be all right?' Will asked, as they sped along the unlit motorway.

'I hope so,' Emma replied, concerned that she was already feeling tired, with over a hundred miles of darkened road still to go.

'We've been too hard on her, haven't we?' Will commented. 'She didn't deserve getting caught in the fallout between Dad and us. We should have kept her out of it.'

'I know,' Emma agreed. 'I just hope for her sake – for all our sakes – that Dad doesn't get himself into trouble.'

'He's trying to make things right,' Will commented. 'I think he's trying to make up for the past few years.'

'He could make things a hell of a lot worse,' Emma said grimly, 'if he goes storming in there with a gun. Who knows what could happen.'

'Do you think there's a chance that Dan and Lizzy are okay? Do you think whoever has them might just have kept them, and not have hurt them?' Will's questions were almost pitiable.

'Ever since this began I've been praying that Dan is okay,' Emma said. 'But I don't know. We've just got to hope that they're both all right.'

'I won't forgive myself if anything has happened to them. This is my fault – someone's taking revenge for what I did, and you're the one suffering.'

'You didn't kill Stephen Myers,' Emma stated. 'Remember that.'

'But I was part of it,' Will replied. 'And whoever sent Dad that newspaper cutting knows that.'

'I wish the police had taken me seriously,' Emma lamented. She had rung them earlier, but been told that Gasnier wasn't in the office. 'I don't think they're going to send anyone to the Myers' house, are they?'

'You could have told the police the whole story,' said Will. 'If you tell them everything, they might be more ready to believe you. I'm ready to take responsibility for what I did.'

'They'd have wanted to bring us in for questioning – I know what Gasnier is like. We don't have time for all that. Anyway, I need your support; I don't want you locked up in a police station.'

'But I'm just saying. I've been holding on to this secret for too long.'

'You're a good person, Will,' Emma said. 'Don't forget that.'

It was one o'clock in the morning by the time they reached Stephen's parents' house.

Emma slowed the car to a stop on the opposite side of the road. She and Will sat there for a few seconds, looking up at the house. There were no lights visible.

'I can't see Dad's car,' said Will, scanning up and down the street.

'No.'

'We might have got here before him,' Will offered. 'We did make good time.'

'Maybe,' Emma replied. 'Are you ready?' She reached for the door handle.

Will nodded.

They crossed the road, with no sign of movement along the whole street, and knocked on the door.

There was no answer.

Emma tried another few times, before knocking on the front bay window.

'What now?' Will said, when there was still no movement.

'I don't know,' she replied, looking up at the top window. 'Maybe we've got this all wrong. It might not have anything to do with Stephen's family . . . anyone could have found out what happened to Stephen and could be doing this.'

'You're right,' Will agreed. 'Dad might not even have come up here, might he, if he suspects or knows that it was someone else?'

Emma paced up and down the pavement, clutching at the back of her neck. 'Why won't this end?' she shouted in frustration.

The door of a neighbouring house opened.

'I'm sorry,' said Emma, as the neighbour, dressed in striped pyjamas, glared at her.

'You looking for Mrs Myers?' he asked sternly.

'Yeah,' Emma replied.

'She's gone,' he said. 'They took her away a few days ago, into a hospital. She's been getting worse recently.'

'Oh, right,' Emma said. 'Is Mr Myers around? Doesn't he live nearby?'

'Used to. Peter moved to London a few months ago. I think he just wanted to get as far away from her as possible. Can't say I blame him really – she fell apart after her son died. I know it's all been extremely difficult for him.'

Stephen's dad has been living in London? He has to be behind all this. 'Do you have an address for him?' Emma asked.

'Why do you want to know?'

'I just need to see him,' Emma said. 'It's really important.'

'Funny, that,' the man noted, suppressing a hint of a smile, 'because you're the second person to come looking for Peter Myers in the past hour. Never knew he was so popular.'

67

'Eh?' Emma lifted her head from the passenger seat headrest and turned towards Will. She felt dizzy with tiredness.

'Hi,' said Will, his hands wrapped around the top of the steering wheel.

Emma noticed that they were parked in a residential road: houses tightly packed on both sides, a couple of homes boarded up with green metal panels. The sun had come up and birds were singing. 'Are we there?' she asked, rubbing her forehead.

'We're here,' Will confirmed.

'What time is it?' Emma peered at her watch. She'd been asleep for over three hours. 'You've driven all the way back down to London yourself? You should have woken me up.'

'You needed the rest.'

'Have we just arrived?' she asked, trying to shake off her grogginess.

'We've been here a couple of minutes. I was just thinking about what we should do.'

'Which one is it?' Emma asked, looking out at the street, house by house.

'That one just there.' Will pointed. 'I did a drive-past when we first arrived.'

'Any sign of Dad's car?'

'None,' Will replied. 'It's not in the street.'

'This might still all be a wild-goose chase.' Emma looked across at the house. 'But there's only one way to find out. C'mon.'

'Maybe we should wait,' Will said, putting his hand on Emma's arm.

'For what?'

'I don't know. Maybe we should wait and think about what to do.'

'We haven't got time. Every second we wait here increases the chance that something bad might happen. Are you coming?'

'It's open,' whispered Emma, as they reached the front door. It was ever so slightly ajar. But no light was coming through the gap.

They looked at each other, wondering how to proceed.

'Maybe we shouldn't,' Will said quietly back, as Emma went to push at the door. 'Maybe going in there isn't the right thing to do.'

'You don't have to come in.'

Will shook his head at her. 'I will,' he replied.

'Thanks,' she said, pushing the door.

They both slid into the darkened house. As Emma pushed the door to behind them again, it became apparent that at least one light in the house was on. It was coming from one of the back rooms, down the end of the hallway in which they were now standing.

They moved slowly along the wall, aware of each other's breathing. The place smelt of damp and dirt, and it was a strain not to cough.

As they passed a door to their left, Emma heard a tapping sound. She stopped.

'What is it?' Will whispered from the darkness.

'Someone's in there.' Emma pointed at the door. Edging forward, groping her way in the darkness, she slowly opened the door. The tapping sound stopped. 'Hello?' she said. 'Who's in here?'

And then they saw.

In the corner of the room, consumed by the darkness, was a human figure, hunched forward on a chair.

68

'Your phone,' Emma directed, as she got her mobile out of her pocket. 'Use the screen as a light. We don't want to alert anyone.'

Will nodded, using the illuminated display to light the way.

Emma moved across to the figure.

'Lizzy, oh my God.' She knelt down in front of her friend.

Lizzy raised her head, a gag tight across her mouth. Her face was bruised and her eyes hollow and vacant. It was as if she didn't recognise Emma.

Emma untied the gag whilst Will stayed back, glancing at the door, ready for whoever might enter the room.

'Em,' Lizzy mouthed, gasping for breath. 'Stephen's father.'

Emma cupped Lizzy's face. 'Everything's going to be okay. Have you seen Dan?'

Lizzy shook her head.

Emma smiled supportively, then looked up at Will. 'You untie her. I'm going on.'

'We both go,' Will said.

Emma thought swiftly, then nodded. They untied Lizzy and, walking either side of her, moved her out of the house, across the road and into the car.

'We'll be back,' said Emma, feeling a sharp shard of pain shoot up her back; Lizzy was exhausted, and supporting her weight had been hard work.

'I'll go first,' said Will as they entered the house for a second time. This time they moved a little more quickly, past the staircase on their right and towards the door at the end of the hallway.

They stopped at the door, able to hear muffled voices.

Will looked to Emma for direction, his hand on the door handle. He was just able to make her out in the light that came from under the door.

Emma nodded.

As they opened the door, a gunshot rang out.

69

'Dad,' Emma said from the doorway. 'Put the gun down.'

Edward stood over Peter Myers, the gun aimed at his head. Peter Myers was clutching his knee, which was a mass of pulp and blood.

He was strangely quiet for a man who had just been shot through the leg.

'I'm going to finish it,' Edward replied.

'Please, don't do this,' Emma begged, edging into the room. 'It shouldn't end like this.'

'He deserves to die,' Edward said. 'First his son ruined your life, and now he's done the same. Do you really want to save the life of the man who murdered Dan?'

'Dan's dead?' Emma said. Suddenly, the floor seemed to tilt and all she could hear was a high-pitched ringing in her ears.

'In the kitchen.' He nodded to a door over his shoulder. 'His body has just been dumped there on the kitchen floor. I'm sorry, Emma, but this ... *monster* has killed your fiancé.'

'No,' Emma said, shaking her head and bringing a hand to her mouth as Will put an arm on her back. She felt as though she was going to be sick.

Peter Myers looked at her, grimacing, but offering no hint of remorse.

'I'm sorry, Emma,' Edward repeated. 'Can't you see now why this man doesn't deserve to live? He just wanted to hurt you and everyone you love. He deserves everything he gets.'

'No,' Emma said, tiredly, trying to push the images of Dan out of her mind. 'He's just a victim like the rest of us.'

'How can you say that? He's not a *victim*,' Edward spat.

'He's suffered, too,' Emma said. 'Stuart Harris began this, but you're not the one to finish it – not like this.'

'Em's right,' Will said, taking a step forward. 'Put the gun away, Dad. Miranda needs you. You're going to have another child who'll need you. And we need you, too.'

Edward gave a sarcastic laugh. 'If he lives, then you'll go to prison.' He took neither his aim nor his eyes off Peter Myers. 'Has he told you, Emma? Has your brother told you what he did? He was an accessory to murder.'

'He's told me everything,' Emma said. 'We can work this out.'

'No,' Edward replied. 'As long as this man is alive, it could all still come out.'

'Who do you really want to protect?' Will asked. 'Me, or yourself?'

'You, of course,' Edward replied. 'I want to protect my son.'

'Then you might as well put the gun down, because it's already too late for me. I've told the police everything.'

'What?' Emma glanced around.

'I called them when we first arrived here, while you were still asleep. They should be here any minute.'

'You idiot!' shouted Edward, taking his eyes off Peter Myers for the first time. 'You stupid idiot!'

Emma saw her chance. In one smooth movement, she spun towards the floor, sweeping Edward's legs from underneath him. He fell to the ground like an uprooted tree. 'Get the gun,' she shouted to Will, as she held Edward in position with a carefully placed knee. Will picked up the gun and stood guard over Peter Myers.

'I'm sorry, Dad,' Emma said as he lay motionless and defeated on the floor. 'I just can't let you do it to yourself.'

70

'Don't do it,' Will said, the gun still aimed at Peter Myers as Emma reached for the kitchen door. 'Don't look.'

'I have to,' Emma replied, her hand shaking and tears falling. 'I have to see him.'

'It could haunt you for the rest of your life,' Will responded. 'Let me—'

But Emma had already opened the door.

The first thing she saw was Dan's bare feet, blackened with dirt. Then, as she opened the door wider, the horrific scene became clear.

'Oh, please, no,' Emma cried, as she saw Dan's face. Dried tracks of blood snaked down from his hairline and spread out across his cheek.

As she slid down onto her knees, she heard voices. One of them was Gasnier's.

But it all seemed so far away. Blinking through the tears, she stroked Dan's hair, something she had done thousands of times before but never really appreciated until now.

'I'm so sorry,' she said. 'I'm so sorry. I love you so much.'

She placed her head on his chest and closed her eyes. Her heart was in overdrive, pounding through her body and into her head, dominating her senses. But then she noticed something else.

It was Dan's heartbeat.

Acknowledgements

First of all, thank you to my wonderful family for their support and encouragement over the years. You've always been there for me, and without you I wouldn't have the happy bedrock in my life that enables me to write. Thanks also to the friends who have read my books and provided such useful feedback.

I've enjoyed creative writing from an early age, and this was in no small part down to the wonderful teachers who have been there to foster this passion. Creativity is such an important part of the educational system, and I really value the inspiration and help I was given during my school and college years.

Thank you to all the team at Coronet, including my brilliant editor, Mark Booth – thank you for believing in my work. Special thanks to my agent Jon Elek at AP Watt at United Agents, for all his effort in securing the publishing deal. Thank you also to the other publishing professionals I have come into contact with during the past decade or so – you've all, in one way or another, contributed to this.

And finally, a big thank you to all those who have purchased my books, and a special mention to everyone who has got in touch with me via email, Facebook and Twitter over the past two and a half years. It's been an amazing period in my life, making contact with people across the world who have read and enjoyed my work. It's something that I never believe would happen. The kind messages I have received certainly makes writing worthwhile.

Do you wish this wasn't the end?

Join us at www.hodder.co.uk, or follow us on
Twitter @hodderbooks to be a part of our community
of people who love the very best in books and reading.

Whether you want to discover more about a book
or an author, watch trailers and interviews, have the
chance to win early limited editions, or simply browse
our expert readers' selection of the very best books,
we think you'll find what you're looking for.

And if you don't,
that's the place to tell us what's missing.

We love what we do, and we'd love you to be part of it.

www.hodder.co.uk

@hodderbooks

HodderBooks

HodderBooks